THE DARKNESS WITHIN

A Lythinall Novel
Book Two

TIR-LANATH

SILVERSWORD PASS

SNOW PEAK
MOUNTAINS

THE TOOTH
HILLS

THE WINDING
RIVER HAVEN

THE DARKNESS WITHIN

A Lythinall Novel
Book Two

MICHAEL D. NADEAU

THE DARKNESS WITHIN

www.skullgatemedia.com

ISBN 978-1-7355040-5-6

Ebook ISBN 978-1-7355040-6-3

Third Edition: 2021

Second Edition: 2019, Kyanite Press

First Edition: 2017, Michael D. Nadeau

Cover art by Simon Carr

Cover design and internal layout by Chris Vandyke

ACKNOWLEDGEMENTS

To my wife, Sheila, for always being patient with me, even though you want to smother me in my sleep sometimes.

To all of my friends for always having faith in me and reading my stories.

To my gaming group for inspiring me with our escapades. You all made this possible. But wait...there's more.

To Gwen and Lexi Gagne, who were the inspiration for my faeries.

Last, but definitely not least, my kids and grandkids: Amber, Gabriel, Connor, and Jackson —Widdle Dood—.

THE DARKNESS WITHIN

A Lythinall Novel

MICHAEL D. NADEAU

MAP OF LYTHINALL
And Surrounding Regions

THE DARKNESS WITHIN

A Lythinall Novel
Book Two

CONTENTS

Prologue: What Has Gone Before   1
1. The Long Journey Home   5
2. Together at Last   18
3. Flight   36
4. Common Ground   52
5. Almost Home   82
6. All Paths Lead In   119
7. Reunions   150
8. Revelations   189
9. The Coming Storm   219
Epilogue: Through a veil of doubt   249

The Adventure Continues   255
About the Author   257

PROLOGUE: WHAT HAS GONE BEFORE

Once sealed away, the incarnation of death and corruption is loosed, crawling his way out of his earthen prison. This being causes things to wither and die just by touching them and can pull power from the very earth around him. He marches towards civilization and descends upon the frontier villages without mercy. At the same time, a young warrior named Rhoe has a dream in which he watches this evil being destroy a village and start towards his own; but it wasn't a dream. Strange powers have awoken within him and his life is about to change forever. It's then that the legendary bard Karsis arrives to train Rhoe in his powers and teach him of the wider world. They travel south to warn King Arian of this great evil

Meanwhile, at the capitol city of Everknight, Princess Allissana has dreams of this young warrior, and sees him coming to her rescue. The princess hears of the evil at a council meeting and takes it upon herself to go and fight it, so it does not come into the capitol. High General Carana, who has trained her to be one of the best fighters in the kingdom, goes with her, sneaking out of the castle in the early morning hours. She goes to the bridge and faces the incarnation of corruption above the spring fed waters of the river. Then it happens. Assisted by magic, Rhoe runs right around the incarnation and stands with the princess. Together they fight the being, but after a short bout, his anger corrodes the very bridge they stand upon and they all crash into the roaring waters below, getting washed downstream.

They are found by faeries and the unicorn Avaryn, who takes them to their queen, Lurien. The incarnation is washed further downstream, but finally makes his way up and out of the water, heading towards the faeries. The princess, now going by Liss, and Rhoe attend a revel in which they accidently get married. The next day, the former queen of the faeries, Irilyn, chooses to fight the incarnation with the combined power of the faeries burning inside her, but she also has a plan. Avaryn guides Rhoe and Liss towards a magical faerie ring and they are transported to the Misty Woods, just northeast of Everknight. Avaryn then rushes to Irilyn's aid, arriving just in time to see her fall into her own trap, a faerie ring that goes to a dead end. He impales the Incarnation in the back with his horn, and drops him into Irilyn's trap as well, then destroys the ring so there is no way back. The faerie ring leads the two to the northern most part of the Northern Belt Mountain range, and here Irilyn attacks the incarnation when he appears. She wounds him mortally, but is destroyed in the process, and the incarnation collapses in the snow.

Back at the capitol, King Arian is attacked more than once by southern sorcerers, and in the last attempt, the old priest Ralavin saves the day, giving his life to slay the traitor. Karsis leaps to the priest's side and gives him the Vial of Eternity, which not only restores the priest, but gives him back his youth as well. After the attacks, the king walks into the city on an errand, and finds some homeless children playing at being knights. He believes that he can give them a better home and brings them back to the castle to train them to be the King's Messengers.

In the meantime, Rhoe and Liss make their way south towards River Vale, but are attacked by a Wolvren. They struggle to fight it off, but Liss is wounded severely. Rhoe places himself in the way to save Liss, clawing the things eyes as it shreds him. They are saved by Aeric, the king's marshal, and his patrol, and are taken to River Vale. Karsis travels behind, wondering if the incarnation survived. He looks up and out, far above the clouds with his own magic and sees him far to the north. He is alive but barely, but it will take him months to walk out of those mountains... they have time.

THE LONG JOURNEY HOME

The dragon sniffed the cold, crisp air once more, knowing the other animals were afraid of something. Nothing had ever spooked all of them at once...except for him. Kanthalianar was one of the most feared creatures of legend, sweeping down out of the skies and devouring whole villages at his whim—or so the stories went. In truth, the great dragon hated villagers. They were chewy and didn't digest well, and he detested all the screaming. No, he much preferred livestock, especially cows. *Great, now I'm hungry,* he thought as he narrowed his eyes at the horizon. He hadn't flown over the countryside in well over seventy years, as he had been dozing comfortably in his mountain lair, but now something had awoken him and he might as well see what it was. His great bulk stretched out in a magnificent sight, his glistening, deep red scales covering his massive frame. Dragons scales changed color with age, and Kanth was indeed an ancient one. He climbed gracefully up the rocks, for one of his size, and looked out over the peaks.

His gaze stretched out over the miles as easily as those damned elven mages did with their *sight*, noticing immediately what was scaring the animals of the mountains. The thing that was approaching seemed like a man, walked like a man, but the power radiating off him was nothing like Kanth had ever seen. *Well, I have seen something like that, but that was a long time ago,* he thought to himself as the being came to a stop. It was looking straight at him even though they were miles apart. The thing bowed to the great dragon, then advanced—slower this time. Kanth had to decide what to do, and very quickly if that thing was indeed an incarnation of some sort. He would either flee, giving up his lair, or fight, and quite possibly die in the process. *Either way, every creature in these mountains will know that I no longer hold sway... damn it all to the gods,* he thought, knowing that he had no choice; he would have to fight this thing. Kanth inhaled, building his stores in his gullet for his breath, and beat his powerful wings, lifting into the air and flying to meet this creature.

Dar'Krist had been walking for days when he saw the dragon. He was momentarily stunned by its size, as most dragons he had known were much smaller. He stopped and used his *sight* to get a better look at it, surprised once more by the deep color of its scales. Another hundred or so years and the scales would darken to almost black, which was the oldest these things ever got. He started walking slower this time, to judge what this thing was going to do. He wanted to give it time to *really* think about its choices. Another fifty feet and he had his answer. The dragon started beating its massive wings and came gliding through the air towards him.

Well, thank the Dark One I fed my cloak last night. Wouldn't want it to spoil my fun, he thought as he started into a loping run. He was stepping from one rock to another, leaping ever upwards as he gained altitude as fast as he could. He could keep this up as long as there were rocks to hold him, but he had to move fast; he knew what was coming. The dragon took to the sky and banked around impossibly quick, turning on the currents it knew so well. This high up, the wind was strong off the other peaks, and the dragon soared down towards him, intent on its prey and roaring its challenge.

Dar'Krist ran right at him. As soon as the dragon spread his wings to slow its advance, drawing in a great breath, Dar'Krist jumped once, twice, then surged off the last step with all his strength, cracking the stone beneath him. He soared up beneath the dragon's head and grabbed the dangling claw, holding on tight. He smiled as the fire he knew was coming burned below. Now it was an even fight. It would take the dragon a couple of moments to build his stores back up for another blast, and he was hoping the fight would be over by then. He waited for the dragon to realize that he wasn't down there anymore, then flared his power in a burst that would've killed any normal being. Hells below, it probably would've killed ten. It took a bit out of him to throw that much power out, but this *was* a dragon, and he wasn't taking any chances. The dragon shuddered and started to descend, and Dar'Krist looked for a good place to leap down.

Kanth felt the concussive force of death burst outward from the man, and it took all his fortitude to remain conscious. Even though he was resistant to most magic, this was something else altogether. He glided down, unable to find the strength to stay aloft, and finally caught sight of his foe. The being was seven feet tall with a long mane of black hair and robes that looked tattered. *Now I know which incarnation it is at least...and by all the gold in the mountain I am in trouble.* The dragon landed roughly, hopping around so he didn't lose sight of his opponent, and saw him roll to his feet after dropping from the dragon's leg. *Tooth and claw it is, then,* he thought as he prayed that his natural healing would get him airborne in enough time. Dragons healed a little faster than most beings, as they were one of the first beings. Still, that would take a little bit, and he may not have a little bit. That power the man had hit him with was devastating, and he could feel it eating it away at him even now.

The dragon lunged forward, claws grasping around the huge rocks that made up their battlefield. He was at home in this terrain and he thought that gave him the advantage. He swung his claw at the enemy and followed up with a bite that should've caught the man in his razor-sharp teeth. Both missed. He swept his tail around in case the man was behind him, and even buffeted his wings to throw his foe off balance. His neck twisted around to search for him, and he kicked out with his back leg, catching the man in the chest. The incarnation flew back into a rock wall, shattering it, then smiled at the dragon. Kanth spun to face his opponent, trying to keep the growing fear out of his stance, but something must've betrayed him because the man stood slowly and flexed his arms, mocking the great dragon.

"Well, well. It seems that there is still some fight in you after all. I was afraid that my power would've ended the contest before it began in earnest." Dar'Krist said, shifting his feet just a bit. He leaned upon a rock casually, examining his nails as if bored. "You realize this fight can only end one of two ways—" he started to say, but had to leap sideways as the dragon lunged and tried to catch him in his gaping mouth once more. The dragon only hit rocks, pulling his head back in time to catch a glancing blow on the snout by Dar'Krist. The incarnation laughed aloud as he danced from boulder to boulder, looking for an opening. "One way is with your rotting carcass draping the mountainside, your great life ended prematurely." He rolled over a small ledge and came up under the great beast's chest with a powerful uppercut that should've done absolutely nothing, but with his power behind it staggered the dragon.

Masking his pain, Kanth beat his massive wings, throwing up a small dust storm and used the burst to lift him up onto a higher ledge. "And what of the other way, oh powerful lord?" he spoke, his mighty voice echoing off the rocks and caves. "Does it end with me slaying you and throwing your body from the highest peak?" He swiped again and caught the man in the arm, spinning him into a wall face first. Kanth was surprised to hear laughter after that strike.

"No, foolish beast, the other way is with you fleeing this fight and feeling your life ebb away anyways; it will just take longer." The being licked blood from his lips and shook his hair out, staring at the huge dragon. He showed no fear in his cold, empty eyes.

Kanth backed up a little, gaining room for his swishing tail, then came in with a claw. As the man rolled under it, closer to the dragon's torso, Kanth beat his wings to lift him up momentarily and swiped. This too met with only air. Now it was the dragon's turn to smile. He saw the man roll backwards, leaping up to his feet just in time to take the tail full in the chest. The dragon heard bones snap under the impact, and the rag doll that was his opponent was flung up onto an overhanging cliff. Kanth landed softly, taking a deep breath into his shuddering lungs. He was not without his own power, but it was taking all that his healing could do to resist this growing rot coursing through his scales. He felt a surge then, in the very rock bed around him, and his concern grew as he considered what it may mean. He flexed his wings again, testing them, and was not pleased by the weakness still there.

Dar'Krist should've seen that tail coming. His ribs were telling him so, very loudly for the past twenty seconds or so, and his sternum wasn't even speaking to him. He rolled over, biting down at the pain that flared up. Usually, Dar'Krist would be angry, but this fight was just what he needed to take his mind off of the long walk home and how angry he was with that elfling boy and that cursed bard. Let the beast think he was down; it would be his last mistake. He closed his eyes and pulled power from the rocks underneath him, seeking that deep essence that rests within old foundations. Deeper and deeper he pulled, gathering it into himself, then he sat up as his bones began to knit together. He heard the flapping of great wings and saw the dust kick up, so he rolled painfully into a somersault. When the dragons head crested the cliff edge, Dar'Krist lashed out with a powerful two-fisted blow to its head.

Kanth's world exploded. The blow felt like the mountain itself had come down on him. He tried to roll with the hit by whipping his head with the force and following with his whole body, but it still blurred his vision and sent waves of corruption straight into his face. The dragon roared, albeit weakly, and landed over one-hundred feet away. He cursed the incarnation under his ragged breath. The man was right; he had to flee and hope his own power was enough to hold off the destruction eating away at his very soul. He heard the man chuckling behind him, up on the cliff. When Kanth turned his badly bruised head towards him, he saw that this powerful being was standing straight—showing no signs of pain.

Dar'Krist smiled. "Well, that was a good fight, but I'm in a hurry and this has taken long enough. I'm truly sorry to slay such a magnificent beast, but you can't be trusted not to come after me and delay me further." The incarnation's cloak fluttered in the breeze as he hopped down onto a boulder mere feet away from the dragon's tail. The great dragon gathered himself up and collapsed once more in a shudder, and Dar'Krist thought it was over. When the beast's leg shot out and rammed the cliff behind him, he was truly surprised.

Kanth saw his only recourse. This wouldn't be victory, oh no. This would be survival only, and that was if his wings would hold him aloft long enough. As the man jumped down, and Kanth made like he was struggling to get up. As his body fell again, he gathered his strength and lashed out at the cliff behind the figure with everything he had left. The rock shuddered and came raining down on top of his foe, burying him under the entire cliff side. As the dust settled, Kanth felt that familiar surge deep inside of his gullet. His flame was almost ready. He may have a shot at escape after all.

He scraped himself up onto all fours and dragged his bulk over the rocks and jagged edges of the mountain to the large ledge overlooking the valley. One of the secrets of dragon kind was that they were immune to their own breath. This is one of the reasons they are very hard to kill, as they can use it to boost their already fast healing to regenerate wounds. As Kanth raised himself up on the ledge, he breathed deep and expended the fire inside his throat and lungs, breathing it in instead of out. Leaping from the ledge and spreading his weakened wings, he soared down, trying to catch an updraft, feeling his fire battling the rot spreading within him. Kanth's body was ravaged, as he had taken quite a beating. Though he only got hit a couple of times, they were solid blows, and each had a devastating power behind them. Kanth started to feel a little better, but just when he thought he was going to be fine, the fire went out. He pumped his wings, climbing higher and higher, knowing this was his only chance. He had to get high enough so that when his wings wouldn't support him, he could glide down to safety somewhere, preferably near the elves.

Oh sure, the elves would be furious with him, and probably come at him faster than he could explain himself. But of all the races, only they had a chance at stopping the monster that did this to him. As he crested the cloud cover and saw the bright rays of sun, he saw how far the forest of the elves was from him and his heart sank. He closed his eyes as he felt the strength finally run out of his wings; it was too far away. Well, he would give it his best shot and try to get as close as he could. His fire wouldn't be ready now for a couple of minutes—it got longer and longer between times the more he used it—but he would fight until he couldn't anymore. As he sank back under the clouds, gliding and aiming for the mountains near the elves, he felt his eyes start to blur. Fantastic, now his sight was going too. He offered a silent prayer to whatever god would hear him and fixed where he wanted to land in his mind before his vision faded. This had not been his best day ever, and it didn't look like there would be many more days to compare it to.

Somewhere over the Northern Belt

Rhoe saw the land below him as if he were flying, the rows of mountains flashing by beneath him quickly. He had done something like this before, but at least this time he knew it wasn't merely a dream; he was here in spirit. But why? Karsis said that he had *tranced* before, and if he remembered rightly, this could be what that was. The training he had received on the way down the Northern Run road was mostly a blur, but he was sure that was what the bard had called it. Yet, he was sure that Karsis had said that only powerful wizards did this—which made him feel like throwing up, if he could even do that in spirit form. He decided to not think about it and concentrate on what was going on around him.

The mountains blurred together and then he started to slow down again. Remembering the last time that he had done this, he tried to think of how he could remain hidden, but he wasn't sure how to do that. He did not want to draw unwanted attention from whatever he was going to find way up here. He focused on himself, finding his center, and pulled everything else inward. He felt a calm wash over him and as he looked down at his "body," and saw that he was almost transparent, his grey robes seeming translucent. The young warrior also noticed that he was fully healed. *Didn't I get mangled by that wolvren? What if I'm dead?* He decided that this was another thing he didn't want to think about and looked around at what was coming towards him: a great beast with wings and deep red scales. *A dragon... great. First faeries, now this. I should've stayed lost in thought.* The dragon was fighting something, and when he felt a familiar concussive power he went cold with dread; the great beast was fighting the incarnation of death. Rhoe glided down, trying to stay high enough so that he was out of the incarnation's senses, but still observing the fight. Rhoe had to be here for a reason, he just didn't know what that could be.

The battle raged this way and that, and Rhoe finally felt the powerful man draw power from deep within the rock itself. *I wonder if I can do that? If I remember this, I'll have to ask Karsis.* The dragon came up and the hit that was landed upon his scaly head was enough that Rhoe felt it way up here. He watched the beast lay there and felt a pang of sadness for the magnificent creature. He hated that he had to watch this evil thing destroy more lives while he floated here, powerless, but before Rhoe could make any rash decisions the dragon kicked out.

The cliff face was smashed and the whole thing raining down on top of the incarnation, burying him in tons of rubble. Rhoe stifled a shout of victory, and wasn't sure why his form still hovered here. He had assumed that with the incarnation beaten, he would automatically be pulled away, but so far nothing felt different. The dragon flew off towards the Snow-peak mountains and Rhoe made another mental note to let Karsis know about this as well. Before he could get too deep in his thoughts, his form pulled back, stretching out impossibly thin as he was whisked back to his own body. The countryside was a blur and his head was spinning. *Why did I see that, and will I remember it all?* That was all he had time to think before he was back in the cold comforting darkness that was within himself.

Boarder Road, North of Alrin

THE WOMAN STOOD at the crossroads and looked to the west. Down that road lay Keragan Hold, and to the north, Everknight. She had received the note to travel to the castle with haste, but surly she wasn't supposed to wear herself out doing so? She was beautiful and she knew it, with long, brown hair tied up in twin ponytails and piercing green eyes. She was small and thin, cresting a little over five feet, and weighing only eight stones. Her harp was slung on her back, and her clothes were cut to show more skin than fabric. She looked exactly like what she was: a bard. "Well, I'm going to rest up and have a drink or six, and damned that note." She flinched inwardly as she waited for a lightning bolt to strike her down. When none came, she smiled and thanked Ollian, goddess of love and beauty, for allowing her to have her way.

Thunder rumbled in the distance. She chuckled aloud, "I know, I know. I'll shut up and get some rest, then It's straight there. I promise." She turned on her heel, spinning seductively for absolutely no one but herself, and started the walk to Keragan Hold. The hold was one of three across Lythinall, all run by former members of that famed group: The Companions of Everknight. They were meant to be bastions of defense against threats faced by the capitol city of Everknight, but Keragan Hold had the worst of it. Situated near the border of G'harr, they were under constant lookout for spies and sorcerers that meant the people of Lythinall harm. That being said, the garrison of Keragan Hold really knew how to drink and have a good time when they were off duty, and that was just the type of evening she had in mind.

"Then, I'll make my way north." she said convincingly, and she knew that only meeting the legendary bard Karsis could keep her from her destination. She had seen a good many years and had never met the famed hero. If she finally got the chance to meet that man, not even a goddess would stop her. As walked down the packed earthen road, her hair suddenly stood up on the back of her neck. She slowed, but didn't stop, and started singing a merry tune. She swung her head back and forth with the song and noticed dark forms in the high grass watching her. She didn't get a good look at them, but if they were hiding, they were up to no good. She absently fingered the sword that rested on her slender hip even though she didn't really need it. Instead, she pulled a thin dagger out and spun quickly, launching it at the side of the road near where they were hiding. This was meant to startle them into revealing themselves. It was an old trick, and one she had used for many years, but she got a different reaction all together. The three large rats scurried away through the high grass and were gone in a blink. She let out a breath that she was holding, then looked around again. *Why would they all be on one side of the road?* Something didn't feel right. It was then that she heard a crackling sound behind her, like bones breaking.

The rat that came onto the road was transforming rapidly from animal to small, wiry man. He was formed in seconds, with a blade out at the ready, smiling a toothy grin and naked as the day was long. "Well, missy, you scared away my little friends."

"Janna, not Missy." she interrupted casually.

"What?"

"I said: Janna, not Missy. You called me Missy, and if you're looking for her, I can inquire along my way as to her whereabouts." She moved forward quickly, keeping her hand off her sword, but always ready to reach for it. "You must be so worried about her. Look, I know a guy at the hold up ahead, he will help us find this poor lost Missy, whoever she is."

"No... wait. But..." He was flabbergasted at her prattling as he tried to make sense of what was going on.

"It's all right, I'm sure you're overwhelmed with despair. Here, allow me." Janna picked up a small piece of rock and started to inspect it, and the man leaned in to see what she had found.

"What is—" That was all he had time for as the woman whispered soft words and touched his arm with the rock. "Crap," he said as his eyes grew wide with realization of what was happening.

"Crap indeed, my lycanthropic friend. You decided to abscond with the valuables, and possibly life, of the great Janna Suris." She ended this in a flourish, still keeping her distance. After all, that spell took a minute or two to finish and take hold.

"Who?" He shook his arm, likely trying to work the numbness that was spreading up it. He couldn't be hurt by most weapons, but magic was another story all together. All he had wanted to do was rob her, and possibly have his way with her. Now here he was, naked and trembling and wondering where the hell Missy went, whoever that was. The man was not very bright for a wererat.

"You have not heard of me?" Janna was hurt. Hurt and stunned all at the same time. How had her name not spread this far? "Well, no matter. You won't be around to pass it on anyway." She had played with him long enough. Fast talking was her specialty—it kept adversaries off balance—and now she had him right where she wanted: helpless. Janna whispered a plea for the earth to speed up its process, and watched the look of horror spread across the wererat's face as his flesh slowly morphed into stone. He tried to turn and run, but he only got three steps before he stopped in his tracks, a complete statue. Satisfied that he was dead, she pushed him over and watched as he crashed to the ground and broke into pieces. She shrugged and turned back the way she was going. Janna walked towards Keragan Hold once more, singing a merry tune as she sauntered down the road, and knew that this was going to be a very entertaining night.

❦ 2 ❦

TOGETHER AT LAST

The morning light came through the lazily drawn curtains. It touched the woman's feet as she nodded off once more in her chair next to the bed. Karsis smiled knowingly at his old companion and remembered the good old days when they would ride together. She was naive then, thinking the whole world was good and just. Boy, the times they had laughed at *that* over the years. Lady Caerlyn was not pretty—she was radiant. Her long, flowing blond hair was braided down her back with golden ribbon intertwined, and deep emerald eyes that could see your faults just so she could forgive them. She was short, only barely cresting five feet, and weighed all of seven stones soaking wet... while holding a bag of marbles.

She was attired simply, in a long white dress adorned only with a gold belt, and her delicate feet stuck out of her sandals. At her modest thirty some odd years, some found it utterly amazing she hadn't found anyone special in her life. It didn't amaze Karsis; he knew why: her god hadn't told her she could yet. He chuckled at his own wit and shook his auburn curls out as the sun came further into the room. Karsis turned his gaze over to his young charge, healing in the bed, and his smile faded away. Rhoe was gravely injured, and it was all Caerlyn and he could do to keep the boy in one piece these past five days. The bard sighed and crossed his other leg as he leaned back in his chair, his burgundy longcoat swishing in the quiet of the room. That was one hell of a fight they had, by princess Allissana's own words.

Karsis had grilled Allissana for three days about the events that had occurred after she fell into the river with Rhoe. She probably thought he was angry, but he was impressed by her ability to recall details. She got that from her father. What worried him the most was the attack when they came out of the Misty Woods. He had known it was a wolvren chasing them, but he didn't think they would actually have to fight it. The thing should've run after taking a good hit or two, unless it was starving; and by the carcass he had found when he saw the tracks, it shouldn't have been.

Caerlyn stirred. "Mmm, is it time to check his bandages again?" The soft voice came from tired lips. Caerlyn hadn't done that much healing on one individual in a very long time. Thank Davalar that Karsis was here; he was always a good steady hand and center for her. Too bad he was as mad as a purple squirrel sometimes.

Karsis yawned, shaking out his arms and standing. "No, dear, he's all right for now. It's morning though, so maybe you can finally eat?" Gone was the sarcastic quips that Karsis usually heaped upon anyone near him. With Caerlyn, he was polite, and it irritated some of his old companions to no end. It wasn't because he wanted to seduce her, like Tanan thought. Or because he was secretly religious, like Arian assumed. No, it was because she was pure. That's all, just pure. That quality was so rare nowadays, that when one found a soul as clear and pure as hers, you showed it the respect it deserves—even from him. "You said he was almost out of the woods last time we checked an hour ago. You've been nodding off ever since."

Caerlyn slapped his arm playfully at this last part, smiling pleasantly as always. "I didn't nod off; I was recharging my spiritual energy." She giggled at this witty repose and broke into full on laughter as she watched him roll his eyes. She calmed down a bit and looked around the room. "Where's the young princess?"

Karsis smiled once more at her mention. *Oh, how the princess looks like her mother, and carrying that sword makes it even harder to tell them apart. If it weren't for the hair...* he thought as he looked out the window. "She took a walk to clear her head. I told her the sunrise would help, and I was only partly lying." She had sat here and worried for days, loudly, and he needed the peace and quiet for a bit. *Besides, it's not like she needed to heal.* She didn't have a mark on her. He had talked to the healer that found them outside of the city, as they were leaving with the King's Marshal, the man was astounded that she was fine; she had looked pretty bad when they arrived. Of course, the man chalked that up to things like the boy's blood all over her, or that it wasn't that bad, but Karsis knew better. He had seen the ring she was wearing, and having seen that on her father for years, knew *exactly* why she was fine. It seemed fitting, since he had found Tanan's ring hooked onto Rhoe's rope belt as well. He could handle prophesy, but this was going a bit too far for his liking.

"Will she be all right out in town alone?" Caerlyn asked.

"Seriously?"

"What?"

"Caerlyn, sometimes I really miss the conversations I can have with you. It brightens my day. Yes, she should be fine. She's a canny fighter, from what I saw; and if she has Deathsong, then anyone will hear if she is in trouble." He had a momentary flicker of concern though, remembering that sometimes Caerlyn *saw* things that others didn't. It wasn't the same as the elven wizard's *sight*, more flashes from her god—Davalar the Protector.

It was Caerlyn's turn to roll her eyes. "Anyway, he should be awake by high sun the latest, then we can get him to my hold, and I can *really* check him over." She hadn't gotten out of her hold much and she was going to savor the ride home, especially since the travel here was so fast and fraught with worry. "You could sing your songs on the trip, to keep me awake." She smiled at the bard and sat forward to check on Rhoe's breathing.

Karsis laughed. Caerlyn was always the one that wanted him to sing. He sat back down, stretched his legs over the side of the chair and pulled a lute out of his inner pocket, the instrument seeming too large for where it had been concealed. He played softly and sang in almost a whisper, just to pass the time. He dismissed the faint thoughts of her vision. After all, if she *saw* something, then she would've said something. Thank the gods they were almost in the clear. Five more days and they would be in Everknight again, then the planning could start.

The Trade Way, River Vale

ALLISSANA WALKED the packed earthen street, called the Trade Way, in the early morning bustle of the city. It was called this because it was twice as wide as the other roads in this city and accommodated some of the larger wagons coming off of the water. River Vale made its living by boat, and if you weren't up at the crack of dawn you lost out on the early morning ferry. She walked slowly, lost in thought, and the people walked by her in a hurry, with a nod here or a 'Morning lass' there. No one recognized her, partly because they had no time to try, and partially because she still looked a mess. Her clothes were torn, and there was blood all over her. Her long, golden hair was dirty, and her copper eyes were glazed. Her father's magical ring may help heal her wounds, but it didn't clean up the aftereffects at all. As she went, she absently scrubbed at some of the blood on her sleeve, worrying about Rhoe. She never had anyone risk their life for her before. *Well, to be fair, I haven't done a whole lot of anything outside of the castle before this,* she thought. It had been five days since the King's Marshal had brought them here. He had gone back out right away to make sure there were no more wolvren lurking, and it was an hour or so later that Karsis came strolling through the gate.

She couldn't believe her eyes. Karsis the Bard: legendary rogue, warrior, and general hero of the downtrodden. His name had spanned centuries, his deeds the stuff of legend. His auburn curls were as recognizable as his one-of-a-kind burgundy long-coat. He had played for kings, slain tyrants, even won the heart of an ancient dragon. His exploits with the Companions of Everknight were what she grew up on. Then she remembered that her parents travelled with him, and it was all she could do not to babble. He was kind, almost parental, but he was all business. He needed to know what they had done, what had happened, and especially the fight with the wolvren. He talked with her for three days, off and on, while he was helping Lady Caerlyn with Rhoe. Liss was pretty sure he was angry with her, but Caerlyn had told her later that he was just worried about the young boy.

She hadn't seen Lady Caerlyn in over a year, but she was just the same as she remembered. Saintly. Liss looked up from her daze and saw how far she had come in her reflection. She was nearing the merchants' quarter when she heard a noise from the nearby alley. She stopped to see what it was, knowing that this was probably a *very* bad idea, but doing it anyway. The sound was curious—not a whisper exactly, but like a whistle.

She entered the alley and saw only piles of clothes and refuse; then she heard it again. Wary of what could be hiding in the garbage strewn alley and remembering the chance encounter with the gnome at the hunting lodge, she pulled out Deathsong. The sword seemed dormant, as it was dead quiet coming out of the sheath.

"You won't need that, lass. The only weapon I have is a dirty rag, and I'm not very good with it at all." The muffled voice came from a larger pile of rags, and she stepped back as the whole pile seemed to rise.

"Slowly there. I've had a bad couple of days, and my trust level is low enough to live in this alley." She spread her feet apart a bit and switched her stance so that the way out was a quick roll.

"Don't worry, I'll stay back here if you want." The figure seemed to shrug and most of the pile of filth rolled onto the floor. It was a man, and as he straightened his back he rose above her and flexed his shoulders. He was about six feet tall, but whip lean, and his black hair was long and tangled. The thin rags he wore seemed to still be in good condition despite being under all that other ruined clothing. His hands were open and his arms out wide as if to show her he had no weapons. "Why have you come in here? Were you looking for somewhere to sleep?"

Liss hid her disgust with the practiced face her mother taught her to use with the lords and ladies at the castle, impassive and neutral. But her nose twitched at the smell involuntarily. "No. I thought I heard something, just a faint something on the wind."

"Ah, that was my whistling, sorry. I sometimes do that to lull myself back to sleep when I wake up too early." He shuffled backwards, stepped over the large pile, and picked up bits of the refuse once more, donning the rag-tag scraps like a mighty wizard's robes in the stories.

Except no wizard I ever read about in my children's books smelled like this! she chuckled at the thought and drew a curious glance from the man. Feeling like she should at least offer some help, she searched her pockets for anything she may have, and came up dry.

"Listen, I don't need any handouts from nobles."

"No, I know, I..." She was caught off guard. How did he know she was of noble stock? Did it show that much? She didn't want to offend him, but she didn't want to seem like some of the nobles that he was referring to. "My name is Liss. What's yours?" She stepped deeper into the alley and sheathed her sword as a gesture of sincerity.

"Heh, okay, I'll play. My name is Graf." He curtsied a little as he said this, mocking her. "Sorry the place is such a mess, *milady*. The maid was fired yesterday." He laughed, then sputtered as he saw her face. He took a step towards her as she turned on her heel and stormed for the street. "Wait, don't... I'm sorry, that was wrong of me."

Liss stopped and waited, not turning around. With everything else, this was not something she needed right now. She was furious and should be getting back to Rhoe. Then she noticed the man across the street, and her hair stood up on the back of her neck. He was just standing there, pointing a crossbow at her with a deadly smile, and she saw it recoil as he fired. Her mother's leathers wouldn't stop a bolt going that fast; she was in trouble. She tried to throw herself out of the way, but strong hands grabbed her and covered her in something that reeked of wine and urine.

Graf threw rags on top of her to deflect the bolt. "Hold on Liss. It might smell, but you'll be alive." He was trying not to laugh as he threw the rags on top of her to deflect the bolt. It struck the massive pile of clothes and stuck there, hanging limp. He saw the man scowl and draw a sword. It seemed like he was signaling to someone else, or maybe a bunch of somebodies. They were smart, they had a backup plan. He would've had one if he was doing this, wouldn't he? Sometimes it was hard to remember. Graf pulled the rags back off her, letting them fall to the ground, and tugged her towards the back of the alley. "This way! We're going to have company very soon."

"Wait, who…?" She looked down as he led her back and saw the crossbow bolt sticking out of the bunch of rags on the ground. They were so thick and layered that it just buried itself in them harmlessly. Then she saw the man coming and the others falling in beside him. There were two—wait, no, three men, all dressed in dark clothing and cloaks. *You think someone would've noticed them dressed like this, firing crossbows into alley's at strange women.* Her thoughts whirled as she looked about at her terrain. The alley was only ten feet wide, and the clutter was going to impede her footing if she had to sidestep their blades. She pulled Deathsong once more and the blade rang with a clarion call. When she fought the wolvren it had howled. *If I live through this, I'm going to have to speak with mother about this sword.* The men spread out as much as they could coming down the alley, but the debris was impeding them as well. She looked back as Graf's hands came off her shoulders, and suddenly he wasn't there anymore.

"Your filthy friend isn't here to help you, princess. Now we can finish this." The others started to try and circle around and she saw one start to trip on a pile of rags. Knowing an opening when she saw one, she lunged at the assailant on the other side while keeping her feet set for a retreat once the man talking saw his chance. She was counting on that. She only grazed the man she went after, but her ploy worked. The other man came at her hurriedly, thinking she would be off balance, and Liss sent Deathsong back across in a wide arc, splitting his leathers and slicing into his chest. He cried out and fell back, clutching his wound, letting the others have a chance at the cornered princess. If it wasn't for the many years of Carana's lessons, Liss would be dead already. She just lacked the experience of almost dying that most others had. *Well, not anymore,* she thought as she parried a dagger thrust and kicked another man between his legs after feinting with a slash. That's when she noticed that there were only two men on her.

Liss didn't have the time to look around for the other assailant—the two in front of her were enough, especially since she kept stumbling over the refuse around them. The good news was that they were too. One such mistake was made by the man favoring his precious manhood after receiving a dainty kick. He stumbled forward, almost dropping his dagger, then Deathsong punched in his chest and out his back in a violent burst as Liss put everything into her frustrated lunge.

"Damn," she muttered as she realized her mistake. She could almost feel Carana slap her with the practice sword and hear her yell that she shouldn't put everything into a lunge when there were more opponents left. She let go of her sword— another scolding she always got—and rolled into a pile of rags, kicking out at where the other man might be. She was rewarded with a yelp of pain as she connected with his knee, then she heard a muffled gurgle. *Well, that's new.* She jumped up and saw Graf behind another man, with rags wrapped around the man's throat and a blade into his ribs. She backed away, grabbing her sword and pulling it out of the dead man.

"I know, I lied," he started, letting the body fall at her feet, conveniently between them. He wiped the thin blade off on the rags, then it was gone, without her even seeing that he sheathed it somehow. "I really do know how to use these rags." He stepped back once more, open arms and a wide smile. "But believe me, I really don't mean *you* any harm."

She couldn't help but laugh. She had cheated death again and felt exhilarated. She thought that the man must be some sort of retired adventurer, with his skill, but it was the way he had said that. *You.* She was about to start her eternal question tirade, but when she sheathed Deathsong and looked up, he was gone. Shaking her head, she rushed back to Rhoe and to tell Karsis that they weren't alone, not that she was worried about the bard.

Graf watched her go from the shadows. No one saw him if he didn't want to be seen, he was just that good. He waited until she was well out of earshot and sighed deeply. The voice had told him to protect her, and he never ignored the voice; well, almost never. "This is going to get me in trouble, isn't it?" he muttered to the voice in his head that refused to answer him. It never answered his queries, just whispered sweetly when it wanted him to do things, and that was few and far between as it was. "Fine. I haven't lived this long by ignoring you. I may be a fool, but I'm not crazy." He laughed at that, quietly though, from inside of his filthy rags. If anyone saw him talking to a voice inside his head, they would call him crazy, and they would only be half wrong. He hadn't been stable since that year in G'harr when they caught him trying to free that girl. He had gotten away, but not until they broke something in his mind. He sighed heavily. The voice had told him to protect the princess and get her across the river to Everknight, and he would; but he wasn't going to like it.

Someone else watched the princess exit the alley. He sat atop the building directly across from it and frowned at the utter loss she dealt his trained assassins. True, he didn't count on a homeless man saving her, but they still should've had the upper hand since his magic hid their weapons from lesser minds. He was dressed in all black and had the southern style cloak that could be pulled up to hide his face, without covering his head. His short, blond hair blew in the spring breeze and his black cloak billowed as he turned away. He was already thinking of how to ambush them before they reached Caerlyn Hold—he just had to be careful of Karsis. If the rumors were true about the bard consorting with demons, then he would have to be careful indeed.

Healer's House, River Vale

RHOE SLOWLY CAME to consciousness to the sound of light music floating in the air. A strange voice accompanied the sound in a lilting tone that sounded almost magical. At first, he thought he was still with the faeries. But then his memories slowly unfolded in his mind like blowing the dust off an ancient book. He sat up quickly as he remembered the flight over the mountains, the incarnation, and Liss—then immediately regretted that decision as the room decided that it didn't want to stay still for him until he laid back down, which he promptly did. "Whe — Where is... Liss?" he asked, shutting his eyes and trying to center himself, to no avail.

"Ah, he awakens at last. Do take it easy young one; magical healing is great, but it can leave the body extremely weak," Karsis admonished as he stopped playing his lute. He chuckled as Caerlyn kept singing a bit longer, caught off guard by the sudden absence of music. "Caerlyn, do you have that cranroot tea I asked for last night?"

"Yes, Karsis. I do know how to tend to patients you know," she retorted, her normally light voice edged with a bit of sarcasm; but her smile said that she knew he was not questioning her expertise. She giggled as he frowned in worry at his own question. "I know how cranroot affects wizards," she said. "In fact, you would be amazed at what I know about. I've read almost every book known to man, and three more after that."

"I didn't mean—"

"Oh, how fun it is to tease the mighty bard Karsis," Caerlyn laughed as she brought up the hide skin full of the tea. She helped Rhoe sit up and drink the tea, and watched his eyes as they tried to focus on her hands as she helped him. His pupils came into sync and his hands weren't shaking anymore. Good. *It was bad for a while, and there was no way I was going to tell Karsis how close it really was. If he wasn't here to help me....* She had ridden through the night and almost killed the two horses she brought, once she received the message from the courier that came with Allissana's message. Karsis had arrived and was stabilizing the boy with his magic, but the boy was slipping. That was the longest five days of her life. She would never have been able to look Tierra in the face again if she had failed. She closed her eyes and pushed the dark thought away for the moment.

"We're glad that you are awake dear one." She couldn't believe that this was the child she had delivered all those years ago. He was fit and toned for his age, but his robes hid most of the muscle. It was his white hair that she remembered most, he had come out of the womb with a tussle of it, and everything she had checked for was normal. Now it was well past his waist.

Karsis let her have her fun. Caerlyn was not someone he messed with. He focused his *sight* on Rhoe as he drank the cranroot tea and was relieved that his magical aura was settling back down. That much magical healing had not only left him weak, it had tangled his own magic and knotted it up good. The cranroot would help it to unweave and straighten out by itself in a couple of hours. The only thing was that he had to be conscious for it to work, otherwise it may kill him.

Karsis heard the sound of running feet, leapt up, spun around, and had his sword out and as he slid in front of Caerlyn and her patient. He relaxed as he saw the princess skidding to a halt just inside the door.

"He's awake!" Liss shouted as she started towards Rhoe, but Karsis stopped her with one hand as he put his sword away with a flourish.

"Focus, princess. You didn't come running in here because he was awake. What's wrong?" He knew he should've listened to Caerlyn's *sight*.

Liss took a deep breath and looked the bard right in the eye, then regretted that instantly. He had the eyes that said he had seen it all, and laughed even then. She gulped and started her story, remembering that he wasn't angry with her—just worried. *Well, can he be worried towards someone else now please?* She clamped down on her thoughts and retold the morning's events.

Karsis listened, never interrupting her, and when she was done, he patted her on the shoulder softly and walked by her into the street, scanning the horizon with keen interest. He had done the same after she had recounted their adventure. "Do you think we're in danger still?"

"Why yes, I do."

He continued to scan the horizon like he was looking for something. "And?"

"And what?"

Caerlyn chuckled behind them both remembering the many times the bard had done the same exact thing to Arian. *Where did the time go?* she thought. "Karsis, she wants to know what we're going to do now." She helped Rhoe lay back down after he finished the tea.

"Ah, then she should learn to use her words." Karsis turned with a flourish and winked at the frustrated princess as he walked back in the door. "We have to flee of course, right away, and without informing anyone."

"But we have to tell the duke. He is the only one here that knows who I am." Liss remembered making Aeric Savar, the king's marshal, swear on his oath to keep her a secret to all save Duke Brenscomb. She knew the duke. She was there when he was appointed to govern this city under her father, King Arian.

"No, dear girl, he's not. Further, I would bet fifty crowns that half, if not more, of his guards here were enemies of the throne," Karsis said as he mentally planned their route through the city to the southern gate, realizing there was no good way except to fight their way out.

"Wait, no... how do you know all this?" She was trying to regain control here, but Karsis was a whirlwind of chaos to her order. How did her father ever do this?

"One—you were attacked in the city, then ran all the way here with your weapon out. Even if you weren't the princess, there would be guards following you to find out what happened, as well as an inquiry into the bodies that you must've left behind." Before she could open her mouth, he spun around, letting his longcoat fly out momentarily diverting her attention. "Two—there are at least eight men on the surrounding rooftops watching us right now, probably reporting to the man that orchestrated this entire thing. No, don't go look, that would only make it worse." He sat down in the chair once more and started tapping his feet to a rhythm only he could here.

Liss was stunned. Stunned and extremely perturbed. "So, what's three?"

"What now?"

"Three? You said one. Then two—"

"Oh, I figured three would be a little too much for you, so I left it out," he said like it was a matter of fact.

Rhoe slowly got out of bed and stood up, trying not to laugh.

Mainly because he thought Liss would hit him for it, but also because he was pretty sure he would pass out if he did. "Karsis, I tranced again..." He wobbled and almost went down, but steadied himself and gained his balance. He found his center, closing his eyes, then straightened.

"Rhoe, focus on your memory now and lock it away. We need to flee, and there is no time to go over your journey right now, no matter how much it is killing me that you can do that without trying." Karsis never turned around while he said this, and it was eerie.

"All right, Karsis, but do they even know we're here?" Rhoe took two steps and felt faint again. *Must be that drink, I can feel something tingling all over my skin.*

Caerlyn rushed to his side, ever the healer, and guided him to another chair. "He can't run, Karsis. Hells below, he can't even walk fast. He would need another two, maybe three hours before he is strong enough to be able to try."

Karsis ignored her and focused on Rhoe. "Yes, they know, and they will expect us to flee out the south gate. But then, whoever is behind this will remember that *I* am here. He will assume that I will have a master plan to fool them into guarding the south gate so we can sneak out another one, and leave them chasing their tails. I *am* a genius, after all." Karsis smiled, sure of himself, but deep down knowing if they got this wrong he would have bodies to deliver to the castle instead of children.

Liss smiled, finally catching on. "So, what's your devious plan to lead them astray?" She was ready for anything, or so she thought.

"Nothing. That's the beauty of it. We go for the south gate, which will be guarded by a token force as a show of strength, while his main forces guard the other gates watching for us." He stood up with his hands out wide like he was giving a master speech and realized that only Caerlyn was clapping.

"That's your plan?!" Liss was too shocked to be outraged. They were going to die horribly, she just knew it.

"Actually, it sounds like the perfect plan for this situation. I'm in too."

The voice came from the window on the other side of Karsis. He spun, sword out, and lunged, whispering words of magic and the wind took the sword and sent it like a dart at where the man should be. The bard was already rolling backwards and coming up with hands spread out ready to cast again, when he saw the man holding the slender sword like he was bored.

"Graf?" Liss was shocked to see the homeless man again, and even more surprised to see that he wasn't even worried that someone had thrown a sword at him.

"Sorry, didn't mean to startle you. I figured since you were the great Karsis you would have wards up or something to warn you." Graf surveyed the room and saw the boy's feet move just a bit, ready to defend but not attack. *Well trained, and smart...not bad,* he thought as he tapped the sword against the window with his other hand up.

Karsis had that look on his face that said he could skin the man, and he might already planning what to do with said skin. "I did, that's why I attacked. Only a handful of people can bypass those wards, and I'm three of them. So, who are you, really, Graf?" He didn't like being caught off guard; it was bad for his reputation.

"For now, I'm someone who can help the boy get out of the city, and in one piece, while you three escape out the gate," Graf said, disappearing then coming in through the door a moment later, handing the slim, sharp sword to Karsis hilt first. He did it almost reverently, like he truly did respect the bard. "Besides, the voice in my head said I have to help her." He pointed to the princess without looking at her.

"Then why did you take off and leave me in that alley?" Liss wasn't angry, but her frustration had found an avenue that wouldn't get her a verbal lashing, and she took it. "What, you save me then run away?"

"Um...yes." He cleared his throat a bit and blocked the entire doorway, purposefully. "Now, may I suggest that we head towards the back where the men on the roof can't fully see us?"

Rhoe shook his head. *Great, two people like Karsis. Can the world even handle that without tearing apart?* He giggled a little at his own thoughts, and everyone looked at him, everyone but Karsis. The bard only smiled and shook his head as if to say 'No,' then sheathed his sword and guided the princess towards the back door. Caerlyn fussed over Rhoe some more, once again checking for a fever by holding her hand to his forehead as he walked. It was as if his mother was here. "So, where do the two of us go?" Rhoe asked the tall man dressed in rags. He wasn't sure he wanted to go with the man if he was going to end up smelling like that. He had clamped down on his memory of the journey he had taken, and was confident that when he needed it, he would remember.

"Well, we are going to head out with them, then duck down the alley by the alchemist's shop. While they keep going towards the south gate, you and I are going to take a secret route and meet them on the road near the old dry bridge."

"Ha! So *that's* your plan. Damn that *is* a good one, but is it still accessible after all these years?" Karsis hadn't been surprised like this in a long time—well except when Rhoe tried magic, that always surprised him; the kid was a natural.

Graf eyed him suspiciously. He thought he was the only one that knew about the ancient underground tunnels that the former alchemists used to dispose of their failed potions. They had dug it out all the way to the old tributary of the river and were eventually caught and charged with polluting the water over ninety years ago. It was sealed away and the water cleansed and diverted, but the old bridge still stood. Graf had found it decades ago and used it to get in and out of the city unnoticed. He shook his mangy hair out of his eyes and grinned. "Yes, it is. I use it all the time."

They checked the back door, and Caerlyn grabbed a bunch of cloaks to cover them with so they wouldn't be immediately spotted. Karsis scanned the rooftops and saw only two men. He focused his *sight* and zoomed in, getting a clear picture of them, then whispered to the winds to kick up a bit of the dirt and dust of the packed earthen street, obscuring their passage. He pushed the princess ahead of him, pulling Caerlyn behind him. "Go now, gentleman. And Rhoe, be careful." With that they were off, running down the street, hugging the buildings for what cover they could find.

Graf scooped up the young warrior and threw him over his shoulder without warning and sprinted for the alley just two buildings down. His rags covered his eyes enough so that he could see the mini dust storm and avoid it. In seconds he heard, more than saw, the arrows click and clack off the buildings beside them. Into the alley and all the way into the back he ran, until he got to the back fence. A huge pile of refuse was sitting there, and Graf, who was more afraid of that bard's wind than any arrow, dove right into it without hesitating. There was a ladder, but he knew it would take time to climb down with a body on his shoulder. This could hurt a bit.

3

FLIGHT

Rhoe couldn't see Karsis and the others, and he couldn't get air into his lungs to ask the wind to slow his fall. Rhoe realized, in this moment of weightlessness, that he rather hated falling. First, off a bridge with Liss, now this. The man that held him turned in mid-air, placing himself on the bottom of the impending collision with whatever lay at the bottom of this hole, and all Rhoe could do was tense up, ready for the impact. They hit rather hard, and Rhoe felt the air rush out of the man as they rolled down another pile of something that Rhoe refused to identify; it would only bother him if he knew anyway. He lay there for a minute, trying to get his bearings, which were still trying to catch up with him anyway. They were probably still coming down that long fall with his stomach.

"You in one piece, young one?" Graf asked as he rolled up to a knee trying to convince his lungs that he didn't hate them. The boy looked fine; a little queasy, but fine. The amount of control this young man had was astounding.

Rhoe tried to laugh but couldn't. "Yeah, I'll be fine. Breathing is a little disturbing right now, but I'm sure my nostrils will forgive me later." He stood up on shaky legs and did a few stretches to make sure he was stable, then looked around at where they were, and his jaw unhinged. The cavern was about fifteen feet in diameter, and was covered with a variety of flora, all vibrant colors and sizes. There was a slight trickle of water dripping a few feet away from them, feeding a small stream of water that ran away down the tunnel. It was almost mystical.

Graf chuckled. "Yeah, pretty cool, huh? Never ceases to amaze me, and I've been coming down here for years. It was caused when the old alchemists dumped all their failed concoctions down here. It created a bunch of bizarre plants, and every time the duke pays someone to get rid of them, they just came back, even with very little water and no light at all." Graf was walking now, motioning for Rhoe to follow. "Just don't eat anything and you'll be fine." Graf seemed to laugh at some private joke as they continued on out of River Vale, with no one the wiser. He had tried some of the plants years ago and had learned that lesson the hard way.

Up in the streets above, it went a little different. Liss, Caerlyn, and Karsis ran, then the arrows started. Thanking the sudden wind storm, and not knowing that Karsis had done it, Liss couldn't help but think that she had been running for her life ever since that fateful day in the council chamber when she smashed the chair down and took charge. She had decided to fight the ancient incarnation, and things had gone sideways ever since. "Karsis, was *this* three?"

Karsis dodged a flurry of arrows and threw Caerlyn down as another barrage came at them. He rolled over and saw Liss take one in the arm, spinning her around. There had to be more than two assailants now. "Actually...yes. This was three. *Now* do you see why I didn't tell you?" He got up and pulled Caerlyn to her feet, thinking that she was sobbing. He frantically searched her for a wound, then as they ran once more he realized she was laughing. "What is so funny?"

Caerlyn caught her breath and looked him straight in the eyes, stopping their run for just a moment. "The flight out of Terrafar." She whooped again and ran over to Liss, grabbed her arm and guided her down the road, ducking and dodging arrows once more. Terrafar. They had been on a mission to save Tanan, way back when she had first joined the Companions, and their escape had ended just like this; right down to Arian yelling at Karsis because the bard never told them they would have archers. It was one of those moments that she would never forget. Running for their very lives, and those two were arguing about who was in the wrong.

"Syll take me, you're right!" Karsis hadn't even realized the similarities until she had reminded him of that mission. "Oh, gods above, I had forgotten that." He ran after them, once again calling to the winds to try and deflect some of these arrows. "I was right, you know." He laughed as he ran, and they finally came flying around the corner towards the south exit, only to find a full contingent of guards and the duke waiting for them in front of the wide-open gate. *Oh great, how did things get worse when I never even said they couldn't get worse? That's how it always goes,* Karsis thought as he sighed, slowed to a walk beside the girls, and readied his breath for a hasty casting in case one of the guards got twitchy. At least with the duke here the arrows would stop.

"Hold, Allissana!" The duke called out. Duke Brenscomb used to be a warrior, but the years of sitting behind a desk had added some girth to his waist, and to his chubby face. He hadn't lifted a sword in spirit in over ten years, but he still carried one for show. "You have nowhere to go. If you surrender, your enemies will spare the folk of this town. I must think of the people, after all," he said with a sly tone to his voice.

"Duke, why are you doing this? I know you. You were always a good man, and trusted by my father." Liss was at a loss—this was the last person she would've thought wanted her dead. The king had always had good things to say about Brenscomb; what could've gone wrong?

While Liss had the duke's attention, Karsis used his *sight* to look past the duke and his forces, for any sign of Rhoe on the road ahead. His mind whirled at the surprise he saw out there. He needed to keep the duke busy for another minute or so. He whispered to the winds his plea of silence, then sent it out to what he *saw*. When he was sure it had worked, he refocused his *sight* back and eyed the duke as Liss finished her plea before he interjected. "Yes, good Duke, how much is the G'harran sorcerer paying you to detain the princess?"

The duke's face went red and he started to draw his sword, but the princess beat him to it. Despite the arrow sticking out of her arm, she drew Deathsong and its ringing, clarion call sounded across the entire city. "When my father hears of this, he will have your head, Duke—if the king's marshal doesn't take it off when he returns!" she yelled. The duke visibly blanched. Even some of the guards cringed, but they still stood their ground.

The duke took a deep breath and looked around at his men. "Marshal Savar won't be coming back, princess. I had my men follow his patrol and take care of them days ago. So, now you are outnumbered five to one at least, and one of you is only a priest." He thought he was clever, showing how he thought he had outmaneuvered them, but he was caught off guard by the next outburst.

"*Only* a priest?" Caerlyn all but screamed. "Only a *priest?*" She stepped forward and raised her hands, calling upon Davalar for one of the most powerful prayers she knew. She could only do this once, then she would have to wait for at least a tenday, but she needed it now. Her form shimmered and she was encased in a golden hue. She strode towards the duke, and Liss fell in step beside her, readying her sword.

Karsis chuckled and walked on her other side. Five to one odds, and the girls didn't even know about the surprise. This was going to be good. "Now you've done it, Duke. Lady Caerlyn may be a priest, but she was a Companion of Everknight." It looked like he didn't need to distract the duke as the girls had that under control. *Just a few more moments...*

The duke called for his men to attack, and they gave a cry as they advanced. Then there was blood. They attacked Caerlyn head on, and every sword that came down on her rebounded with a shrill cry, never touching her in the slightest. In fact, the guards were so close that when their swords rebounded, they often hit other guards, throwing them off balance, and even slicing into them on occasion.

Caerlyn's eyes never left Duke Brenscomb. Her normally meek smile was gone, replaced by a fierce grin that showed she could do what needed to be done when lives depended on it. Liss, on the other hand, seemed to be having more fun.

After facing trained G'harran assassins and the incarnation of death itself, a few city guards were unimpressive, even in these numbers. If she were alone, she would've been in severe trouble, but every time a guard came at her, she used the unbalanced guards trying to fight Caerlyn as cover, then ran both through with Deathsong. She laughed, but more guards were flanking them as they slowed in front of the duke. Then a guard came down on the arrow in her arm and broke it off. She screamed but realized that without the piece sticking out, she had more maneuverability. "Thank you!" she called out as she ran her sword across his neck and kicked. The duke's men had gathered in front of him as a shield against Caerlyn, and Liss slowed as they bunched up.

Karsis was having his share of fun as well, slashing and stabbing at any who came near him. Not one blade even came close to wounding him, and everyone that tried came away bloody. After the first few minutes, the odds were more balanced. In fact, there were only five guards left in front of the duke when Karsis saw the surprise enter the open gate at full speed. "Goodbye, dear Duke," Karsis called out over the yelling guards, grabbing Caerlyn. He kicked Liss hard in the side, sending her sprawling the other way, then leapt backwards holding onto Caerlyn.

The Duke frowned, thinking that some spell was coming for him, but then the lance burst through his chest, spraying his guards with his blood and throwing everyone aside as Aeric Savar, the king's marshal, came tearing through on his bloodied warhorse. The man was covered in a dozen wounds and drenched in blood. Only two other men came behind him, their stallions making absolutely no noise as they galloped around the guards, hacking and slashing with abandon. In seconds, the southern gate was quiet, and Aeric held his fist to his heart and bowed to Liss. "I'm sorry for my late entrance, princess. The duke thought to ambush us, and it took us a couple of days to get back here."

"How did you know we needed you here?" she asked.

Aeric and his men looked like they needed to lie down for a tenday, but they were still straight in their saddles. Liss nodded to Caerlyn, and the priest slowly let go of her protective aura and started to try and heal Aeric, but she looked drained.

"Well, when we were attacked, we kept one of the men alive to figure out who wanted us dead. He talked shortly after we started asking with our knives." Aeric waved Caerlyn away to one of his other men, then continued. "He talked about ambushing the princess at the southern gate, so I took only the men that could still ride and went around the city to catch them. Imagine our surprise when our horses stopped making noise halfway down the road." He looked at Karsis, knowing that he was probably the culprit, and nodded his thanks silently. "Then, Duke Brenscomb decided to be here in person. Well, that was the icing on the cake, and I do love cake." He let his head fall and added softly, "I lost seven men to that bastard, and two more might not make it here, even with the healer."

"I'm sorry, Aeric. They died in service to the king, and I will never forget that." Liss was angry now, and if what the duke said was even partially true, the people here were in danger. "Unfortunately, we have to leave immediately, and get to Caerlyn Hold." She sheathed her sword and surveyed the bodies. These men may have tried to kill her, but how many were just following orders?

"Then, give us a mere moment, princess, and we will be ready to ride." Aeric sounded tired, but resolute. He would die to protect the king's daughter, and he almost had.

"No, good marshal." Karsis intervened. "The city needs you now, more than the princess does. The duke said the people would suffer if the princess went free, and now they have no leader, and a much-lessened guard presence." He looked around at the dead and dying and shook his head; the guards never had a chance. *So, what was the sorcerer's goal here? What am I missing?* His thoughts spiraled away as he walked slowly towards Caerlyn. Then, he stopped dead. "Marshal Savar, we need those three horses, now!" Karsis's voice was ice, and his eyes were dark points of hate.

"What is it, Karsis?" Liss was afraid to ask, but it came out reflexively. She saw Caerlyn automatically take a horse from a wounded armsman and mounted without a second thought, like she trusted him completely.

Karsis, took the horse from the other man, just as Aeric dismounted in front of Liss. "The sorcerer knows about the old tunnels. This was to delay us, not detain us. He's going for Rhoe. We have to ride *now!*" He leapt up into the blood-stained saddle and kicked the horse around. He couldn't use the winds to speed up all three of them, it was too dangerous to control that many, going that fast, so they would just have to push these great beasts as much as they could. But he could make them quiet at least, so he whispered again as he rode to mask the sound of their hooves upon the road.

Liss vaulted into the saddle and turned the horse in one fluid motion, and with a last salute to the kings marshal she bolted out of the city after Karsis. *Hold on Rhoe, were coming!* her thoughts were spinning, she just wanted to get home to see her mother and father. They thundered down the road as fast as the horses could manage, making hardly any noise. "Is this you Karsis?" She looked over and saw his determined look and realized that he really *was* that dangerous; just like all the stories said. She didn't ask again.

MILES UP THE ROAD, a pile of broken branches in the dry riverbed moved aside, and two figures emerged. Graf came through first, testing the air like it could be poison. He held up his finger as if testing the wind, then nodded and motioned for the other figure to come out. Rhoe stepped out in his tattered, bloodstained grey robes and squinted at the sun rising in the sky. While the flora was beautiful, the tunnel had been dark and cramped, and he was glad to see the sky once more. "Is that the old dry bridge?" He asked, his throat dry and parched. He realized that they had walked in relative silence and didn't even know this man's name.

"Yes, now stay low." Graf snuck towards the bridge, using the dry riverbed as cover from anyone on the road, then he jumped with a start as the young boy was right next to him out of nowhere. *How did I not here this one coming? Is he that good?* his thoughts had been distracted, maybe that was it.

"By the way," Rhoe whispered, "my name is Rhoe. What's yours?" He was trying to be quiet, and didn't mean to startle the man, but he also wasn't sure why they were hiding, or from who. He still felt drained, but he could walk with ease now, and his thoughts were clearer than in the city. He still didn't dare try running just yet.

"Pleasure. Mine is Graf. Now shush, someone might hear you."

Graf looked up at the bridge and caught a glimpse of something that he had seen when they came out of the tunnel. He didn't want to scare the boy—what was his name? Rhoe?—but something was on the bridge, and he didn't think it was this kid's friends. He noticed some scrub under the bridge and leapt into it when he heard a man's voice up above them.

"Well, well. I was expecting the princess to be smuggled out by that old tunnel, not a young boy..." S'ren Dro, a southern sorcerer, stood tall upon the bridge, at least twenty-five feet above the riverbed. He was dressed in all black with a southern style cloak. His short, blond hair blew in the spring breeze. He scowled in annoyance that his plans had not gone as anticipated, but he loved to improvise. "I guess you will have to do, young one. You may have been a decoy, but I'll use you to slay the princess." He laughed as Rhoe crouched down, ready for a fight. "Oh, come now, little one. I'm just going to take over your mind, like I did to that irksome duke." He closed his eyes and felt the power come alive within him, its dark festering throb a reminder that it had grown around his heart. "Obren ethir mist dosit a'ren!" he said with fervor so the ether would respond quicker and cloud the young man's mind so that he could be controlled.

Rhoe knew what he was facing, even if he couldn't fully see him with the sun at the man's back. A sorcerer. He crouched, waiting for which element he was going to face, and was shocked when he heard the elven word for ether. *Oh crap, now I'm up a creek. Oh wait, I really am.* He pushed his thoughts aside and concentrated. He would have to fight ether, and there was only one way he could think of. "Ash'anti ethir, sran ea!" Rhoe called for the ether to shield him, and grinned when he heard the sharp gasp from the sorcerer. He rolled under the bridge then, trying to stay out of sight, and immediately regretted it. Walking was one thing, but this made him dizzy.

S'ren was dumbfounded. This young whelp knew how to call upon magic? Not only that, but he had countered it? Angrily, he gave in to his rage and decided to wipe the earth clean of this upstart. He would collapse the earth down around the boy, caving in both sides of this dry riverbed. "Obren dir frein dwoen!" He heard the earth obey as it started to shake, then heard the boy chanting as well.

Rhoe knew he was in trouble. Graf was nowhere to be seen, and he heard the sorcerer speaking again. Without waiting to hear what was coming, he limped out the other side of the riverbed and whispered to the air. "Ash'anti fra hadar ea ubel." He rose quickly, supported by the air itself, and grabbed the rail of the bridge as he canceled the spell and pulled himself over the side. He landed hard and stumbled as the man spun around and raised his hands, startled by the appearance of the young warrior.

"You!" S'ren spat out. The bridge was shaking as earth slid down the banks of the creek, so he cancelled his spell before the bridge went out and took him with it. He reached inside his coat and drew a black dagger from its stone sheath for the first time.

The stone had to be broken to liberate the cursed blade, and once freed it would hunger for a soul. He pulled that darkness from his heart and felt it pulse down his arms. He hadn't fought with weapons in a long time, but already it felt like an old friend.

Rhoe saw the dagger and was cautious, but not worried. He had fought the incarnation of death and corruption; what could one sorcerer do to him without magic. That's when he noticed that the blade was whispering... loudly. *This is just not my day.* He took a defensive stance, worried now about what that blade could do. *Come on legs, don't lose it now.*

⚜

Karsis had his *sight* out as far as he could while riding this fast, and it was giving him a headache. It was the bouncing. His *sight* was fine when running, because he could control his own balance. On a horse, he got dizzy as the horse bounced him about. Then suddenly, he *saw* them and his heart fell. "Caerlyn, get ready. The sorcerer has a Xalrin blade." She would know what to prepare in case Rhoe got cut by that blade—if there were anything to prepare. Gods knew it didn't go well the last time they encountered one.

"*No!*" Caerlyn screamed and started a prayer to Davalar. She hadn't done this astride a horse in decades, but her need outweighed her worry. She hadn't saved that boy to lose him now. She prayed for speed and swiftness, and then with a burst of light from the clouds above she was away. The wind flailed her hair and cloak as she moved faster than any bird could hope to fly, and probably any dragon as well. She held on with everything she had, but she would get there faster than the others. She had to. It felt surreal galloping that fast with no sound, but after a few minutes she saw the two people grow nearer through windswept tears. Then she saw the one with the long white hair forced back against the railing of the bridge. She could feel evil radiating from the blade. The sorcerer cocked his arm to throw it at the young warrior, and she knew in her heart what she had to do. Closing her eyes, she grabbed her small wooden shield and rode between them. The Xalrin blade was stopped with a dull thud.

Karsis saw the burst of light and knew she was going to try something stupid—brave and courageous, but stupid. The worst part was that she had left him out of it, and he loved those kinds of plans. He looked at the princess next to him, her mouth wide at everything happening at once and nodded to her. "Just keep going and meet us there." He tossed her the reins of his horse and closed his eyes.

He had never tried this moving quite so fast, but that was the best part of magic for him. The *'What can I do this time?'* feel of it. He spoke clearly and precisely. "Ash'anti ethir, sistren ea car'cen!" Asking the ether to bring you somewhere—in this case, 'there'—needed the *sight* to work in conjunction. It used the image you had formed in your mind when you asked, and if you didn't keep a level head and calm mind, you could end up torn apart by conflicting images. Attempting all this while riding a horse at full gallop was foolhardy, and he was loving every minute of it. A grey tunnel appeared in front of him and he went right through it, disappearing from the horse and reappearing past Rhoe and the sorcerer.

Unfortunately, he was still traveling as fast as the horse.

He hit the road hard and rolled over and over, bouncing to a stop as he struck a boulder with a sickening crack. He probed his side and shoulder with delicate fingers. *At least six ribs broken, and I think the shoulder is dislocated. That's a new record, I believe,* he thought as he tried to stand. His leg was bashed but whole, and he was a bit dizzy; but all in all, not bad. He got up just as the fight ended.

Rhoe looked up just in time to see Caerlyn, or what he thought was Caerlyn, fly by him on a horse. The horse was moving faster than he had seen anything move, but the knife missed her shield and thudded into her side "Caerlyn!" Rhoe screamed as she slumped over. His gaze settled on the man without a weapon, and his eyes spoke volumes. He couldn't go to her and leave this man to escape.

S'ren Dro knew a lost battle when he was in one. He turned around to flee, saw another horse coming, and thought to jump over the rail. He was about to utter a command to the air when he felt a sharp pain in his side. He looked down and there, hanging on the rail of the bridge, was a man. *How did he get—?* and that was the last thought he had.

Graf leaped over the rail and onto the bridge and let the body fall, "Sorry. I climbed up when the earth started to shake and was waiting for him to lean over." Then he saw the commotion and knew something bad happened. "What was that evil I felt?" he asked as he saw Karsis limping from the other direction, and the princess coming at them from the city.

Rhoe ignored the strange man as he ran to stop Caerlyn's horse.

Karsis reached her first, easing her out of the saddle and onto the ground in his lap. He could feel the evil siphoning her essence away with every ragged breath. "Hold on, Caer. I'm here, and you know there isn't much I can't do, right?" He tried to get her to respond, to keep her engaged while his mind ran in circles trying to think of what he could do.

Caerlyn coughed, trying to smile while barely conscious. "Is Rhoe alright?" She had her eyes closed, knowing to save what strength she had, and lay still. She could feel the blade trying to dig deeper, and her will was focused inward, fighting the growing darkness spreading like a sickness throughout her body.

"I'm here, Caerlyn" Rhoe limped up to them, his breathing ragged as well. That fight drained what little he had saved up, and walking was tough again. He knelt down hard in the dirt and brushed her hair away. "By all the gods above, why did you do that?" First his parents, then Tanan, now Caerlyn. Why was everyone close to him being taken away?

Karsis felt tears coming to his eyes, but he wasn't giving up yet. "Rest easy, Rhoe. I've got her, and I think I may have a plan. But you're not going to like it very much." He squeezed her shoulder, anticipating what her reaction was going to be. When they had first encountered this type of blade, wielded by the sorcerer Xalrin, Tanan had gotten sliced by it. A little cut really, but they had found that it resisted healing. When it started to get worse, Karsis took the wound upon himself and tried to purge it with magic from the inside. That time it was only a small cut, and it almost killed him; this was going to be much worse.

Carelyn drew Karsis closer. She was losing her strength fast. She pulled him down to her face with the last of her strength, then whispered, "Come in h... here, and... he... help me... fight." She turned inward fully then, trusting that he would listen to one of the best healers in Lythinall, next to Ralavin.

Karsis sighed and turned his gaze upon Rhoe and saw that Liss and Graf were coming over slowly, fearing the worst. He waited till they were all there before he told them what he was going to do. "All right, this is going to be bad. To save her, I have to either take the wound into me and fight it with magic—and I could die horribly doing that mind you—or Caerlyn thinks I should go inside *her* and help her fight the evil leaking into her very soul. Again, possibly dying horribly."

"So, shot or hung?" Graf tried not to sound callous, but he

hadn't been around people for a long time, at least those that weren't in his head, so he wasn't used to it yet. Give him a couple of weeks and maybe. He pulled the rags up and over his head. The wind was picking up again. Great.

"He's not wrong." Karsis said, when he saw Liss's head snap around towards him. "I have to do something right now, so listen up all of you." He used his *Listen or I'll stab you* voice. That was his favorite. "I'm going to be out cold, and she will too, so it's up to you three to get us to Caerlyn Hold in one piece. I'm not even sure we will be better by then, but that's a start. You guys will do fine, you survived the faeries, right?" He laughed and gave no time for them to argue. *I'm coming Caer, hold on.* He channeled his thoughts inward, then whispered softly to the ether to take his soul into hers. Not just anyone could do this, but he wasn't just anyone. Thank all the gods above that Caerlyn knew that.

Rhoe saw Karsis go limp and let out a breath he didn't know he was holding, then wiped a falling tear from his cheek. He had just met Caerlyn, but she had fought hard for days to keep him alive and knew him when he was born. Then there was his teacher. The bard Karsis had never been anything but alert and ready for anything, and to see him like this... "Okay, let's get them on a horse or two. It's about thirty miles to the hold, and we'll be walking slow."

After they got Carelyn and Karsis on horseback and fastened in place, Liss walked over to Rhoe and said, "It's been so crazy, I haven't had time to say thank you." She wrapped her arms around Rhoe and held him tight, feeling close to him regardless of how little they've known each other. It was like she had known him all her life.

"For what?"

"For saving me from that wolvren, for saving me in the river, for coming to my rescue on that bridge. All of it. I may have been trained to be a great warrior, but I've never actually *done* much of it till now." She laughed at how stupid that may sound to the man standing beside them, but he wore rags soaked in wine and urine, so what was he going to say?

"Well, I've never had to do any of this either. I just knew that I wasn't going to let you face that thing alone. After everything we've been through, we don't have to say thanks anymore." He felt complete with her, and if that felt weird, well, so was the fact that he was learning magic from Karsis himself.

"So, you guys met faeries?" Graf asked.

"Let's get on our way and we'll fill you in as we walk. I hope you like a good story?" Rhoe didn't fully trust Graf yet, but the man had ample time to attack him when he was at his weakest and hadn't. Then again, maybe he was waiting for Karsis to be out of the way.

"Yeah, it'll do us good to take our minds off of what is going on inside these two." Liss said, then shuddered at the thought of the evil blade that was sticking out of Caerlyn. Even the incarnation didn't feel *that* wrong, and he was death incarnate. They walked and talked, keeping an eye out along the way for danger, all the while their friends were fighting for their very souls.

4

COMMON GROUND

Lan stomped down hard and raised his shield just in time to absorb the blow. Even with perfect timing, it still rocked him back on his heels but he rolled with the force of the blow and came around, sword at the ready, poised to strike if there was an opportunity. Unfortunately, his sparring partner wasn't leaving any openings. He shook the sweat out of his short, curly hair and pursed his lips in determination, advancing once more. His practice armor felt heavy on his lithe frame, but he swung his sword with skill, nonetheless. Thrust, step, slash, parry, back step. He was just about to thrust again when he saw the sword coming at him from an impossible angle and speed. Without a moment to think, he impulsively ducked into a roll towards his opponent. The sword arced over his head, barely missing, and he brought his own blade up as he tried to steady himself on one knee. He met a firmly planted boot to his chest instead.

"Good thought, Lan—but your roll was too predictable and slow in that armor." Carana sheathed her practice sword and held out a hand to the winded boy. He took a while to regain the air she had knocked out of him, winced as he took her hand, and grabbed his shoulder as he stood. *Another injury that I didn't give him. I know that some of the knights are beating him for not being a noble, and god help them if I ever catch them.* She was furious but couldn't prove anything, mainly because the boy refused to implicate anyone. "Fall down again? You may never make it to knighthood if you keep hurting yourself." She saw the horror on his face and couldn't help but laugh. "I'm kidding, Lan. Take it easy."

"I'm fine, High General. I can perform my duties." Lan worked out the pain in his shoulder and considered his goal once more. He had always dreamed of becoming a knight. His mother, before she had died, had told him stories about the father he had never known—a knight pledged to the king of Lythinall that had gone away on a mission and died in service to the land. He thought she was just making it all up, to make him feel like he was special, until she died and he found a nameless journal. The journal was vague, but definitely from the hand of a knight. That's where he had found the pledge; a pledge he had memorized over time. "Shall we continue?"

Carana sighed and readied her stance once more. She was easily six feet tall with short, dirty blond hair. It matched well with her sun-darkened skin and brown eyes, but even these features paled in comparison to her physique. The woman was built slender, but had packed that slender frame with every ounce of muscle possible. "This time, try coming at me with the shield first," she advised, circling slowly now. "Bash my weapon aside, then thrust." She purposefully left her sword out front, like most knights did, even though her reflexes were screaming to pull it in a bit and to the side. She started training this young boy a tenday ago, and already he was catching up to the first-year knights—which was why they probably had it out for him.

He said he was homeless, but he must've been practicing every day to be in this kind of shape. At only fifteen winters, he was lean, but the practice armor wasn't slowing his footwork down. Neither was the weighted practice sword. He may be able to join field tests in another couple of days.

Lan came at her with his shield raised, but his eyes darted to her left before he bashed the sword she was holding. Then, she heard the scrape of a foot behind her. She read his eyes and foot placement, let him bash her sword wide, then circled to the left while concealing a smile. He was grinning as he thrust, but she knew what was coming. You didn't live for well over a century without picking up a few tricks here and there. She quickly side-stepped the thrust and his sword slid harmlessly by before thudding into the boy sneaking up on her from behind.

"Oof!" Tomas doubled over as the weighted practice sword went into his midsection with the full thrust from Lan. He slowly fell to his knees, the wooden club he was holding falling from his hands that were holding his stomach instead.

Lan's eyes went wide, then he remembered his opponent. Too late. His shield arm was kicked out wide, just like the move he was trying to do to her sword, and her kick came inside faster than he could see. His practice armor took almost none of the blow, partially because it was designed to protect from slashes and cuts, not pure force. He folded in two and rolled for at least ten feet before coming to a stop. His air was gone from his lungs, but he was still trying to gulp for air.

"If an opponent can't stand, they can't fight. If an opponent can't breathe, they can't fight. Now, boys, what did we learn today?" Carana was trying not to laugh, but it was very hard with these kids. They had a determination that astounded her, and that was rare. Tomas recovered first.

Tomas was a big boy at over five feet and only eleven

winters, and growing fast. He usually favored the hammer, like the one that had been in his hands early in his life as the son of a blacksmith. "I'm sorry, Mistress Carana."

"General." Carana's gaze was hard. She hated being called 'mistress'.

"Sorry, *General* Carana." Tomas shuffled his feet, feeling embarrassed. "I just thought that I'd try and help out Lan," he said, hoping that she wasn't too angry.

Lan got to one knee, finally breathing again. "General, my apologies. That wasn't very knightly of me, and I will accept the consequences." He stared at the floor, waiting for the harsh words of finality that would end his dream.

"Oh, for Davalar's sake, you're only children. Get up, the both of you." Carana walked over and placed her practice sword on the rack. "You're not expected to abandon all your emotions, nor are you to be expected to never have a mischievous thought. The purpose in this training is to get you ready for what you will be doing in the name of the king." She turned, saw their incredulous expressions, and almost laughed out loud. Clamping down on her mirth at the boys in front of her, she put on her stern face and walked slowly towards them. "However, you will be expected to keep all playfulness to your off hours, because once you are in the field, those actions can get you killed or worse."

"What could be worse than being killed?" Tomas wasn't going to ask, but the thought of something worse was raising his anxiety. He may be a quiet boy, but that didn't mean he wasn't curious.

Carana looked them both in the eyes. "Worse? What could be worse is that your foolhardy fun may well get someone *else* killed, and then you would have to live with that for the rest of your life." She saw the realization set in, more in Tomas than

Lan. He already seemed to know that by his crestfallen look. "All right, let's not dwell on that right now. Tomas, it isn't time for your training so what brings you here?" She was training most of the new messengers, all except Sprout. She had to think about what she was going to do with her.

"I'm here to take Griff's place this morning Mistr— uh, General." He caught himself before upsetting her again. "He's still with High Priest Ralavin, and might be until well after high sun." He waited before going over to the armor rack, in case Carana dismissed him.

"That's fine, I'll catch him tonight. Get ready and pick out a weapon, I'll be with you in a moment." She turned and walked with Lan as he started to take off his practice armor. "Lan, you're doing good, but there is one thing you need to work on."

"What is that, General?" He knew he was far from perfect, but this was the first time she had said anything. He wasn't nervous per se, but...

"You need to be a little easier on yourself." She saw his frown, not understanding her criticism, "Listen, you have been living on the streets ever since your mother passed, and who knows how long ago that was. No, don't answer, that's not the point. The point is that you don't have to walk in here and prove to Arian that you're knight material in a tenday." She took a deep breath and turned him so that she could look right into his eyes. She needed him to really listen to this, she had seen too many young knights get killed in situations exactly like his. "You have already impressed him, trust me. Do you think he would have the high general of Everknight train a bunch of kids if he didn't think you had something special?"

"I know, It's just..." He looked aside, not wanting to bare his soul to those deep brown eyes. "It's just I've always wanted this, and now it's so close. I don't want to fail." There. He said it. It had been in his mind for the last tenday, ever since he started training with her, and getting thrown around like a rag doll. Failure was his greatest foe. He pulled out of her grasp, and placed his armor upon the stand, keeping his back to her so she couldn't see face.

Carana placed her hand on his shoulder, knowing just how he felt. When Davalar had chosen her to be his incarnation, she had feared that she would fail— but she couldn't exactly tell that to the boy. "I understand, Lan. Just know that I think you're doing fine, and in a couple years you are going to be one of the best. You just have to live that long." She walked away, giving him some time to compose himself before leaving the training room. "Okay, Tomas... No, you've got the armor on wrong. Here let me show you..."

Lan straightened his shoulders and left feeling better. He could do this, he just had to keep at it. He walked down the hallway with a spring in his step that he didn't realize was there. He was so focused on his renewed sense of purpose that he never saw the knight staring at him from the distant corner with a scowl on his face.

Davalar's Temple, Castle Everknight

RALAVIN LOOKED AGAIN at the boy and was pleased at his recovery. Rythal had been a broken mess. His collar bone, arms, and his right leg had healed, and in the last tenday he had gotten a lot of rest. Physically, at least, he was doing much better; mentally though, Rythal was a mess. No, that was an understatement—more like his mind had been tossed into barrel and kicked down a long hill. What he had seen had blasted his reason to a far corner of his mind, and there was no map to recover it.

Rythal was fourteen winters old with sparkling blond hair

and golden eyes, but the energy he used to have had gone out of him after the incident at Daelyn. He had lost his twin brother Innal to the incarnation of death and had been stuck like this ever since. Ralavin hadn't given up yet, though. "Griff, can you get me another cool cloth from the back?"

"Yes sir." The young boy ran back and grabbed another cloth, soaking it in the bucket that had the big block of ice. "Is he fevering up again sir?" he called from the back. He had been helping with the healing of the refugees, mainly the former Companions of Everknight. He was still in awe at meeting these larger-than-life heroes he had read about.

"No Griff, but I want to try something else to reach his mind." He had tried simple methods, now it was time to involve prayer. Most of his time was spent healing physical wounds; wounds of the spirit were more Lady Caerlyn's bailiwick, but he wasn't without knowledge of it.

"He told me to save you." Rythal had only spoken those words since he had been found in Daelyn, and no others.

"I know Rythal. Now let's see if I can get in there and find out what's stuck." He took the cool cloth from Griff and draped it around the boy's neck. Griff smiled and Ralavin couldn't help but feel at ease with his young student. His freckled face always had a smile that matched his wavy red hair and green eyes "Now, hold his arms, like this." He waited until Griff had a good grip then started chanting quietly. He called upon Davalar to help penetrate this darkness and to reveal what was in the boys shattered mind. He felt the power build then he channeled it into the boy ever so slightly. *Just a little farther...* The concussion of the blast threw both of them like a child's doll in a windstorm.

Griff couldn't hear anything except a ringing in his ears, and his sight wasn't much better. He was in the back room, sitting in a puddle of very cold water. His legs were not being very helpful at the moment and his head wasn't in the mood to argue. He felt, more than saw, the blast that had thrown him off of the boy and back into the other room, and as his eyes started to focus, he could see the boy still standing right there. Guards were piling into the Temple, with drawn swords, but couldn't see anything wrong. "Ral…" He couldn't make himself heard, so he tried pointing instead and found his arms were on strike as well. He started to panic, his breath coming in short ragged bursts, then he remembered his training. He took a deep breath and focused inward.

Davalar, God of Life and Honor, bless me with your wisdom and power to heal these wounds, so that I may serve you. He felt his hands grow warm and tried to move them to his legs. He touched himself and felt his back tingle, then crack in pain. *Oh, that's why my legs weren't moving.* It frightened him that he could do things like this, but after the last tenday of healing the wounded, he realized that it was truly a blessing. It scared him even more that his back was damaged that badly. He shook his head and put that thought out of his head for now

"Wounded!" one of the guards called out as Griff stood on shaky legs. The man sheathed his sword and moved to take his arm. Two others went towards Rythal, but were still cautious.

"Ralavin is over there." Griff said weakly, trying to point. He went to Rythal as well, looking over the boy without touching him.

"He told me to save you."

"Yeah, good job you're doing of that." Griff was growing annoyed at this kid, broken mind or not. He walked around the boy, giving him a wide berth, and went to Ralavin as well.

Ralavin was startled awake. He was sitting in the council meeting, nodding off again. He looked up to see what jostled him out of his slumber and saw that Trost, that meek scribe with the tiny glasses, was standing up and had changed almost completely. He was no longer cowering, but commanding, and then the flames grew around the room. Ralavin called for Davalar to protect him, and then drew his ceremonial dagger. He shook his head as he slowly got to his feet, his old bones creaking at the sudden movement. He knew that this dagger was only for show, but his king needed him. Hells below, everyone in the room needed him by the looks of it. He gathered up his strength and lurched towards the scribe, putting everything he had behind his two-handed swing into the man's chest. Upon impact the flames overcame his wards and he felt himself burning with every breath...

"*No!*" Ralavin sat up in a rush, fighting off the hands that were holding him, until he realized that he was in his temple. *Just a dream. It's over, and I'm still alive.* his thoughts were almost always on that fateful day. That day when Karsis had used his faerie vial to save him, and had brought him back from the brink of death. It helped that it had also given him his youth back as well. He was no longer the bent, broken old man of eighty winters. No, now he looked as if he were only twenty-some-odd winters, and with a physique that he almost didn't remember having. His long white hair was full and black once more, and he had cut it shoulder length just last week.

"Priest Ralavin, are you all right?" One of the guards was trying to help him up, not noticing that his leg was bent the wrong way.

"Stop!" Griff rushed in and tried to stop the guard, but his partner pushed him back, thinking that the boy was trying something. "His leg. Don't move him." Griff hated being small, and just wished for once he could push others around instead.

"Oh gods, Raeric, look! Put him down." The guard that stopped Griff was pointing, and the other guard, Raeric, eased him down gently. It all happened so fast that Ralavin was still trying to figure out what was the matter. "Sorry Father, um Minister...uh." He was at a loss as to the head priest's proper title.

"Priest Ralavin will do; it always has. It's okay, thank you gentleman." They sat him back down, and he looked at his leg curiously. *That was some blast if I don't even remember that happening. What in the hells did that anyway?* He moved his fingers cautiously over his leg as he thought it over, and he came up with nothing. Griff was holding his hands on Ralavin's lower leg waiting for the signal, then Ralavin nodded and bit down hard on his shirt. Griff pulled hard, setting the bones and quickly inhaled, focusing his energies and calling to Davalar. Ralavin tried not to scream, but his muffled cries sounded in his ears against his wishes. Once the stars cleared from his watery eyes, he marveled at the boy. He had seen others try to heal like this over the years, and while there may be only a few people that have their prayers answered, many more can still heal minor wounds without Davalar's blessing. This boy however, channeled the god with ease. He may even be better at it than Lady Caerlyn, and she was a master healer.

"Done. How does it feel sir?" Griff slowly opened his eyes and saw Ralavin staring at him with his mouth open. "What?" Fear overtook him. "Oh gods, did I not set it right? Is it crooked? Oh no, please. Somebody, help!" He tried to stand to go get the guards, who were already on their way back in at the commotion anyway.

"Griff stop, it's fine." Ralavin grabbed his leg as he tried to stand and pulled him back down. "Easy son. Guards, it's okay— we're fine." He laughed at Griff's expression and sat him back down. "It's nothing bad. Look. When I healed Gareth, that big man with all the broken ribs?" He waited for Griff to nod, and saw the boy was fighting back tears. "Well, it took me, what, almost three hours to fix him up? Well Griff, you just healed my leg, that was fractured in at least three places, in about three minutes. *Minutes.*" He let that really sink in. Gods, he was still trying to let it sink in *his* mind.

"So, I didn't screw it up?"

"No! Far from it, my young prodigy. Lady Caerlyn is going to have her hands full when you go to study with her." He got up, effortlessly, and stretched the leg. Minutes! He was almost jealous. "I taught you how to channel the power, but I haven't really explained how it all works, have I?" He saw the boy try and work out an answer to the rhetorical question and kept going before he could. "Come over to the alter and sit. I'll try my best to give you the basics." He got up and walked over and flexed his leg once more, just for giggles.

"First, you have to understand that there are two ways we classify healing: soft heals and hard heals. Soft heals are the easier wounds to heal and can be accomplished in minutes, especially if done cooperatively. Cuts, slashes, and stab wounds, even those that could be fatal, are called soft heals."

"Even when someone is dying?" Griff interrupted. He couldn't believe they called that "easy."

Ralavin smirked at the question, not at all upset that this young man cut him off. He loved that he wanted to learn and not just glaze over like some of his other students over the years. "Yes Griff. Like when Sprout was dying and I had you help me, that was a soft heal. It was her flesh and blood, specifically her heart, that needed repair. Well, that and a dozen other little things that you will learn later, but all in good time." He turned around and looked up at the statute of Davalar as he continued. He remembered when he had this lesson from his instructor all those years ago, and he was just as inquisitive.

"The only difference with Sprout was that we also had to

coax her spirit back just a little bit, but that's another bucket of coins altogether." He held his hand up to forestall any questions on *that* subject, as it was a very long discussion and he wasn't ready for that yet. "Hard heals are more solid—like bones and structure—and it takes quite some time to graft them back together again. It takes patience and endurance to heal someone with broken bones, taking sometimes two or three hours of healing, over days sometimes, and letting the body rest."

"So, that's why you were shocked? Not because I did it wrong... but that I did it so quickly?" Hearing Ralavin talk about how hard it was made him a little more worried about how he healed himself. *What if I healed my back wrong? Will I be crippled?* He slowed his thoughts and took a deep breath. He shouldn't panic, but he had to tell him.

"Well, yes, young Griff. That *should* have taken a true healer at least two hours." He noticed the look on the young boys freckled face and frowned, trying to figure out what he may have said. "What is it Griff? that look seems serious."

Griff felt tears welling up in his eyes again, he was so scared. "Ralavin... when I was blown back, I couldn't feel my legs. I couldn't even get my arm to work either, so I called to Davalar and healed myself, and my back tingled...then I was fine." As he finished the statue started to glow softly, filling the room with light.

Ralavin stared at the representation of his god, glowing softly before him, mouth open wide at the implication of both the boy's words, and the manifestation before him. "You really are touched by His hands, aren't you?" he asked softly, not even meaning Griff to hear him. "I'll guide him I swear. He will learn all I have to teach him and more," he said to his god, in solemn promise, then turned to the petrified young boy and placed his hand upon his shoulder. "It will be all right Griff; I'll take a look at you and make sure you're all fixed up." He smiled then, wiping a tear that refused to fall from the boy's water filled eyes; he was trying so hard not to cry. "Now come on. Let's clean up this mess and see about getting young Rythal here into his room." He clapped the boy on his shoulder and went about picking up the debris from the explosion. The explosion! In the excitement of Griff's seeming miraculous healing powers, he had forgotten about the way he and his student were blown away from Rythal without a reason. Well, at least a reason that he could think of. He was *definitely* going to have to ask Karsis about this one.

Standing there by himself, Rythal saw everything; he always did. He screamed again for the thousandth time for his brother —but Innal was dead. His brother was just a pile of ash and dust, and he wouldn't hear anything anymore. It didn't keep Rythal from screaming though. That's all he did now inside the broken mess that was once his mind. Gone was the fun, carefree life he had known with his twin, along with his sanity. That thing, that *incarnation*, as he has heard everyone call it, was responsible, and the voice told him that he was to be its down-fall. He couldn't even control himself anymore, and anytime he did try to speak, all his body did was recite the words that the voice had told him to. That day, they had both heard the voice tell them to go back to Daelyn and save the people that fought the man in black. Had he known that he would lose his brother, he never would have. He saw the young boy picking up a statue and screamed for Innal again. It echoed inside of his fractured mind and seemed to go on forever. He would be free someday, and on that day he would take all his pain and suffering and deliver it to those responsible.

Servants Hall, Castle Everknight

SHE CREPT IN SLOWLY, slipping around the corner and trying to stay out of sight. If they saw who she was, half of them would bolt and the other half would prostrate themselves. Maressa, queen of Everknight sat down slowly, like she was watching wildlife from the bushes, trying not to spook them. The young boys in front of her, eating their meal and talking in hushed tones, were pages. These boys delivered messages, carried notes, and even cleaned clothing on occasion. They ranged from seven winters old to about thirteen; once they turned fourteen, they were given a stipend of money and went back to their families. While they were at the castle, they were schooled in manners and court etiquette, and even basic reading and writing. At fourteen, with money and being literate, they could do better than most people in the city.

"Well, here you are." The man's voice was loud and boisterous, and it turned into a yelp as the queen stood in one fluid motion and grabbed him. Tanan was quick, but he had not expected attack here in the mess hall. He was pulled down hard, and when he tried to ask what in the hells was going on, her hand was clamped over his mouth.

Maressa glared at the rogue with her piercing blue eyes, and held her hand over his mouth. With her other hand she held one finger up to her mouth and made a shushing noise. "Quiet, you'll spook them."

His reply was so soft, it was little more than indecipherable mumbling.

"Oh, for Ollian's sake," she whispered as she released him, continuing to glare. Lord Tanan Norhil was dressed in a black silk tunic with black breeches, but his trademark long dark blue cape was missing. Broaches and pins adorned his clothes and his high black boots clicked when he walked. His thin wiry frame was in perfect form despite years of easy living. "But keep it down."

"What is going on?" Tanan whispered. He was into it now—he loved a good sneak play, and once he got into something... well, he was all in. "Who's getting nabbed or grabbed?" He looked at the queen and wished again that she had chosen him instead of Arian. She had curly brown hair, shoulder length, and eyes that could read your every move, sometimes before you made one. She was lithe, but her stare could turn aside a dragon.

"I'm trying to observe the pages in their natural habitat." She was only half joking.

"Okay, I'll bite. Why?" He had a smirk on his face that said he didn't believe her.

She turned to stare at the boys sitting there and smiled bitterly. "Karsis had an idea to use them as a kind of spy network. They hear everything that goes on in this castle you know, and they are practically invisible to nobles." She tried not to sound resentful, but she should've thought about it before Karsis did. That really burned her. She turned to smile at Tanan, then her eyes went wide as he was no longer sitting there.

Tanan started walking over to the pages, very surreptitiously, hunching himself over to look completely different. He stopped a table away from where a couple of pages ate, and sat down, pretending to fix his boots. "One of you chaps have a pin?" he asked in a small voice, almost like he was scared. He watched as the pages gave a start, then calmed down when they saw he was hunched over.

"Here." Page Fenton walked over and handed Tanan a small pin. "Have this one. I've got another." He was turning around but caught a whiff of perfume. His eyes went wide and he made a small click with his tongue, and the others started to move instantly. Perfume like that was only for the nobles or the rich. They packed up their trays, gathered their things, and started to leave the room in three different directions. Nobles in hiding equaled retribution, and they didn't want to be anywhere near that.

"Damn." Maressa swore under her breath at the sight of them fleeing—it was as if they were being hunted. They were well organized, but she might stop them yet. *Yes but I wanted to observe them some mor. Well, when the Dark One drives...* she thought, standing and throwing back her cloak. "Hold!" Her voice rang throughout the room, and even Tanan froze where he was. "Stay here, all of you. I've got something to say to every who is here, and you can pass it along to the others that aren't." She walked forward and they started averting their eyes. "No, no, stop. Look at me please." This last wasn't in the commanding voice of the queen, nor was it in the lighter tone of a bard. No, this voice was just a woman asking for a favor, and they heard her.

"It's all right guys, we can trust her." It was page Fenton who spoke. He remembered the queen and how she had asked him where to find the high general that day. No one had ever talked to him like he was a person before. Well, except Carana; she always did. The others slowly came back and sat down, some seeming eager to hear what the queen herself could want from them.

"You all know that there have been attempts on the life of the king—most of the city knows that by now—and I need your help." She paused for effect and let that sink in. She saw Tanan move to the back door silently, as if to cover escape; he was still into this as, if it were a job. "You all see and hear more than anyone can possibly know, and proof of that was the help that we got from page Fenton. His knowledge helped Karsis hold off an attempt that would've killed not just the King, but the entire council." She watched him blush, but he stood a little straighter at the same time. He would be the key to getting them all. "So, I want to offer this to you all, starting with page Fenton." She turned and bowed her head, going to one knee. "Fenton, please be the first of the pages to join my cause. I need stalwart heroes that look and listen for king and queen. You will be my secret hand among the nobles, and I can keep us safe with your help. What say you Fenton?" She was relying on this boy who had to be all of twelve winters, if that.

Fenton looked down at his feet for three long breaths, feeling the quiet of the room weigh on his little shoulders. He had seen what the council room looked like, and he had heard the stories of Grason. He didn't want to get his fellow pages hurt, but at the same time, he wanted so much more than what he had. He looked up at his queen to see her kneeling at his level, and the breath rushed out of him. "I'm yours, my Queen." He didn't even know he had said it before it was out, but he meant it. He turned to the others. "I know that some of you just want to be invisible, and that is fine, but if you do this with me, we can change things, maybe even help the king." He held out his hand to the queen, and helped her up, then dropped to one knee. "I pledge myself to you as one of the secret pages..."

"The Queen's Hand!" Tanan interjected from the back of the room, and his sudden outburst startled five of the young boys. It sounded more like a secret society, but it flowed better than the secret pages.

Fenton didn't miss a beat. "The Queen's Hand." He stood and pulled out another flat pin. These were used to hold fabric in place sometimes, or even just clean under fingernails. Every page had two or three of these on them from time to time. Now he tied a bit of red cloth that he had from one of his clothing repairs to one of them and pinned it inside of his jacket. He showed them all this, then folded the jacket back so it was hidden. Then the queen placed her hand on his shoulder and spoke to them all.

"Nobles never see you; you're nothing to them. So when

they talk, you listen. And when I ask, you tell me what you heard. No heroics, no fighting—just be where you are all the time. In plain sight." She smiled and of the eleven boys in the room, eight of them were coming forward now. The first two were only seven or so winters. *They could get killed, but I need them right now. How much of a monster am I?* She smiled through her dark thoughts but remembered that Arian's new recruits were mere children as well. At least she wasn't the only monster. She caught Tanan's eye and he was smiling at her, silently clapping. Somehow having this devious man applauding her made her feel even worse. "By the way Fenton, how did you know Tanan wasn't a servant?"

Fenton kind of smirked, looking at his feet again. "He smelled nice." The young boy looked at the back at Tanan and shrugged his shoulders apologetically. "Like perfume."

"Thank you... I think?" Tanan walked forward now, no longer pretending to be anything but himself. The boys peeled back from him like he was a plague victim out of habit, such was his aura of importance. *If they only knew that I had started out just like them,* he thought as he recalled the old days, before he ran into Arian that fateful day. He swirled around to sit, but realized he didn't have a cape so the effect was wasted. "So, I was made 'cause I smelled... nice?"

"Sorry, but yeah. Servants don't really smell like flowers." Fenton spied Barris coming in the far exit and held his hand up as if to say it was all right. "Not that they are dirty, but even clean we don't smell *that* good. I thought it was coming in through the windows at first, but when I turned, I saw that they weren't open."

Maressa was laughing so hard it hurt. "All hail the Lilac Lord!" she burst out, and when she saw his frown, she laughed even harder. Of all the things to give him away, this was by far the best.

"All right, laugh it up." He was silently amazed at young page Fenton for noticing something like that. Usually that took training, or years of experience at least. He looked around the gathering of young ones to see that they were all smirking and smiling, and finally joined in. He bowed deep, in mock acceptance of his new title. "Actually, I rather like it—The Lilac Lord. I can be a secret liaison..."

Barris walked over to the happy gathering and shook his head. He was never late for a meal, and the one day he was the world turned upside down. The queen, here with them laughing? "What did I miss?" he asked, dumbfounded, as the group laughed all the harder now, and it was quite a while before he got the story, and after he did, he pledged himself as well.

Throne Room, Castle Everknight

ARIAN WALKED into the throne room with heavy steps. He was tired and had been dealing with nobles all day. He even had to eat alone, since his wife was off sneaking around the servants' halls doing Davalar knows what. Now here he was, the King of Lythinall, answering some last-minute nobles request at an audience late in the evening. He should've had guards with him, what with all the attempts at ending his life and all, but the page had used his secret password that only trusted nobles knew, and only a handful at that. To call him here like this was truly important, and could even be a clue as to who was behind all of this. Besides, he could handle himself... as long as it wasn't magic. He shuddered at the memory of that sorcerer taking all the air out of the room, stealing his breath and almost killing him and Maressa. He had felt so powerless. He heard a woman's voice behind him in the hallway and turned as someone came through the door. His weary, forced smile disappeared instantly.

Gareth was huge, well over six feet tall, and his corded muscle stood out prominently through his woolen shirt, stretched tight over his barrel chest. He had shoulder length brown hair that always looked like it could use a combing, but no one dared to get close enough to try it. His blindfold was the only thing out of place.

"Tierra, are you sure I need to be wearing this thing?" Gareth couldn't see anything, but when his wife said it was a surprise... well he hated to disappoint her in anything; besides, she could get ornery when she didn't get her way.

Tierra smiled, then noticed the king staring at them and shoved her husband into the room and bolted back for the door. "Well, have to run! You two play nice." She turned and slammed the door closed, sliding a chair over and blocking the door from being opened. Then she remembered the strength of the two men inside and sat down in the chair for good measure, though she hoped it didn't come to that. She had a slim build and long flowing hair that gave an almost dainty look to her short frame. She always kept her platinum blond hair in twin braids, straight back, and set with two-inch steel balls that would click and clack whenever she was about.

Arian frowned deeper and turned to exit the throne room the other way. He wasn't dealing with his past right now, and he was angry that he had been obviously deceived. He reached the doors and pushed, but they wouldn't budge. Shaking his head, he shoved harder, thinking they were stuck, but they groaned and creaked, holding fast. The king was tall, well over six and-a-half feet, and it was all muscle. His golden locks fell short, brushing his ceremonial armor but lightly, and his piercing blue eyes seemed to hold one's attention involuntarily. Even though he was now past fifty winters, Arian could still keep up with all the day-to-day activities that came with being the King of Lythinall, yet he could not budge the door. "What foolery is this!" he yelled to the door, "This is your king, open these doors!" He was thinking to give whoever did this a fright so that they would yield a bit and he could shove harder, but then he heard his favorite giggle and knew that he was doomed.

Maressa giggled through the door, quite pleased with herself. "Dear, you two have been avoiding each other for a tenday; get it out of your systems. We will have you healed up afterwards, don't you worry!" she yelled through the closed doors. She was having a very hard time not laughing, imagining his face right now. She just hoped that Tierra could hold her door until she could get there and use her music to seal it like she had this one. "Love you!" Then she was off, running through corridors that she had practically grown up wandering around.

Arian sighed and turned around reluctantly, seeing Gareth taking off the blindfold and staring dumbfounded at the throne. He shook his head and walked over, putting on his Kingly smile that he used with the nobles he didn't like. "Gareth, what brings you?" He tried to sound nonchalant, but it came out strained anyway. So much had happened since that day, but it was still vivid in his mind.

"What brings me? My wife tricked me, that's what brings me." He stormed angrily back to the door he came in and pushed, but though it gave a little, it didn't open. "That's it." He backed up a good six feet and lowered his shoulder, but felt a hand on his back and snapped around before he could charge. "Don't touch me!"

"Gareth..."

"Don't even try your placating words on me. We both know you don't care." He pushed the king away from him with everything he had, focusing his anger at how powerless he had felt lately with everything, especially his son. The king went backwards, but kept his footing, turning around to try and stay balanced.

"Don't placate *you*?" Arian was usually the calm one, but with all that had been going on in the city and against his family, he finally lost control. He rushed his one-time friend, anger twisting his features. "*You* are the one that struck *me*!" He swung, his fist connecting with the man's jaw loudly. They were both big men, but in different ways. Gareth was shorter, but had more strength, while Arian was taller with better skill. All in all, they were well matched.

Gareth took the hit and turned his head with it, never losing a step. He came back around with his own fist as his head turned to glare at his king. He saw the king throw his arms up in front of his face to block the hit, and opened his fist at the last moment, grabbing an arm and pushing out and up with the momentum. This threw the king back off his feet a little, so that he couldn't keep his balance at all. He stalked after the man and watched him land and roll to his knees to get up, facing away from him. "You're damned *right* I struck you. You had it coming, Mr. High and Mighty, talking down to me like I was one of your lowly subjects." He placed his foot on the King's back to shove him down, but Arian spun, grabbing the foot and lifted it up high, with effort, sending Gareth up in the air and sprawling to the floor. Gareth hit flat on his back and felt the air rush out of him.

"I was trying to... I needed..." Arian saw his old friend lying there on the floor of the throne room unable to defend himself. He *was* placating him back then, trying to defuse a bad situation with his office, instead of talking to a trusted friend. The king sighed and stood slowly, offering a hand to the breathless warrior on the floor. "I'm sorry Gareth—you're right. I let my pride get in the way all these years, and I never even thought about how wrong I was. I only focused on how hurt my pride was when you hit me in front of my entire court."

"Laid you out," the big man said quietly, just getting his breath back.

"Yeah, you did, didn't you?" Arian laughed at the memory. It was all he could do, now that he had given in to being wrong in the first place. The man could hit like a runaway horse.

"I shouldn't have though, not there. I should've just accepted that you chose the thief over me." He hung his head, remembering how hurt he felt when his closest friend had not chosen him to guard the people of the north. Back then Arian had just proposed that the people needed bastions of defense in each of the three outlands of Lythinall. To the East, North, and West. He appointed one of his trustworthy companions to each post, but when it came to the north, Arian choose Tanan over Gareth.

"Gareth..." Arian knew his friend was still hurting, but he didn't know how to explain it without hurting him even more. He had thought long and hard over that fateful decision. With it being newly manned and the fields planted late, there was a good chance that the winters would be very hard for a couple years. It was a hard post, and he knew that Tanan would've done better, mainly because he cared *less*. The position needed someone that could make the hard choices and not always the right ones. Gareth cared too much about the people to make those kinds of choices. It had devastated the kindhearted warrior.

"No, don't. I know why you choose Tanan. He is charismatic, charming, and smart—all the things you think I'm not." He turned his back on his king. He had thought about having this conversation for the last eighteen years, but now that it was here, he didn't really want to.

"That's not why..."

"Arian, Tierra was pregnant for heaven's sake! I was counting on you to help us!"

"I know Gareth. That's why I sent Caerlyn to help with the birth, but you don't understand." Arian hadn't thought about this, had tried not to think about it, but it was weighing on him now. "Will you let me explain? Please?"

"You didn't even come to see us! All these years Arian..." Gareth walked over and leaned on the throne, resting his head. "You were my closest friend, the brother I never had."

"I know, and I let you down. But hear me out." He put his arm around his old friend and explained that fateful decision. After that, they sat there, well into the night, talking and catching each other up on eighteen years of missed memories.

On the other side of the door, the two women sighed quietly, knowing the worst was over. Maressa let her scrying spell fade and smiled at Tierra, still sitting in the chair blocking the door. "Well, we did it. They will be talking for a while now so we might as well go get a drink or three." She was so relieved that Arian and Gareth were talking that she might cry. It had eaten her husband inside and out all these years, and they had missed so much, over something pride built.

"I'm just glad Gareth didn't charge the door. When I heard him say 'that's it', I thought it was over." She smiled and jumped up, taking the queen's arm and leading her down the hall. "Now we just have to root out the conspirators, defeat the great evil, and stay alive doing it."

"Yeah, thank the gods the *hard* part is over. Fixing men's pride was the hardest thing I've ever had to do!" They laughed all the way to the king's sitting room, where all the best bottles were kept.

Outer Courtyard, Castle Everknight

The older man walked out and shielded his eyes against the bright sun. He looked around for the children that he had yet to add to the castles list of occupants, and he was tired of them evading him. Othren Lawkland was the old seneschal, and he knew everything about the castle that there was to know. He had been appointed to the post back when Arian's father had married, and he had performed the ceremony as a high-ranking cleric of Ollian, Goddess of beauty and songs. He had deep knowing eyes, short close-cropped hair, and a wit that was sharper than Carana's sword. He had just passed his seventy-sixth winter, and boy he felt it. He heard the children before they came into view, and when he turned the corner, he saw that one of them was training with the hunts master. Othren slowed his walk, trying to stay unnoticed ere he spooked the children into running; he didn't want to lose them again. A couple more feet and he would be within snatching distance of the little one. *Sprout, I think was her name, if I recall,* he thought. He reached out and grabbed a handful of her shirt, trying not to seem menacing.

"Children, it is so good to finally catch up with you," he said, putting some cheer into his tired voice, to no avail.

"*Ah!* He's got me!" Sprout wailed as if she was in the clutches of a fire breathing dragon. At only eight winters old, she was four feet tall and barely weighed over six stones. Her short blond hair was still dirty despite being washed, and her skin was a dark tan from being on the street for years. Everyone knew that when this one grew up she would be a force to be reckoned with. "Help Vance!" She couldn't keep a straight face anymore and started laughing uncontrollably.

Vance was aiming his bow, with his arm pulled all the way back when she called his name. He released the arrow and turned his head, sending his shot wide of the target, and frowned at the distraction. He shook his sandy brown hair out of his face and looked to his trainer with an apologetic smile. He was only ten winters, but he was as good with a bow in his hands as a second-year hunter. "Sorry, Master Breich."

The hunts master shook his head and smiled. No one could remain irritated at Sprout, no matter what she did. "That's alright boy. You've done good for today. Kari, you're next." He looked to the young girl sitting on the bench with her hands folded politely and wondered again why she wanted to learn to shoot. She had long brown hair, tied up in twin braids with red ribbons intertwined. At twelve winters, she looked the most grown up of all the children, except Lan. "You sure you want to try this?" His question seemed to shake her out of whatever daydream she was having.

"Oh, yes!" She stood and saw Othren for the first time and smiled awkwardly, laughing at how Sprout was struggling playfully. She turned her attention to Hunts Master Breich. He was a stern man with a kind heart, short and stocky with black hair and dark eyes. "I want to try everything at least once." She stepped up and put on the leather armguard that she saw Vance use, then selected a bow from the rack and tested it.

"Here, like this." The hunts master took her aside and talked quietly, giving Othren a little room.

"Now, you two," Othren started, seeing his opportunity. "All I need to do is get your full names for the registry. Is that so terrible?" He released the little one and she sat down quickly, as if he was burning her.

Vance shrugged and cocked his head to one side. "Sorry, we are just used to hiding from anyone with authority."

"Yeah, authoritieze." Sprout still had some trouble with some words, but she was doing better. She had been on the street for longer than all of them, and learned from watching and listening more than anything else.

"It's all right, I understand. I'm just old and can't chase children like I used to." He took out his rolled parchment and sat down. Out of his pouch he pulled a quill and tiny bottle of ink, setting them aside and getting ready. "Now Sprout. Is that the only name you go by?"

"Yes sir, I never knew any other name since my parents died in a fire." She looked down at the ground as she continued, refusing to cry. "I was called that a lot by the flower lady down in the city."

"Why was that?" Now his interest was piqued. Not at the death of her parents, tragic as that was, but he had assumed it was a self-given title, or at least bestowed upon her by the other children.

"'Cause she always caught me sneaking around the discarded flowers in the back. I liked to decorate things with them, so she called me Sprout."

"I see, thank you." He turned to the other boy, sitting next to the little one protectively. "And you, good sir? Do you know your full name?"

Vance eyed him suspiciously. Something about the older man made him nervous, he just couldn't put his finger on it. Maybe it was because he reminded him of the officials that gave the kids so much trouble when they were on the streets. "My full name is Vance Blaine, though I haven't used it in quite some time." He scratched his head absently, "My mother told me that before she... before she passed. I never met my father."

"Lots of that going around." Sprout joked. She never did well with jokes, always said them at the wrong times. They laughed anyways, but sometimes she saw them look at her funny.

"Did you all meet around the same time?" Othren wasn't going to ask anymore, but these kids were starting to intrigue him, more than a little.

"No, I came along and met Tomas, Kari, and Sprout about

two years ago." It seemed like a lifetime ago, living in alleys and foraging for scraps to eat. "Then Lan showed up with Griff and Meri." He frowned then, remembering poor Meri.

Othren knew that look, and knew better than to ask. Life on the street for children was harsh, and it was a miracle that these children survived as long as they did. Especially in the winter months. He looked to Sprout and saw that she was trying not to cry. "There, there little one," he started, but she brushed his hand away with a look that should never be seen on one so young. It was contempt. Taken aback, he sat back and just looked at them for a while. Finally, Vance shifted and looked at his feet.

Sprout took a deep breath and looked Othren right in the eye. "She was kilt when a fancy man hit her with his horse in the snow. You all think we're nothing. He never even stopped when we called for help. No one did." She stood up and ran for the castle, holding back tears.

After a slight pause, to let the little one get out of range, Vance spoke up, breaking the silence forming after the girls flight. "Meri suffered for a long time, sir, and Sprout was right there, holding her hand and telling her that she would be okay. It hit us all hard that day." Vance was looking down, his fists clenching and unclenching in frustration at the memory. "By morning she was gone, and we couldn't even bury her cause the ground was still frozen. Lan and I dropped her off at the North gate later that evening. We heard they burned her up."

"Cremated. They probably cremated her." Othren didn't know what else to say. He knew that the nobles thought themselves above the peasants, but he never thought they would ignore a child that badly wounded. *Poor thing must've had bleeding inside that they couldn't see, or worse.* His thoughts drifted back to when he took the oath to be a member of Ollian's faith. Long and long ago. He vowed to always help those in need of song, story, or life. "I'm sorry, Vance. That should never have happened. It is even a miracle that you all survived the winters together. Thank the Goddess that Sprout had you all, being that young."

Vance laughed, shaking his head. "You don't understand sir. We all had Sprout to thank. She had been on those streets far longer than any of us. From what we can tell, she was barely talking when she was abandoned. She knew all of the hidden places to stay, the best places for scraps, and knew half of the guards that would help us out in the cold." He stood, and bowed to the older man, brushing his cheek of the tears that silently fell. "We owe our lives to that little miracle." With that he walked back to the castle, needing to find Sprout and hug her for no reason at all.

Othren sat there for a while longer, originally telling himself he was waiting for the older girl to finish her lesson, but he was fooling himself. He didn't want to get up because he felt ten times older after that entire conversation. *This is exactly why I'm trying to change things; these self-righteous nobles think they can walk all over everyone.* He clamped down on his emotions and guarded his thoughts once more. It was going to be hard, but change was never easy. He got up and walked back to the castle himself, thinking about what he had started. It might work, but he would have to change his focus. He never noticed the man watching him from the high window.

❧

Frenir Darkshadow turned away from the window when he could no longer see Othren and swore under his breath. That man would have to be dealt with very soon. The black haired, bearded man was a sorcerer from the southern lands of G'harr, and as councilor of foreign relations, he was here to try to win little victories for his homeland whenever he could in the interest of peace. He walked quickly through the upper hallways, his polished boots clicking across the stone floor. Othren was going to be trouble, he could just feel it. *You won't ruin my plans old man, I'll see to that.* His thoughts were troubled, but he couldn't dwell on that right now. No, now he had to anxiously await the arrival of the princess and she was overdue.

5

ALMOST HOME

K arsis sat up slowly, his head feeling like it had been hit by a small mountain. He surveyed his surroundings, marveling at what could only be described as astounding. The sky was a deep azure color, dotted with billowing white clouds, and birds trilling their songs as they soared high above. Statues dotted the lush green grassland as far as the eye could see, placed here and there among shrines or pools. Every statue was the same however, and that clue made him frown; they were all of the God Davalar, pristine in his glory as a protector and healer of the races. He got to his feet, testing his balance and realized that he had appeared in Caerlyn's head somewhere different than Caerlyn. He had never seen another mind this lonely. Oh sure, it looked positively gorgeous, but there was no one here. No memories dancing by, no favorite people mindlessly repeating their trademark moves, nothing. Nothing except the statues of the God she served dotting a serene, but deathly empty landscape. He started walking and thought of her face, her hair, her smile. He knew how to travel in this place, and suddenly his surroundings changed.

Between one step and the next his steps went from the soft,

lush grass to a hard, unyielding stone. He was in the throne room in Castle Everknight, and there against the wall were his former travelling companions. They were still as statues, but seemed real, except for the fact that they were all behind a glass wall. Everyone was there, even himself, posed like they were talking. *Arguing more likely,* he thought as he neared the throne. Sitting on the throne was a young girl, maybe six or seven winters, with long blond hair and dressed in a pure white dress. The dress was very plain and had folded edges, no frills at all. This had to be little Caerlyn. Karsis stood staring at her for a long while, his mind racing at how bad this was. While it looked very innocent, seeing herself as an innocent young girl like this had implications to what they were trying to do. If Caerlyn started reverting while they were fighting this darkness, he would be on his own. *Oh Caer, you are so lonely that you put your memories away under glass to keep them still all the time. Do you fear what they might say?* His thoughts turned inward at what someone might see in his own head and he shuddered.

"There you are," Caerlyn said as she walked in behind him, a note of embarrassment in her voice. She hated that he was going to see things about her that she had kept locked away from everyone. Well, everyone except her god. "Come—I can feel where it is, and it's growing stronger." She placed her hand on his arm and got a flash of something long and white... hair? Why did she get a flash of Rhoe when she touched Karsis? Were they that close?

"Yes, yes." Karsis reassured her by patting her hand and turning to walk with her. "Do you feel like you've been hit by a mountain as well?" he asked, shaking his head as if to clear it. Something was trying to distract him. Could it be the evil penetrating her soul?

"Yes, as a matter of fact I *do* feel like that." She smiled as she thought about the deep, dark evil burrowing into her very fabric, and suddenly they were somewhere else, and she regretted it instantly. Before her was a massive temple of Davalar, complete with pillars of gold, and marble stone steps. The high stone roof was starting to cave in as a huge, black, monstrosity dug into it with raking claws and tentacles. "Oh, gods above, why did it have to have tentacles?" She asked no one in particular. Then she remembered who was beside her and waited for the sarcastic retort about tentacles... and got nothing. She looked to her right and saw that Karsis was staring at this beast with narrowed eyes. She didn't even think that he had heard anything she had said. "Karsis?"

"Hold on Caer... busy." The minute they had appeared that thing shot out at his mind and he threw up the quickest, and strongest, shield he had ever had to use. He had been rein-forcing it, second by second, as he continued to hold that thing at bay. *No, not a thing. That thing is called Xilquiliv, and he is very old... older than me or my entire race.* He realized that he had backed up at least three steps. He could feel this thing's thoughts as it tried to punch through his shields. Karsis smiled. He could feel its fear. "Caer! Hit it hard and fast. We're kind of linked, so it is going to hurt me a bit, but he's scared."

"Linked? Karsis, I don't want to blast you clear out of my mind; you might not even be whole again." She hesitated as she lifted her hands, but she was so used to trusting him that she almost did it while she was talking to him anyway. Old habits die hard. "And what do you mean he?"

"Caerlyn, later! He is going to needle his way into my mind, my shields are only slowing him down... If I can feel his fear, then he has to be scared of you, not me." He fell to his knees, barely holding his thoughts together. Xilquiliv pushed harder, adding mental probes to all sides of his shields, almost like the tentacles that he had. Karsis had a plan, but she had to do some-thing now. "Please Caer... *now!*"

She flinched at his harshness, and turned her head to the thing, narrowing her own eyes and focusing her energy into her arms. She didn't need to call upon Davalar here; it all came from her mind. She thrust her arms out at the main bulk of the thing and screamed. "In the name of His light, be *gone!*" Light burst forth from her arms, slamming into it and burning away a good chunk of the side of it. She heard a scream and saw Karsis stand quickly and fling his fingers out at the monster right as her beam hit. Something detonated between the two of them, throwing the bard back and making the thing on the roof utter a moaning screech that chilled her spine, then it was gone.

Karsis was rolling again. When he finally stopped, he realized that his chest was burned clean through his shirt and blistered the skin. *That was close,* he thought as he struggled to stand. He had waited for the creature to try and shield himself from her attack, then launched himself mentally at it with a pulse of force from his own mind to give them some space. It had worked to shield himself from the blast, well most of it at least. Caerlyn was racing over, concern all over her face.

"Are you all right?" Even though she knew that healing in this place was just as easy as traveling, she was still worried about his injuries. Too severe and his mind would be forced out without his control.

Karsis smiled at her and suddenly his chest was healed. He looked down, and the shirt was back a second later. He twirled around for her, just to make her feel better. It worked, as he saw the smile spring to life on her face. "Now, let's think about this. That being is old, older than I have ever encountered, and it is not gone, just pushed somewhere else for now."

"Yes, I can still feel it, him... whatever it is." She glanced back at the temple and its crumbling roof, she winced as a slab of marble choose that moment to collapse inward. She closed her eyes and the whole thing vanished. She couldn't fix it now.

That would take too much energy, and she had to conserve. Caerlyn could still feel herself being eaten away bit by bit. She opened her eyes and looked at the bard with determination. "Now what or who was that thing, and how did you know its name?"

Karsis smiled, glad that his friend had found that old fire once more. Now if he could just keep her in this mood. "When we were linked mind to mind, I got a glimpse of who it was. It's a demon." He saw her eyes go wide with a mixture of fear and loathing, but continued before she could interrupt him. "Its name is Xilquiliv, and once it touched my mind it remembered me." He counted silently to three.

"Demon!" She couldn't even fathom that there was a demon after her soul. This changed things. Then the rest of his statement sunk in and she grabbed his jacket and pulled him closer. "What do you mean he *remembered* you?!" Her voice raised in pitch until she was almost squeaking.

Karsis gently pulled her hands off of his longcoat, brushed the wrinkles out, clearing his throat, trying not to laugh. "Calm down Caerlyn, it will be all right. Now, remember that time I took Tanan's wound? Well, apparently this demon is tied to all the blades made like that, and he could tell me from the smell of my soul." He should've known that the thing in here was a demon, after all—what else could be that old, or that evil? "I threw up a shield, but even that barely held him out."

Caerlyn was pacing now and had her thinking face on. "I've studied a lot of books Karsis, and I know that the elven archwizards dealt with demons, but other than that, I don't know anything about them." It seemed hopeless. Even the great bard Karsis had his limits, though there were rumors of him having pacts with demons.

She knew they didn't have a lot of time, yet she needed to know what they were going up against, even though she did really well blasting it like that. He could only assume that it was busy with his shields so couldn't defend against her as well. A mistake it would not make twice. "Okay, I'll try and make this quick so listen carefully. Demons are tricky and not at all like the stories make them out to be. Most people think demons are horned creatures with tails and wings that were covered in flames. The stories say they were summoned with magic into chalk outlines that supposedly kept them bound and restrained. Rubbish, all of it. Demons are beings with immense power that dwell in-between worlds and can only reach out to this world through magic conduits, like the Xalrin blade. They come in varied shapes and sizes, and they only want one thing: souls. Once they get inside your mind, they attack your soul and devour it, then leave you an empty husk, fleeing back to the space between worlds." He knew that she was going to keep asking questions, but they just didn't have time to go into what they could do, or how best to fight them. "Before you ask, just do what you did back there, over and over until it screams for you to stop."

"What do I do when he does that?" she asked, knowing how this was going to go. It was an old trick he used to keep his comrades calm. Tanan and Storn always fell for it. Every time. While she was waiting for his answer, she homed in on another focus of evil and closed her eyes, concentrating on its location.

"You hit it again." He laughed as they appeared near a small village. He looked at it and recognized it as one of the farming villages east of Alrin. *J'ren, if I'm not mistaken,* he thought as he saw the monstrosity laying across the fields and digging great furrows in the barren ground with its tentacles. The demon did not look like it was frightened at all, and Karsis was working furiously on what had scared this ancient being. This was going to hurt; he just knew it.

Caerlyn ran to the left, trying to put distance between her

and Karsis, her old training and reflexes kicking it once more. She raised her arms pointing to the beast and willed the light to come forth. She didn't need to shout the words, it just made her feel better. She saw the lance of bright light slam into the things side and burn a huge line across it. The howl it made bore into her head like an avalanche, but it wasn't like before. Now it just seemed angry. She called up another blast, but never got it off as she was slammed to the ground with two of those tentacles. She cried out and tried to roll with the hit, but they pinned her tight to the earth. She could hear Karsis calling for her to do some-thing, but she couldn't hear him with her head being pushed into the ground. Then she remembered where she was. Suddenly she was where they started, at the edge of the field, about a hundred feet away from where she was. She spit dirt and grinned at the thing that was trying to devour her. *Let's try that again.*

Karsis saw the tentacles slam her down and fired a line of energy blasts that pelted into the beast's side. It was pure magic energy, and should've burned the thing to ash, but they were only burning parts away. He saw her travel away and smiled, smart girl. He rolled under a reaching tentacle, then came up with a jet of flame coming from both hands. He was switching his attacks to keep the demon off balance. Not that it would work, but it made him feel clever. It screeched so loud when he hit this time, that he felt blood trickling from his ears. He kept moving and firing; then a tentacle smashed into him, sending him flying through the air. *Aw hells below, this is going to hurt...* he thought as he crashed into the dirt and rolled for at least fifty feet. He got up and jumped to the left as a tentacle slammed down where he was. This was going about as well as trying to out-drink a dragon. He sprinted towards Caerlyn and prayed he could get to her before she was crushed. They needed a new plan. It knew their thoughts from being in here with them.

Karsis had to get her to do something new. He needed her to lose restraint; it would never see that coming.

She dodged and fired again and again, then saw the tentacles coming down for her and sidestepped, blasting it with her power over and over again. *Why did it flee the last time? What's different?* It was hard to keep ahead of it, but this was her mind and she could almost sense when this demon was going to swing at her. Then she saw Karsis fly through the air and hit the ground. She winced, knowing that there were very few things on this earth that could do that to him. *Oh yeah, it's not of this earth.* She laughed out loud at that thought and it must've caught the demon off guard because its attacks stopped for a second. Then Karsis was there, grabbing her and whisking her back away from the demon.

"The little girl, Caer—bring us there now!" he yelled as they ran across the barren fields of dirt. He was missing something again, and that was getting tiring. He needed time to think and work through some of this before he lost his friend, and as he held her, he could tell that she was getting colder. One second they were on dirt, the next they were stepping on the cold stone floor of the throne room. they stumbled together and collapsed, breathing heavily. He saw that the little girl was still sitting there, but now she was smiling at them fondly. It made him feel a little uneasy.

"What now Karsis? I can almost feel him before he attacks, but I can't keep it up that long." She felt ragged, torn, but her spirit was still fighting the demon off. She saw him looking at the girl with those eyes that said he was almost onto something and she giggled; the girl on the throne giggled at the same time.

His eyes went wide. Not because he figured out how to beat the demon—no he wasn't quite there yet. No, what he just realized was where they had been going and what everything represented. It was why he and his friends were encased behind glass, and why she was a little girl watching them. "The Temple, the fields, and here... they are all parts of you." Usually in a person's mind, it was made up of memories, but in here, at least what he was seeing, was the most important parts of what made Caerlyn who she was.

She looked down at her feet, thoroughly embarrassed. To be laid bare in front of her friends, especially this one, was almost more than she could handle. Caerlyn was always very private, but now. "Yes Karsis. The girl is my youth, my playfulness."

"And you have us behind the glass because you grew up watching us." As the youngest of the Companions of Everknight, she was the last one to join the group, and she was only fourteen then. "But what did the fields represent? I can see that the temple was your faith, but what could the barren..." He stopped as he saw her face fall in utter despair, *Sometimes I'm too damn smart for my own good,* he thought as he stepped closer and she backed away.

"No, it's all right." She sniffed away the tears that were forming and raised her head to meet his gaze directly. She would not cave in front of this man. "I learned years ago that I could never have children. It was that wagon accident on the Southern Run road." She had saved a small child, pulling her out from under an overturned wagon, but then it collapsed on top of her, crushing her entire lower half. In fact, it was Karsis that half lifted the entire thing with magic so Gareth and Arian could push it over and pull her out. She didn't remember the trip to the castle, just that they got there in record time. Only her healing, and Ralavin's got her up and walking again after that, but they couldn't restore some of the damage.

"I'm so sorry Caerlyn, and don't worry, you have my silence." He wouldn't tell a soul, except maybe Ralavin. With his youth returned, he may be able to help her better now. "But now to the task at hand!" he shouted, to no one in particular. He smiled and did a turn, spinning his coat tails, trying to make her smile again. It worked, and the little girl on the throne smiled too. Was it him, or did his clone just frown at him?

"Yes, yes Karsis. Now what was different between when we fought that demon at the Temple compared to the fields?" It was bothering her that she hit it with one blast and it fled, then later it took a dozen and Karsis's magic as well with no sign of slowing down. Except when she laughed.

"Well, the temple was representing your faith, right? So, we were linked and then I told you his name...*ha!*" *Syll be damned how did I miss that?* He must be going senile. The oldest trick in the book, and one that had a solid basis in all of his teachings of magic. He knew the thing's true name. Xilquiliv was as good as dead.

Caerlyn laughed at the revelation as well. She didn't even think of that, but it made sense. Karsis had said it was afraid of her, and it was. It was petrified that she would've said his name before blasting him, which is why it fled as quick as it did. When they showed up at the fields and didn't say it, the demon just went on the offensive as fast as it could before they figured it out. "I know where it will be going next." She skipped over to the bard and grabbed his hand. She didn't expect him to pull away like he did. "What's wrong?" The bard looked like he had seen a ghost.

Karsis saw her coming, and when she touched his hand, he felt the cold of the grave. When he pulled away, he saw that he could almost see right through her. He was not going to lose her. "Listen, you have to find some way to surprise this demon, Caer. He knows you intimately now—your faith, your life—and now he is going to take away something else." He was so angry that he could tear apart a mountain, and after this, he just might.

Caerlyn knew as well. The strongest part of her. "He's going after my love." She wrapped her hand in her dress, thinking that it might help him grab her. She reached out and he took it without a second thought.

"Take me away my lady, and remember, do something unexpected." He readied himself as well, then they arrived where he first showed up. He tried to hide his puzzlement, but hearing her laugh again clued him into his failure. Xilquiliv was there, smashing statue after statue across the wide grassy plain. The demon was pulling himself across the grass with great heaves and left a massive trench behind him. "Oh, I get it. The only room you have for love is Davalar." He should've known that one, but it had been a busy day. That's when he heard her say his name softly. He turned in time to see her glowing hand reach for his left arm, and he pulled away to the right.

Exactly where she wanted him. Caerlyn touched her other hand, which was also glowing, to his shoulder and whispered to him as he started to fade away. "I've got this Karsis, you helped me in the only way that you could, the way I knew you would. You found out how to win, you always do. Go, I'll be right behind you," and as he faded back to reality, he stuck his tongue out at her. She had to laugh; if she didn't, she would start crying. She turned, once her friend was gone and started walking towards the demon that wanted her soul. She was almost gone now, only her youth and memories that were locked away were left. If she lost here, she was gone forever. The demon must've felt something different because it stopped mid smash and slowly pivoted, moving towards her. She couldn't do this too soon, or it would flee again, then she wouldn't have the element of surprise. "Come on you evil, repugnant bastard," she said, remembering some of the things that Tanan had said to his opponents in the past. "Let's get this over with, I've got a date with your mother later." It sounded awkward coming from her, but she hoped that would it make the sly thief proud.

It came at her with a hunger that seemed insatiable. He had

lived for eons off the souls of these pathetic beings, and this one seemed delectable. Too bad the wizard was gone; he was powerful, and he remembered that smell from just a little while ago. Time was fleeting to Xilquiliv, but he never forgot when he lost a soul. He hadn't expected that shield to pop up so fast, or for it to hold him out of his mind. He was sure that they had known his name, but they never used it. Closer and closer he came, his tentacles smashing into what she considered her most treasured part of her being. He wanted to consume her with his great maw, devouring her essence all in one. Then he noticed that her whole form was glowing, radiating a smell of *delectable* goodness. He knew that she wasn't the type to put all her power into one shot, she just wasn't that type of person. He had devoured enough of her essence to know what she would do. She would hold back and conserve her strength, trying to wear him down little by little. She thought she could sense him, knowing when he would strike, but he was feeding her ego so that she would gain confidence. He thought it might be a trick, luring him in, since she had done some of those things over the fleeting time she had been with this soul. These beings so liked their tricks. He raised up, his gigantic bulk towering over her small glowing form. He would crush her quickly, not toying with her anymore. He was about to lash out, then everything changed to pure, unadulterated *pain.*

Caerlyn drew in everything she had, all of *her* and focused it into her core. She was glowing from the amount of power coming off of her now, and he was too close to stop her. She thought of her friends, and all of the people that she had saved, and smiled. This had better work. "Xilquiliv! Be gone into the darkness from which you came! Xilquiliv, be banished by His light!" Then she let go. She let go of the shame of Karsis knowing her utter most secrets, she let go of the pain of missing the adventures of the road, even the pain of never raising children. Her form exploded into a thousand pieces of glowing shards that sliced into the demon a million times, each one carrying the echoes of his true name. He melted away, screaming, back to that place between worlds. Then she woke up.

Caerlyn Hold, Eastern Lythinall

RHOE, Liss, and Graf had travelled for two days, trudging along the packed earthen road with the bodies of their unconscious friends draped over the horses. Rhoe was exhausted. He was running on reserves that he was pretty sure he stole from someone. He was still trying to recuperate from healing and then the fight with the sorcerer. Add to that the stress of his friends being close to death, and that made for the worst two days of his life. Thank the gods above that the king's marshal had provisions in the horses' packs, otherwise they would've fallen over dead by now. He hadn't eaten real food for days, and these rations were barely keeping him on his feet.

"Are we there yet?" Liss smiled at Rhoe as she asked, mainly to make him smile back. He was ignoring her with practiced ease. She could see that he was barely standing, yet he was still walking with a determined step. Walking, ironic really since they all had horses. They had to lead the horses since Karsis and Caerlyn we're still out of it, fighting some evil darkness inside of Caerlyn. It was all too much for her to understand. She watched Rhoe lead the horse with Karsis on it and smiled again, more to herself this time. She admired the way he took charge, even though she should've been the one since she was the princess. *Enjoy it now; this will all end when we get back to the castle,* she thought as they came over a rise and saw Caerlyn Hold. "Oh, hey! We really are there." She walked a little faster leading her horse, so that she could be in front. She knew most of the people in charge here and knew how to deal with them. "I'll get us in Rhoe, just head to the right once were in and you'll see the stables."

He nodded to her, trying to smile, but he just didn't have it in him. He looked back for Graf, but the tall man had disappeared again. He was very good at that. Over the last two days, Graf would periodically vanish without telling them, then just be there later out of know where. Rhoe would be more suspicious, if he weren't worried to death over the two people pretending to be saddle bags at the moment. He shrugged and just led the three horses in as Liss talked to the guards. She was pointing and smiling, and they just opened the gate. This world was so different from the one he grew up in. He led a simple life in a frontier village and had never had to deal with courts, kings, or castles. He had no idea what was going to happen when he got to Everknight. *I hope you wake up soon Karsis, I don't think I can do this without you.* He had come to depend on the legendary bard, even though he did pretty well on his own. As he neared the stables, two older boys came over and helped him tether the horses. He accepted their help with a polite nod, and they stared at his long grey robes with amusement. He took Caerlyn down reverently, then Karsis, and laid them down on the hay.

Liss walked over with two guards behind her and smiled at the stable boys. They immediately recognized her, blanched, and bowed their heads as they walked off. She had seen the way they treated Rhoe, and that would not be tolerated. "Okay, I told the chamberlain that we needed help with the bodies, and after he almost fainted, he sent me these two men." She pointed to the bodies on the ground. "Take them to Caerlyn's chambers and put them on the bed if you could gentlemen."

"Both on the same bed miss?" The man just started at her,

clearly not understanding. His partner just shook his head in embarrassment.

"Yes, on the same bed. It's fine—the man there is Karsis the bard." She saw their mouths drop and had to laugh. She turned to Rhoe and saw him lean on his horse, eyes turning up into the back of his head. "Rhoe!" She caught him as he started to fall and eased him down. This was not going well at all. She put her hand on his chest as she pulled him over into her lap and felt his heart beating steadily. "I've got you Rhoe." *But who is going to catch me?* she thought, feeling tired and worn herself.

An hour or so later, all four of them were in Caerlyn's chambers. Caerlyn and Karsis were on the bed, still out, with Caerlyn growing colder by the moment. Rhoe was in the big chair, snoring lightly after being brought up from the stables. Liss sat on the floor watching them all as the sun's fading rays came through the window. They had made it, but she had this growing fear that they were far from safe yet. If Brenscomb could be turned to the will of these evil sorcerers, then who else was working against them. *Was there anyone* here *waiting to kill them?* She had a pair of guards outside of the door, but Deathsong was still on her lap, just in case. She was tired, but she daren't try and sleep with everyone else out of it. *And where did Graf go?* she thought as another yawn forced its way out. She had noticed that he liked to hide around people, but she could really use the company right about now. If only to let her get a cat nap. She had grown fond of the tall, wiry man on the road from River Vale. They had kept him amused by telling him about the faeries for the first day, then discussed the events leading up to their predicament on the second day. She had started to trust him; when he was around, that is. She could still remember the look on his face when they mentioned the incarnation; all of the blood drained out of his face.

A knock on the door signaled the food the chamberlain said

was going to be brought up for her, and quite possibly a healer to look in on the Lady Caerlyn once more. Everyone in the hold was worried about their lady, and it took all of her princess-like authority to get them to leave her alone, lest they interrupt what she was doing with Karsis. Whatever that was. Liss got up and walked quietly to the door, but a sound at the window stopped her. She turned and saw a figure hanging outside of the second-story window, and he was waving at her as if to warn her. It was Graf, and he looked like he had dragged himself through every mud puddle he could find. If he was warning her, then it was bad. She was getting very tired of all the bad lately. She didn't dare draw her sword, lest it sound out to her enemies, so she backed up to the window, cautiously lifting the latch that kept it closed, keeping an eye on the door. She could see Graf outside pointing to the door. *But how would he know who was behind the door?* Her thoughts vanished as the knock became a crash, splintering the door open and off the hinges. Three men flooded into the room with drawn knives and black hoods. Liss had just enough time to see the bodies of the guards lying in the hallway, possibly drugged or dead, then she drew Deathsong, its ringing call echoing off the close walls.

"Duck!" Graf yelled as he pushed open the window and threw his slim knife past her head. It buried itself in the chest of one of the men as Graf dove over her and rolled up to his feet, kicking out at another man. He had followed Liss and Rhoe in, using the shadows that he was so adept at, and saw the men dressed in black hiding here and there throughout the hold. After hearing the stories about River Vale, he thought he would scout this place out. He was not disappointed. Finding the right room was problematic, but he got lucky on the third try.

The first room was empty, but the second one was a bit of a surprise. The woman that was undressing didn't even scream, and if he wasn't pressed for time. *Who am I kidding, smelling like this? She would've slapped me once I got within ten feet of her.* He reined his thoughts in and slid to the side as Liss lunged with that cool sword of hers and slid it right into the last man's chest. He watched the man's eyes lose their light and then went to check the guards.

"How did you find us?" Liss asked, wiping the blade clean on the man's cloak. The sword felt very heavy in her tired hands.

"I got lucky," he said curtly, not wanting to get into it. He bent over the guards and checked their neck for that telltale throb of life. With all the blood on the floor he doubted it, but he always checked.

She scoffed at his 'getting lucky' statement, but didn't pry. She hoped that the guards were drugged, but then she saw him shake his head as he felt for a pulse. She spun and kicked the wash basin out of anger and sent the water bowl flying. "I am going to find out who ever is doing all of this and slice them apart very slowly." She slid Deathsong into its sheath and walked out of the door. "Watch them Graf, I need to ask the chamberlain about this, and he *will* give me some answers."

"But Liss there's probably more..."

She spun, angry tears falling quietly down her strained face. "Just do it. I'm going to hope that I get attacked—that way I can beat someone until I hear them scream. Oh, and be ready to leave when I get back because it seems that we can't stay here any longer." She turned back and stomped down the hall towards the front of the hold, trying to keep her anger in check and failing miserably.

Graf watched her go and smiled. That girl was a firecracker, and he liked the way she took charge. He wasn't originally going to follow them any farther, but now he almost wanted to make sure she got home safe.

You will *make sure she makes it safely to Everknight, or else...*

Graf grabbed his head as the voice echoed loudly. He hated when the voices got all lordly in his own head, like they were better than him. He muttered something about how the voice smelled like a sheep, and why, then heard a cough behind him.

Rhoe came awake slowly, like he was swimming out of a deep-water pool, climbing for the surface. He heard Graf talking to someone, but when he finally opened his eyes, the man was alone. He cocked his head to the side, trying to hear what the man was saying, but he couldn't catch any of it. He coughed politely and saw the man turn quickly. He laughed at Graf's expression, then Rhoe noticed the bodies. "What?" He jumped up and spun, seeing the open window, then turned back to the door in alarm. "Where is Liss?"

"She's okay. She went to the chamberlain to let him know about the bodies. Yes, I tried to tell her not to; and yes, I told her there were probably more assassins. But that one is stubborn." He walked over and started to gather up the packs that they had placed in the corner. He tightened straps and made sure everything was there, just trying to look busy.

"I take it we have to go?" Rhoe asked as he saw Karsis and Caerlyn still out and wondered how long he had slept for. He was more embarrassed then angry with himself for passing out, but he felt ten times better. "How long have I been out?"

"Not long, I guess. I just got here myself, but it's been like five hours since you guys came here if that helps." Graf went over to the window and looked out over the courtyard. He could spot at least three people hiding from here. This was going to be about as much fun as a sword through the throat. "I'll start getting these two down to the stables if you can get the packs." He grabbed Karsis and flipped the slender bard over his shoulder and slipped out the window. He was gone in a heartbeat, sliding down his anchored rope.

Rhoe stared out the window for a minute, amazed at the

man's ability to simply disappear, then he turned and grabbed the packs. He heard footsteps and turned, expecting Liss, and was shocked when a well-dressed man came through the door. "Oh, hello sir, how can I..." Then he was leaping back, dropping the packs and throwing out his hand to slap the blade away from his chest. The blade sliced his palm, but it was angled enough so as to not cut too deeply. He saw the man's face, his eyes distant and unfocused, and knew that he was being controlled. He wondered if he could use magic to free the man, but he just didn't know how to break it. He ducked another sideways swing, then jumped up on the bed where Karsis had lain. Caerlyn's body rolled over onto his foot, and he almost lost his balance when the man lunged in straight with his blade. The man then looked at the body at Rhoe's feet and smiled. "Oh no you don't." Rhoe knew what the man had to be thinking, and quickly whispered to the Ether to free the man's mind. It was all instinct now, as a life was in the balance. "Ash'anti ethir brek dosit a'ren." Rhoe hoped that his use of the elven word 'brek' wasn't going to do the man any harm. It usually meant break or free, but he was worried that it might take 'break' literally and destroy his mind forever, but with Caerlyn as the man's target, he didn't have time to debate it with his conscience.

The man stumbled, then his eyes focused and a look of pure horror passed across his face. He dropped the sword like it was poison and backed away from everyone slowly. "What have I done?" He turned to run through the doorway, but was grabbed by the shoulder before he got three feet.

"It's all right, just calm down, I'm not going to hurt you." Rhoe was just glad that the man wasn't drooling on the floor after his impromptu spell. He really needed to practice more with Karsis, but everything had been a whirlwind since the bridge. He was a little scared that it was coming to him easily though, casting the spells with instinct rather than study. "Sit down, tell me who you are, and try to remember what happened to you." He sat the man down just as Graf came through the window once more. Rhoe made the gesture to the tall man that everything was all right, and tried to keep the man focused on him. "Don't mind our friend, he doesn't like bathing." Rhoe smiled at Graf as the dirty man lifted Caerlyn and scowled, then vanished out the window once more like a spirit.

"My name is Renferd, and I am the chamberlain here at the hold. I was marking in the books that you all had checked in, having just written the names down and then...Verice." He shook his head in disbelief before continuing, "Verice came to me and asked what room you all were staying in, then she said some strange words." He started sobbing into his hands, his memory coming back to him finally. "I kil...killed so many. Oh ...oh my God...wha ...what have I done?"

Rhoe didn't know what to say, but he knew that they had to find Liss, and fast. "Show me where."

Liss stalked the halls and eventually made it down to the main antechamber. The chamberlain was usually here, taking notes or checking the inventory books, but all was quiet. In fact, the hallways were quiet as well, which she would've noticed if she wasn't so damned angry. She was starting to get that feeling. The feeling that said she was going to really regret this day and probably the next three as well. She took a deep breath and turned, jumping as a girl was there right behind her.

"Can I help you, milady?" Verice curtsied slightly, then bowed her head a bit to show deference. She didn't want to try controlling the princess just yet. She was too angry still; better to calm her down first. She put on that fake smile and tried to look complacent, but she wasn't a good actress. She had been taught magic from her master S'ren Dro, in River Vale, but hadn't had a message from him in a couple days, so she was a bit on edge.

"Actually, yes you can." Liss said, trying to calm down. The girl had to be almost twenty winters and was well versed in courtly etiquette apparently. Everything she did was perfect, but it was weird that she wasn't even a *little* nervous standing in front of the princess. Liss looked around the room, seeing if she missed anything before meeting the girl's stare. *Was that blood on the carpet by the chamberlain's desk?* Her thoughts were in a whirl, with the attack still on her mind. "I'm looking for Renferd, the chamberlain."

"I don't know where he went milady, but I can call for him if you wish." She walked over to his desk without waiting for a response and reached for the long rope hanging from the ceiling. She pulled twice and then turned to the princess, waiting for the echoing gong of the bell to stop before speaking. "Have a seat and he should be right here. Can I get you anything?" Verice glided closer, confident that she could take her if she got comfortable and let some of that anger subside. Emotions were tricky with controlling magic, and you had to tread carefully around strong minds. Unless you were a blood born sorcerer like S'ren, then it didn't matter.

Liss eyed the girl closely and walked to a comfy chair. Graf was watching Rhoe, Karsis, and Caerlyn so she could wait a couple of minutes for the chamberlain to arrive. As she sat down and crossed her legs, she saw that spot again by the desk. This time, because she was sitting, she could also see an arm under the desk. There was no way that the girl didn't see that when she pulled the cord. Every instinct told her to jump up and pull her sword, but she closed her eyes and took a breath. She wanted to surprise this killer.

Verice saw her take a breath and smiled, walking around the

chair. She took a quick breath and leaned in, whispering in the princess's ear. "Obren ethir..." That's all she got out before her world was turned upside down, literally.

Liss reached up and grabbed the girl's hair and neck pulling her straight down, yanking her over the back of the chair and onto her lap. Liss rolled out of the chair while holding her, wrapped her arm around the girl's throat, and started punching her in the side as they tumbled to the ground. The girl was fighting desperately, but was no warrior. In another couple of hits, Liss was on top of the girl, straddling her waist and landing blow after blow into her face, bouncing her head off the carpeted floor. She heard her name being called faintly, then arms grabbed her from behind.

"Princess, it's all right—you got her." The young boy was trying to get through to the princess, but she was so angry she couldn't hear him. He had hidden when the chamberlain started killing people, but came out when he heard Allissana's voice. He ran around behind her and tried to pull her off, and then he felt his lungs explode as her elbow seemed to go right into his chest and do a little dance.

Liss threw her elbow back and connected, but when she heard the young voice cry out, she snapped out of it. The young boy was bent over, trying to breathe but without any air he was having a hard time. She felt horrible for hitting him like that. "I'm so sorry. You'll be all right, here sit down here." She guided him to the chair. "I've got to get back to my friends to make sure they are all right."

"No, you don't, silly," Rhoe called from the door way, "We came to you." He walked in with Renferd, who was still a sobbing mess, and a young page carrying most of the packs. "I take it you found Verice?" Rhoe looked down at the girl and was shocked at the violence with which she was subdued. Her face was bloody and swollen already, but then he remembered that the girl could be a sorceress and how bad that could've turned out.

"Who is Verice?" Liss was dumbfounded. The last thing she knew Rhoe was out cold, but now here he was, and he knew more of what was going on than she did. *How does he make me feel so powerless, yet so important at the same time?* she thought as she eyed the bawling mess that was the hold's chamberlain. There was blood all over his clothes and the boy in the chair was whimpering at the sight of him.

Renferd saw Verice on the ground and seemed to snap. He launched himself at her and started kicking her mercilessly, over and over, crying all the while. "You made me do this! You made me kill them. Why did you make me kill the *children?*"

Rhoe quickly grabbed him and pulled him away, but he just kept kicking at the air. *Maybe I did break his mind,* Rhoe thought as he dragged him away from the unconscious girl. "That is Verice. She took control of the chamberlain and made him kill a bunch of people." Rhoe didn't know that he had killed children; that must be horrible to have on your conscience. "He came in to kill me and the others, but I broke him free of the magic."

"Where are the others?" Liss asked, finally calming down now that it seemed to be over. Servants were slowly peaking in to see if everything was all right, and then the healers came in shortly after.

"Graf brought them to the horses. He said we had to leave fairly soon, so I brought everything else down." Rhoe smiled at her, feeling that warmth that he always felt now when he looked at her. It was getting easier to talk to her without feeling stupid.

"Yes, I just have to find out who is going to be in charge once we leave. I don't think they are safe here anymore." Liss looked around at the assembly in the antechamber and saw only lost looks. How could she leave them?

"Well, if they aren't safe here, why don't they come with us to Everknight?" Rhoe thought it was a simple thing to say, but judging by the look she had on her face you would think he just invented the wheel.

Liss couldn't believe that she didn't think of it. This boy, who led a simple carefree life, could see things that she couldn't. No, not simple. He was raised a warrior and his training was probably just as extensive as hers. Not simple, but rather, uncomplicated. "Rhoe that is an outstanding idea, but how are we going to know who is innocent and who is trying to kill us?" She just didn't know who to trust anymore.

"Oh, well, I don't know." He hadn't thought of that. He hoped that they had found the one behind it all and that the rest would... *Would what? Run into the night with their tails between their legs?* He felt stupid. He didn't know how to rule over people and make decisions like this. She was raised in the castle and probably made decisions like this every day. "Well, on the bright side, they would be right there with us so they couldn't plan to ambush us later."

Liss was surprised with his every thought. Karsis said he was special, and gods above he was right. "Rhoe, that is a great plan. You," she pointed to the oldest healer there, hoping she had some authority, "gather supplies and get everyone together in the courtyard, we are evacuating to the castle." She looked down at the young boy and smiled. "And you. Go make sure everyone is told that they must leave. Take two healers with you just in case you find any injured." She felt a bit guilty asking him to do this, but if he had hidden that good when they were attacked, then he maybe he knew his way around this hold better than anyone else. She turned to Rhoe and smiled at his confused expression. "Let's go see Graf and tell him that were going to have company on the road." She grabbed some packs from the other young boy and led them out of the hold into the courtyard.

A little later, everyone was assembled in the courtyard and two wagons were hitched with teams of horses. All in all, there were twenty people including poor Renferd. He was being consoled by the poor boy who was Liss's new friend, and it wasn't helping at all. If any of these people were still trying to kill her or her friends, then they would have a harder time at getting to them being watched all the time.

"I still think this is a bad idea, Liss." Graf tried to keep his voice down, but he wasn't used to doing that, so it came out louder than he wanted. He could be silent as death, or loud. There was no middle ground.

"You're uncomfortable around people, I know Graf." She could see his face and how twitchy he got with all these people around. He kept licking his finger and putting it up checking for the wind he was so anxious. "Hey, I know. Would you scout out ahead for us? It's a couple hours to the bridge and if anyone were going to strike it would be along this route."

Graf looked at her with suspicion. He would sooner believe that ogrann bathe before he would believe that line, but he *would* be the best to spot an ambush. "Fine, but keep them moving." He started to walk away but turned back and looked at her again. "You know, the assassins that were here at the hold might have left before you. Just an observation." He turned back and loped off ahead, moving gracefully for one so tall.

She frowned at his statement. That hadn't occurred to her either. Damn it all to the hells, why did her father make this look so *easy?* She looked at all the people that were counting on her to get them to safety and the weight on her shoulders seemed to press down a little more. Gods above she was exhausted.

"I heard, Graf. You know if we leave them, they might not

be safe either." Rhoe put his arm around her and pulled her in close. They had been on the move for so long that moments like these weren't precious, they were rare.

"Thanks, Rhoe. As long as you're here I feel like it all might not fall into flames." That probably didn't come out right, but she was babbling. She looked up and saw that everyone was ready. "Let's go. It's still two days to Everknight, and a lot can happen in two days." She desperately needed sleep, but it was only a couple hours to the bridge, and they could camp for the rest of the night. They pulled out of the abandoned hold, well past sunset, and made their slow way down the dark road towards Everknight.

An hour after he had left the hold, Graf was moving quickly through the grass on the side of the road. More of a shadow right now than a man, he was almost invisible to anyone that might be looking. He had seen at least three other black figures around the walls of the hold when they were attacked, and those figures weren't with the wagons. He stepped around a dark rock and came to a halt, his long hair falling into his face because he had stopped so fast. He had heard something, and that something wasn't familiar. He scanned the dark road with the fleeting moonlight that was trying to pierce the clouds, but saw nothing. His instinct was to stay put for a moment longer before running on, and it paid off. Graf saw a large shape on the other side of the road lumber into the moonlight and sniff the air. *Crap! It's a troll. They track they're prey by scent. I'm in trouble.* His thoughts were racing as he looked around for another vantage point. He couldn't attack until he had a perfect shot. These things didn't go down easy.

Trolls were ugly things, standing roughly seven feet tall

with long scrawny arms that ended in vicious claws. They had skin that was hard like petrified wood, and sharp teeth bunched up in a mouth that was too small for them all. They had long, scraggly hair. If not killed outright in the first couple of blows, they healed any wound within moments. He would've rather fought an ogrann barehanded. He had to be almost at the bridge, and that's where he was expecting the men in black to be waiting. It was then he had a very foolish idea. It wasn't the *worst* idea he had ever had—there was that time he jumped off that high tower by Whiteleaf Lake and missed the water—but it may hurt just as bad. He leapt out of the shadows and ran over to the troll, who looked at him like he had seven heads, and kicked it right in the shin. The blow did absolutely nothing but enrage the beast, but that was the plan... or at least part of it. The thing howled and swung its arms at him, but he was already away and running down the road. It howled again and lumbered off after him at a colossal speed.

Merchant's Bridge, Eastern Lythinall

BARAND HATED WAITING. They had been here for hours, and all they had heard was a distant howl splitting the night, but it had sounded far enough away that they weren't worried about it. *Probably just a wolf anyway,* he thought as he tried to get comfortable yet again. He would rather be sitting in a warm inn and listening to some bard play something trivial while he drank a good, stout ale. He looked around at the bridge and the other assassins that were waiting for the princess to arrive and scoffed quietly. They probably didn't even need him. There were seven of them, and all trained in the art of stealth and weapons. The princess and her bodyguards were no match for them in their element, even though they had taken out Verice. The moon was hiding behind the clouds and couldn't find enough breaks in the sky to illuminate anything. Then he heard a whistle. He sat upright and drew his blade in anticipation. That was the signal. Someone was coming down the road right into their trap. He heard something right next to him, under the right-hand side of the bridge, and turned expecting to see one of his comrades.

"Here, hold my cloak," Graf said as he threw the rotting, filthy cloak over the man's head and stepped into the road. Graf then tumbled down towards the river and splashed quietly into the water, which would help wash the stink off him, but not all of it. He would watch and wait for his moment. That, and pray to whatever god wanted to listen that this plan worked without getting himself killed.

Barand jumped up and threw off the cloak, but it was too late. The troll came into view and howled as it charged him, its teeth gnashing in anticipation. The dark fighter rolled to the side, slashing the thing's hamstring, trying to drop it, but it turned and slammed two arms straight down into Barand. He felt himself lifted then, and the last thing he saw as he screamed his sanity away was that mass of teeth coming for his face.

The other six men all jumped to the attack, slashing and hacking at the great monster, but their knives only scratched it as they bounced off its hardened skin. The wounds that did penetrate healed impossibly fast. The troll swung Barand's body like a weapon, flailing at the men one by one. One went down, then another, as it clawed and slammed the men around like children's blocks. It started stomping on the bodies lying on the ground, and soon there were only two men left.

Neither of them could get away, lest the troll claw them from behind, so they circled the beast and looked for another way out of this. The troll had dropped the body by now and was turning as the men stalked it. They looked at one another and both lunged at the same time, but only one blade hit home. The blade that hit sunk in to the hilt in the thing's armpit, coming dangerously close to the beast's heart, but it wasn't long enough.

The other blade never made it. Graf's blade came sliding into the man's back, just right, so that he never made another sound ever again. When the troll turned to the other man and gutted him, Graf threw the body aside and sank his own thin blade straight into the troll's neck and up into its brain in a quick thrust. Both the troll and the other man hit the ground in a heap, and Graf rolled clear, laughing at the exhilaration of it all. He stood slowly, wiping his blade clean on the coat of one of the men. and looked around as the moon finally broke free of the dark clouds. Bodies lay everywhere and blood splashed the bridge and road.

I may just be the biggest fool there ever was, but it worked, he thought. He should be going back to warn the princess, but he decided that seeing her face when she saw all this would be even better. He searched the bodies and then got comfy on the bridge, feeling pretty good about himself.

Liss guided her horse over to the wagon once more, answering another question about what they were going to do once at the castle. The people were nervous, understandably so, but she was getting tired of repeating herself. They had been on the road for well over an hour and were almost at the bridge. Graf hadn't been back yet, but he probably hadn't had anything to report anyway. They had all heard a distant howl or two, but it hadn't gotten any closer, so they relaxed a bit. It was slow going this late at night, but the guards had torches in front of the horses so they could keep going. Once they were at the bridge, she knew there was a merchant's circle they could camp at, so she was pushing them through the night to get there. She sighed once again. She was pushing more than just the people—she was pushing herself as well. She was trying to not nod off and fall face first in the road. *Wouldn't that impress the people, if their princess face down in the dirt.* She shook her head and slapped her thigh to wake herself up.

"Almost there, Liss," Rhoe said from beside her. He had brought his horse right next to hers and had seen her troubled look. He knew that she was tired, but she wouldn't ride in the wagons. He was also worried about that howl as well, and had flashbacks of the wolvren. He had sent his *sight* out ahead, but it was too dark to see anything without the moon to guide him. Once it had fallen silent, he had breathed a sigh of relief.

"I know, but I dislike traveling at night with the wagons," she said as she smiled at Rhoe then kicked her horse forward a bit and took the lead near the torches. She just wanted to crawl in the back of one of the wagons with him and sleep, but she had to lead them. *I am going to apologize so much to my father when I see him again,* she thought as she felt the weight of everything on her shoulders for the hundredth time.

"Bridge!" one of the guards in front called as he held up the torch to signal the rear. She came up next to him as they came over the last hill and then saw the carnage. Deathsong cleared her sheath in a heartbeat, but was eerily quiet upon being freed.

"Arms!" called the guard again, and a symphony of swords clanged in the night. There weren't many guards, but the sound startled the rest of the people and they started to crowd together in the wagons.

Liss saw Graf then, sitting on the bridge looking awfully full of himself. He was smiling and kicking his feet like a three-year-old in an oversized chair. Bodies of at least seven men lay all over the road, some of them without arms. "Swords away, men," she called back. She saw the monster on the ground and couldn't help but be impressed. She had never seen anything like it. "Is that an ograrn?" she asked, dismounting near the edge of the bridge.

"No, doesn't look like an ograrn," Rhoe said as he slid off his mount and walked over to it. He was scanning the bridge for any other surprises, but with Graf here he assumed it was clear.

"And how would you know what an ograrn looked like?" Graf asked, genuinely intrigued at the young warrior.

"I killed one on the Northern Run road with Karsis, and they were much bigger than this." Rhoe winced at the memory of accidently killing that beast. He had more control now, but he still had so much to learn. He ran his fingers over the things skin and his eyes went wide. It felt like stone.

"So, what is it then?" The princess started pointing to the guards and then at the bodies of the men in the road. They started to drag them off the road and piling them together. She would burn them after they were all set up for the night.

Graf laughed then hopped down and sauntered over to the gathering near the body. "This is a troll, and I hope there are no more of these around. Killing this one was tough." He spun as there was a shout from the wagons. Someone screamed and he was off like a shot, fearful that another troll had come around. *Why did I say that? It always invites more trouble*, he thought.

Rhoe was right there with him as they grabbed the side of the wagon and vaulted over the side. They landed as Karsis rolled over and grabbed Caerlyn, gently shaking her. The people nearest them were white as ghosts and had all but jumped out of the wagon.

"Come on Caer, you can beat him," Karsis said, his voice the epitome of determination. He had come awake in a rush. Getting thrown out of her mind like that was painful, but his worry for her overrode that pain. At least for now. He felt people behind him, and smelled Graf. That man *really* needed to wash more often. "Come on...come on...*yes!*" he yelled as she coughed violently, turning to the side and throwing up a black liquid all over the wagon floor. People were actually filing out of the wagon now, frantic not to touch whatever that stuff was. He held her as she tried to clear the taint of evil from her body. The demon may have left, but his residue was still in there.

Caerlyn coughed a couple more times, then finally cleared her throat and stopped. She had rid her body of the vile liquid. She turned and smiled at all of them. "Let's not do that ever again all right?" She tried to laugh but she hurt too much. She was helped to her feet and off the wagon where Liss was waiting for her, tears in her eyes. "Oh Liss, no tears! I was in capable hands. Karsis was there with me to help."

"Why do you think I was worried?" Liss said, wiping her tears. She couldn't wait to set camp and sit down to hear this tale.

Karsis made a shocked sound and tried his best to look hurt. In truth, he was just as worried at how they were going to do in there. He leapt down from the wagon and almost lost his footing as his knee decided to argue with him at the last moment. He had forgotten all about his crash trying to reach Caerlyn on the dry bridge. "So where are we anyway?" He looked around and his face grew serious. "We went past Caerlyn Hold... that can't be good. By the look at those bodies over there we have also been attacked more than once as well." He smiled at them and straightened his longcoat, wiping away imaginary dirt like he was some haughty noble. "I say a tall tale is in order all around. Someone get me a campfire, and hurry!"

"Yeah Karsis. It's been interesting to say the least." Graf held up his finger and tested the breeze once more. He had been checking ever since he had slain the troll, and so far, nothing. If it stayed that way for a couple days that would be great, but he doubted it. "I'll go lead the horse and wagons to that circle up ahead." He started to walk away and the people that had abandoned the wagon in fear started to follow him. That made him walk even faster.

It also made Liss burst out laughing. "Guards, help Graf with the wagons and the people." She turned to Karsis and Caerlyn, then noticed Renferd waiting patiently. "Caerlyn, I think there is someone waiting to see you."

Caerlyn turned and saw the chamberlain and smiled. He started towards her then burst into tears. She walked the rest of the way and embraced him, hushing him and stroking his head like a small child. "There, there. It's all right. I can feel your regret and sadness. Whatever you went through, I absolve you of your guilt." A glow surrounded her and Renferd, and he stopped crying slowly, his eyes wide.

"Karsis, she should know what he did." Rhoe looked around and saw that even the people that knew what the chamberlain had done were smiling. "It was really bad, and I had to free his mind."

"You had to what now?" He turned abruptly, shock passing across his usually calm facade. "No, not here. First, Caerlyn is a healer and she instinctively knows when someone needs healing —even their mind. She is one of the best and she can tell how deep that hurt goes once in contact with them. Don't worry Rhoe, I know it had to be bad, and so does she, but everyone deserves peace once in a while." He started walking towards the bridge and noticed the troll. "Ooh, bet that was a nasty fight. Did you use magic?"

"No, Graf killed it before we got here." Rhoe saw Karsis pause slightly and chuckled. "I know. There is something about that guy that is starting to bother me, too."

"Well, that's good; a healthy dose of paranoia is good for the digestion. Let's set up and talk—I want to hear all about every-thing." Karsis was itching to hear about Rhoe breaking the chamberlain free of a spell. This boy was astounding.

They walked to the merchant's circle as the guards helped get the wagons over and the bodies picked up. In a couple of minutes, with the moon high in the cloudy sky, the friends were sitting around a campfire while the people of Caerlyn Hold got ready for some much-deserved sleep. Liss was out cold in Rhoe's lap, but the others had slept too much to be tired right now. Suddenly Rhoe's mind snapped awake and his memories came flooding back.

"*Karsis!*" He whispered, trying not to startle the princess on his lap. "I remembered my trance. The incarnation was fighting a dragon." He was relieved that he didn't forget that, or the questions he had for his mentor.

Karsis held his finger to his lips, then stood up and pulled out a harp. Playing lightly, he turned to the group and crossed his legs in midair, floating silently. "So, tell us Rhoe, tell us the story. And when you are done, someone else can take a turn at what has befallen them—and so on until the sun rises, or there are no more stories left."

"That's no fair Karsis! You never run out of stories." Caerlyn stuck her tongue out at the bard and everyone laughed.

"Well, I *have* been around you know." He looked at Rhoe then and prompted him to start.

Rhoe described the entire experience, and remembered to ask his questions, which Karsis answered with 'Another time, young one.' Then, it was Graf's turn. They traded stories and caught each other up and laughed at each other's jokes. Karsis watched everyone, including Rhoe, and couldn't help but smile. Using ether to break a controlled mind was tricky, just as he feared, but he had done it, nonetheless. Now there was something else nagging at him though.

He watched the way the young warrior stared at Liss when not talking; and for the first time, Karsis thought that it wasn't wholly natural. It seemed that when they were alone, they were drawn to each other. But if distracted, they seemed to forget that connection for a time. He wasn't positive, it would take more time to study them, but it was something he definitely was going to keep an eye on.

Karsis sat back and watched the clouds above, fighting to keep the moon away from lighting the dark fields around them. He should tell Rhoe that his parents were probably at the castle, but he just couldn't bring himself to do that. He wanted to see the young boy's face when he saw them. He wanted him to feel that joy and soar in it, because once they got to the castle, his world was going to turn upside down.

Dragon's Lair, Northern Belt Mountains

Dar'Krist tried to get air in his lungs again and shook with the pain of inhaling. His ribs were trying to heal, but they weren't in the right spots. They were broken, almost all of them, as were his legs, and one arm. He focused his mind once more and tried to draw power from the stone around him. He had been trying to do this for days, but he had already drawn most of it when he fought the dragon, and it needed time to replenish itself. Just like the times before, he got nothing. He tried to shift the rocks around him again with his good arm, but there was just too much on top of him. Only his great strength had kept him alive at all with this weight crushing down on him.

He had moved past anger, which was a long phase, once he had regained consciousness. Now he was on to the *How the hells am I going to get free* phase. He didn't even know how much time had passed, as the darkness was almost complete under the fallen cliff face. He wished that rock decayed like other things, then this wouldn't have been a problem, but stone and earth weren't affected by his power the same way as other things were.

Then, he felt it. A slow current coming up from the depths of the bedrock. He tried to smile, but it ended up a coughing fit as he inhaled some rock dust accidentally. He counted to one hundred, then drew deep again, pulling what he just felt into him. Strength flooded him and he knew he was ready. *Well, this is going to hurt. It's a good thing I heal fast,* he thought as he resigned himself to the pain that was coming.

Dar'Krist braced himself and used his broken arm as a wedge and pushed up with his shoulder as he shoved with his other arm. He screamed as he pushed, not stopping, even when he heard the bone crack once again in his damaged arm. The rocks started to move, and smaller pieces rained down on him as one of the big pieces rolled away. He couldn't get a good breath with his ribs the way they were, but as he straightened up on his broken legs, some of his ribs seemed to pop back into place.

Sunlight streamed in and his eyes burned at the glorious sight. His head was free, and with his good arm he shoved away the rocks to his side. With a final scream, he burst out of his stone tomb and rolled to the ground, breathing in the dirt and dust. He hoped that the dragon suffered in agony as it perished, though he had to admit that *was* a good move.

He laid there, for how long he didn't know, and finally his bones knitted together enough for him to try to stand. He was weak and needed to rest, but he had to find somewhere else— the sun was too hot, even this high up in the mountains. He crawled to a huge cave, probably where that dragon laired, and sat down to think. His arrogance notwithstanding, it was starting to feel like someone else had it out for him. For him to be outsmarted, outmaneuvered, and just plain beaten again and again was unheard of.

The gods were not allowed to meddle in the affairs of

mortals, even the incarnations, but that was the only thing that he could come up with. *Unless I'm just slipping, but this many times doesn't feel like coincidence anymore.* His thoughts were troubled, but it was something to think about later. Once he was fully healed, he would continue his pilgrimage back to civilization—and then woe to anyone who crossed his path, gods be damned.

6

ALL PATHS LEAD IN

The hallways were bustling with warriors coming and going. Regular rounds and patrols happened here like clockwork because of Keragan Hold's proximity to the borders of G'harr. Janna made her way to the main council room where the lord held all his audiences, excited to play for the Lord Storn Keragan himself. She had, of course, heard of the Companions of Everknight. She had been following their stories for years until they retired, but had never met any of them in person. She entered the hall and stopped, waiting for a page or chamberlain to announce her. A man leaned over with a parchment and quill and stared at her, waiting for her to tell him her name and title, if any. She knew the drill. Hells below, she had invented the drill. "Janna Suris, master bard and traveler extraordinaire." She dipped and curtsied flashing the man with her winning smile, and got a bland look back in return.

The man turned and signaled to the small boy to his right and the child played a trilling tune on a harp to get the attention of the room. Everyone pretty much ignored it. "My Lord, Janna Suris, master bard and traveler extraordinaire, is here to meet with you." The man bowed deep and then retreated to his corner.

Janna sighed. No one liked the pomp and flair of the old days anymore. She ignored the fact that she had failed to flatter the chamberlain and strutted her stuff to the middle of the floor. People were talking to the lord and he was trying to answer them one at a time. She thought about which instrument would best suit her in this situation and chose the flute. Janna pulled a small one out of her pack and played a shrill note to get everyone's attention. The room fell silent as they all stopped and stared at her. "That's better," she announced, but then *she* was silenced by the lord himself as he pointed to a bench and went back to answering someone else. She couldn't believe what was happening. She walked to the bench and sat, dumbfounded.

"You here to see the Lord Storn? We're here to see him, too. My name's Dren, and this here is Stard." The other man nodded his head, but his stare was directed more towards her chest. Dren elbowed the man in the side and he flushed, lifting his eyes.

Janna noticed that the man was dressed like a guard, but didn't have the colors of the hold. Each hold sported colors of the ruling lord, just to say that they were his men. She giggled, then batted her eyes. This was more like it. "Yes, and hopefully play for him as well. My name is Janna, and I was hoping that they had nightly gatherings here." She looked around surreptitiously to see if the lord was still talking while keeping her attention on these two guards. "You're not from around here, are you?"

"No, miss, we're from up north. Norhil Hold." Stard said, fighting to regain his failing composure. It was those piercing green eyes that did it. Not that he was drawn to this woman, but her eyes were intense. "We went to Everknight when they evacuated the north, but the king wanted a message delivered, so we were drafted."

"Volunteered."

"Yes Dren, we *volunteered*. You keep thinking that." Stard smiled at his old friend, then smacked him in the arm.

"Why, in all of the heavens, did they evacuate?" This was serious. Nothing like this had happened since they built those Holds. This bespoke of grim tidings indeed. It could also make a brilliant song as well. "Was it a dragon?"

"No miss. You mean, you haven't heard?" Dren swallowed before continuing. He didn't like to remember that day. He could still hear that man's voice over the flames. He shivered but kept going. "It was some guy, black cloak, very powerful. He came right up to the hold and our lord fought him. We tricked him and he ran down the road, but the king wanted everyone pulled in just in case." The woman looked faint, and she was white as a ghost. "You okay miss?"

Janna couldn't breathe. It sounded like an elf, and a wizard at that. This was beyond bad. She would've rather have had it be a dragon... maybe two. They had to be mistaken. If an elf was seen walking attacking a human settlement, that would mean that they were coming back to subjugate humanity. "Okay, so that's bad. Let's forget that for a minute..."

"Or forever."

"Yes, that too." She was starting to like these two. She focused on the lord and shook her head. "So, what do I need to know about the Lord Keragan? He seems like a different kind of man than I'm used to." That was an understatement.

Dren cleared his throat and leaned back. "Well, that there is a sad tale. Most folks don't know it, 'cause it was kept out of the stories that the bards passed around, but that gruff man used to be the happiest man in all of Lythinall." Dren pulled out a small pipe and packed it with a tiny pouch of black leaf. "See, he was with this beautiful woman when he was in the Companions of Everknight. They had a cottage in a small town near the capitol, and he would come home to her after every adventure and bring her trinkets." Dren took a puff and looked at Stard.

"Yeah, then one day he comes home and she's different, like weird." Stard continued for his friend. He looked down at his feet, trying to think of what he would do in the lord's shoes. He hated this story. "He gives her a silver necklace, and it burns her hand. He just stands there trying to think of any other explanation... and she's getting angry."

Janna closed her eyes. She had never heard this—they were right about that—and she already knew where this story was going. She looked up at the lord again and knew what she was dealing with. She waved them to continue anyways; you just never stopped a story, never.

Dren blew out a ring of dark smoke, then sat forward. "You see, he knew that she wasn't *her* anymore. It could only be one thing that could look like someone else and be burned with silver—a gnome. No one knows when she was taken, or what it did with her body, but the story goes that Storn killed her himself as she begged him to love her forever in a cackling voice."

Janna sighed at the sad tale and looked over at Lord Storn and saw him with new eyes. He was dressed casually, a simple dark green cloak over his white shirt and woolen breeches; a stark contrast to his umber skin. His black hair and beard were trimmed but not lavishly so like some lords she had seen, and there were no frills in his court. The table that he and his councilors were seated at was elevated from the floor so as to seem above everyone, but he didn't look down at them, per se. This was a man of action to be certain. She looked back at the two men and smiled tiredly. She didn't expect this when she thought to come here. "Thank you, gentlemen. It is not every day that a bard can be entertained the way that I have been." Sadly, she was being sincere for once.

"No problem, miss. Oh, it looks like we're up. If you don't mind miss." Dren and Stard got up and bowed to her and went forward to greet the Lord. Their walk was slow, not knowing what to expect from the dour man at the high table.

"Okay, men, what does my king wish to tell me this time?" Storn tried to smile to break the mood of the room, but it was so hard these days. He had been arguing with merchants from G'harr for what seemed like forever, and he just wanted to drink quietly in his room. These two and that pretty bard were the last ones of the evening. What could go wrong?

"Well, my Lord, King Arian sends the message that the people of the holds are to be evacuated to the capitol as soon as you can. The north has fallen and..." that's as far as they got.

"*What?*" Storn stood up so fast the table rocked and almost went over. He wasn't a big man, compared to the Arian and Gareth, but he stood over five feet and was well muscled. His attributes were his keen eyes, "What does he think he's doing? We can't abandon the hold! Who would... where...?" He stomped off and came around the front to glare at the two men face to face. He needed to see into their eyes, needed to feel their breath to see what was going on. He took a calming breath and exhaled. "What are your names, men?"

Dren stood a little straighter. Arian had told him what to expect, and this was only the tip of it all. "My name is Dren, sir, and this is Stard. We were Norhil Hold guards, sir. We were reassigned when it was evacuated." There was a slight tremble in his voice as he spoke.

"All right, then. Now tell me; what in all the hells caused you to flee?" He was getting angry—none of this made any sense. Between Tanan and Gareth, never mind that spitfire

Tierra, they should've been able to handle just about anything, a dragon included.

"You mean you didn't get the message that Trost sent over two tendays ago?" Stard blurted out. The king assumed that Storn had gotten the message and just ignored it out of stubbornness, but it seemed that the lord had no idea what was going on.

"What message? Trost hasn't sent word of anything. All right, hold on." He turned to the assembled court and bellowed. "Court's done, go start drinking and leave us alone." He took another deep breath or five as the people filed out, murmuring in hushed tones. He couldn't care less what they were saying. "Now, let's go to my chambers and you can start from the beginning. I feel like Karsis right now. He always says he is missing something— and I think I am —and I bet it's going to be a long night of hard drinking to wrap my head around this one." He started to lead them away, but noticed that the bard was still there. "You too, missy; time to go."

"Begging pardon, Lord Storn, but I've travelled quite a long way to see you, and I'm not the type of girl to take no for an answer." Janna smiled and slid behind Dren as if she belonged with them. She had been doing this for decades and was an old pro.

"Argh! Fine. Keep up and be silent until I know what is going on. My head feel like someone dropped a small castle on it... twice."

They filled in and sat quietly, not wanting to irritate the lord more than he was already. He shut the door behind them and walked around to his desk and sat in silence. He drummed his fingers for a couple of minutes, then looked up at them with eyes that said they had better tell him what he wanted or else. "All right, so tell me what in the hells is going on."

Stard started, retelling the story of the attack on the hold.

Dren filled in here and there, mainly points that Stard was missing, and then they got to the part where Lord Tanan fought the dark cloaked man and Storn crept closer, his hands clenching and unclenching, trying to work through an anger at something he could do nothing about. "Then we went out, after the man took off once more, and all we found was the lord's cloak."

"So, from what you have told me, this man was powerful." He was trying to digest this news. Tanan, dead? He just couldn't believe it. Of all the members of his old company, he would've thought that self-sacrifice would be Arian's thing. "Well, I'm sure that Arian will bring him to heel. Now for the bad news." Storn sat back and pulled a piece of parchment out of his desk drawer. "This was taken from a merchant just down the road. He was stopped coming out of G'harr and was hung for treason." Storn's expression told everyone in the room that there was no greater crime to him at this moment. "It is a writ from someone we thought dead long ago, and if it is authentic, then we are all in some serious trouble." He passed it to the bard as she came around the desk, interest in the parchment alight on her very angelic face. He continued as she read. "I was hoping to get that to King Arian as soon as possible, but I don't know who I can trust anymore. It seems we uncover another traitor every tenday in the hold."

"This can't be true." Janna said slowly, finishing the letter. She had gone white and let the parchment fall from listless hands. She couldn't believe the words that she had read. "Please tell me this is a joke."

"I'm afraid not." Storn saw the confused looks on the guards faces and smiled. "It basically says that the merchant is to infiltrate the hold here and slay me, but that's not the surprise." He handed the parchment to Dren and looked on at Stard as his friend read it.

"No!"

"What?" Stard was getting impatient now, the anxiety in the room was so heavy that it could've crushed his foot.

Dren shook as he held the page. He looked at his friend and tried to tell him, but his mouth was so dry. "It's signed Madam G'harr."

Stard didn't understand. "So... she's bad?" He knew he should've paid more attention to history; he was missing something, and it seemed bad.

"Madam Ill'lyth G'harr was the original elven matron who taught her human lover magic." Janna recited. Her thoughts, however, went somewhere else when she spoke of this story. She didn't even bother with music. "Back when the humans were slaves, there was one who broke the rules and taught her human lover the ways of elven magic. Afterwards, they both were banished. She went south with what followers she could gather to her cause and started the land of G'harr. This, of course, started the second great war—but that's not where this gets scary. She was a vicious woman, powerful in the art and wicked with it. She was slain long ago by one of the last elves seen, and her body burned in the square of G'harr's capitol city." Janna sat down cross-legged on the floor, all strength fleeing her body. She knew how bad this really was.

"All right, so a powerful elven woman rules G'harr. Isn't that what we already have with the Sorcerer King?" Stard knew that much at least. The Sorcerer King of G'harr was said to be the most powerful sorcerer there was.

"Well, with one exception." Lord Keragan stood slowly, this being his area of expertise now. "The Bitch Queen would not honor any treaty with Lythinall. She would be looking for war, which would support the growing number of traitors lately. There would be no 'little by little' with her; it would come all at once, and I fear that it may be soon." He paced around the edge of the room now, itching to shoot something with his bow.

"That's why I can't leave this hold. If we left, she would strike at us on the road and slaughter the people out in the open. No, we have to stay and prepare. But you three can get this to Arian."

Dren stood up, hands at his side and ready. "Yes lord, we will leave right away."

Janna sighed and shook her head. This was Ollian's doing she just knew it. She was heading to Everknight anyway, but now she had company. At least they were good looking. "How about we leave at first light? It makes for better traveling, and we won't have to worry about sleeping on the road at night." *And maybe I can still catch that drink or six...* her thoughts kept going back to that name though, and she cursed under her breath. Why did it have to be *her?*

"First light sounds fine with us." Stard said, standing and saluting the lord.

"Good. Then I will have this parchment rolled and stored in a map case for the journey when I leave here. You will have my gratitude for this, and I will make sure that the king knows that. As for you my lady." He turned to her and smiled for the first time in a long, long time. It wasn't that she was beautiful, no. It was because she had her smile. "I have a room set aside for visiting nobles that you can have for the night."

"Oh, that would be splendid!" She turned and skipped out of the room, with the two guards right behind her. This was shaping up to be one great story after another. The return of Madam G'harr will be a tune to rival all others.

Upper Balcony, Keragan Hold

Egroan watched the lord go with the guards and that woman, and seethed quietly at his inability to get the lord alone. He wasn't going to kill the guards before they got their message to the suspicious lord, mainly because he was just going to kill Storn and be done with it, but that man was constantly watching his back. Egroan had replaced the last G'harran spy, as that man was caught and hung, as were the three before that. This time they sent a sorcerer, and Egroan wasn't going to fail. He had orders to call for an uprising if need be, as there were already over a dozen loyal people infiltrated into the hold, but he had to be able to take the hold if he did that. If he failed, then they would be alerted to their plans before need be.

"You there! Get back to work. Audience is over."

Egroan turned and walked away, cowering under the cloak he wore and picking up the broom as part of his facade. He was a small man, about five feet tall, with shoulder length brown hair and dark eyes. His tailored black cloak was in his room, as his servant's clothes were needed to blend in. He nodded to the guard and went past him without looking. The guard basically ignored him and kept going on his rounds. He was just a servant here, lowliest of the low. Most sorcerers pretended to be lords, or council members, but not Egroan. No, he knew where the real power was. The real power was in not being noticed until it was too late.

He made his way around the upper floor, sweeping and humming to himself for a good hour until he was over the lord's chambers. He leaned his broom against the wall and slowly made his way down the steps on the far side, commanding the air to quell his footfalls. He would wait until the guards and woman left, then it would be over for Lord Storn. He heard talking and ducked around the corner. There! The woman was out, and the two guards were following her like puppy dogs. He waited another minute as their footfalls receded, then warded the room with air to make sure no sound escaped from the room. He came around the corner then, with his hands out whispering the command for the moisture in the air to freeze. "Obren wan fros dost fra!"

Storn heard the words before he registered that anyone was there. He didn't know what they meant, but he had fought these bastards enough times to know it didn't matter. He was in trouble no matter what they meant. He was almost at the door, so he rolled back over the desk and reached under it for his spare bow. There was a catch under the top that held it, and three spare arrows, just in case. *And they call me paranoid, ha! I'll show them. I'll be dead, but I'll be right at least.* His thoughts were always dark these days, but at least he could still joke with himself. He tried to nock an arrow, but frost was growing on his arms and legs making them stiff and hard to move.

"There he is—the lord of worry." Egroan walked around the corner, careful to stay out of the room, lest he fall into his own magic. The elements did what he commanded them to do, without distinction as to whom was there. "Having trouble with your bow lord?" How he loved to mock these self-important heroes. "Oh, and don't bother with calling out to anyone. I warded the room so sound would travel slowly. Only I can hear you."

"I'll have your head yet, sorcerer," Storn said, stalling. He was trying to get his arms to bend and set the arrow straight. He had a solid grip on the bow, his hand was practically frozen to it, he just had to pull it back. Everything in the room was covered in frost now, and it was getting worse. Even his very lungs started to feel cold. *Where's Karsis when I need him? Gods above I really just thought that, didn't I?* He laughed aloud at that thought and startled his attacker.

"What? What is so funny?" Egroan was not used to his victims being so flippant about their death. The lord was obviously stuck and couldn't work a button on his own shirt, let alone fire his bow. What was he missing?

"I'm just laughing at your feeble plan." Storn was lying, trying to keep this arrogant sorcerer talking. You just never knew what could happen. At least that's how his companions used to do it in the past. Unfortunately, he didn't have any of them this time.

"Feeble?" Egroan was losing his temper. How dare this self-righteous lord judge his plans! He stopped his anger from misleading him, smiling at the ruse. He knew what the retired adventurer was doing and it wouldn't work. "Nice try Storn, but it's no use." He spoke again, commanding the sputtering torches to lose their heat faster, dropping the room to freezing temperatures faster and faster. "Soon your heart will grow ice around it and stop beating, and then I will take the hold for my queen."

Storn could feel the cold seeping into his veins. He was shivering so bad and he couldn't move his arms... but he could move his head a little still, and his waist. That gave him an idea. If he could get rid of the frost build up on his arms, he could fight back, but he only had one shot. Literally. He threw his head back and kicked back, sending him flying against the wall with force. His shoulder hit and some of the frost broke free as he crumpled to the floor. With a pain greater than anything he ever felt, he knocked the arrow and fired in one motion. The projectile sailed under the desk and struck the sorcerer in the leg.

Egroan stumbled back screaming at the pain of the frozen arrow shattering into his leg. It had gone in deep, and the cold wood had splintered inside. "I will flay you for that Storn!" He leaned against the wall and snapped the shaft off so it wouldn't hit the wall when he moved. He wouldn't get that out without time, and a little magic. First, he would savor the death of this lord. He took a moment to gather himself and limped back to the doorway. He was trying to come up with something witty, and realized that Storn could already be dead. Before he could do anything else, a dagger slammed right into his shoulder and threw him into a spin that took him into the freezing room.

Stard looked at Dren as they ran and couldn't believe the aim his friend had. "Good shot man!" They had to be at least fifty paces away.

"Thanks, but I was aiming for his head," Dren said as they closed on the lord's room. They had heard someone scream and came running, but never expected the lord's room to be covered in ice. Janna had said it was magic and told them not to let the man speak, so all Dren could think of was to put his dagger thru his head.

"Coming through, boys," Janna called as the men stopped at the door to the room. She ran up to the doorway and called to the heat within the body behind the desk. "Ash'anti fir, halven dosit kithin's shir." She had to heat his heart before it stopped all together. She also had to stay calm so as the heat didn't rise too fast and cook it, but he should be fine in a minute or three. Now to cancel the magic of this impudent sorcerer.

"Do we go in?" Dren didn't want to freeze in his tracks, but he wanted to get to Storn and see if he was all right. He started to test it by slowly pushing his hand into the room, but frost gathered around his fingers the minute he broke the threshold of the doorway.

"Wait." Janna concentrated on the body slumped by the wall. It hadn't moved since it spun into the room with a dagger in its shoulder, but these sorcerers were tricky. She whispered to the heat to stop leaving, and breathed deep when it started to grow a little warmer. Then she coaxed the torches back to life and stepped in. As she came around to see the man, it was apparent that he was already dead. The frost had gone right into the wound and followed the veins right into the heart. Shame—she wanted to have fun finding out what he knew. "All right... it's cold, but safe."

Stard rushed in and threw the desk aside, the heavy wooden piece sliding across the frosted floor easily. "Storn! Are you all right?" Concern gave his voice a rough edge, and it echoed throughout the room.

"Aye," Storn called weakly. He was trying to get to his knees and wondered what had stopped that gods-be-damned sorcerer. "Is Karsis here?" He was feeling a little lightheaded, and wasn't sure he was seeing straight. He had sworn that he was going to be dead. *I would've been with her, but that's gone now too. Oh Kiera, I miss you so much...* He shook his head to dispel his morose thoughts and tried to focus.

"No Lord, Karsis isn't here, but if he were... Well, I'd be half naked and in his arms faster than a noble could turn his nose up to a peasant." Janna smiled and bowed a little as the frost melted from the room. Everything was dripping now, and the torches were burning bright. She chuckled to herself that Storn thought that Karsis was here. Real magic was scarce in Lythinall, being used primarily by bards. Oh, sure there were magicians that could make things glow or disappear, but those were just tricksters. True wizards were only elven, or trained by them. Even bards didn't practice magic in the true sense. They channeled it through their songs or music, instead of asking the elements directly, and usually the effects were practical, not damaging. She was different. She had elven blood way back in her line, so she could do a little of both. "The men here dispatched the evil sorcerer and I helped warm you up with a little bardic magic." She was lying, but didn't want to get into it right now, especially with his distrust of sorcerers.

Guards finally came to investigate the screams and were waved away by Storn. He was more than a little angry at this whole thing, and the guards knew when to let things go. "All right, help me up and let's find that parchment." He looked down and saw that it was a ruined mess. The water dripping on it had made the writing run and it was torn in at least three places. "Great. Well, there goes that plan." He stood up and stretched, then started pacing, slowly because he still ached from the cold.

"We can go anyway, Lord. The king will heed our warning, parchment or no." Stard was gathering up things and putting them back as a way to keep busy. His nerves were strung out like a small child on sugar.

"I have something even better. I'm a bard, and our word is binding in the king's court. If I say it said something, then it did —or my life is forfeit." Janna smiled playfully, still upset that she hadn't gotten her three drinks, though now it was going to be like five.

"Good plan. All right then, let's go." Storn shook his arms out and started walking for the door.

"Lord, where are we going?" Dren asked somewhat hesitantly. He too was looking forward to having a couple of drinks, but duty came first. Always.

"Why? I'm going with you all and having a couple of drinks."

"Or five."

"Yes, Janna, or five." He laughed at the look on the faces of both guards and clapped them on the backs as he walked out. "Don't worry men, we're just normal people tonight. After that attack I plan to get a little wobbly." They went down and joined the other men at the feast and sang most of the night. Janna was a hit, of course, but it was Storn who was the center of attention. He'd never indulged with the other men before, so it was a real treat for the hold to drink with him.

The next morning, Dren, Stard, and Janna were ready to leave. Each one of them felt like they could sleep another five or so hours, but it was worth it. They grabbed horses from the lord's stable and rode out of Keragan Hold early in the morning.

It would take a little over a day to reach Everknight and they wanted to make the bridge by nightfall if they could. Janna knew that the G'harran's would be after them; that was a given, but when they would come was the question. When she knew they were going to have to run for it, she could ask the air to make the horses go faster and possibly make the capitol by evening. She would rather it be a boring ride though.

"We just left, and you are already looking over your shoulder?" Dren laughed at the beautiful lady riding next to him, but in truth he was worried as well.

"Yeah, well, I'm missing that drink I had last night. I've never had a Stinging Volcano before... Not sure what was even in it but gods above it was great." She'd had a lot of drinks over the many years from town to town, but very little surprised her.

"I think it had some of that distilled alcohol from up north." Stard didn't feel good, but he tried to ignore it. His stomach was very upset, and his head felt like it had been kicked by an angry mule. "That, and I heard some of those hot peppers were juiced for it."

They laughed as they traveled down the packed dirt road, moving towards their destiny, and none of them even knew it. They were watched from the high turrets, and the figure smiled sadly remembering a time when he was that carefree. "Gods speed and good luck," Storn said as he looked up at the rising sun burning through the morning fog. He used to love this time of day; when the Companions of Everknight traveled across the land, he always took last watch for just this reason. It was one of the things that Karsis and he had in common. Practically the only thing, now that he thought of it. He went down the stairs and thought of all the times that he would ride home and see his wife waiting for him.

"My Lord?"

Storn looked up and saw the guard's worried expression. He

looked around quickly, and realized that he was in the basement. His mind had drifted again. "Yes?" he tried to sound like he knew exactly what he was doing, but by the look on the man's face, it wasn't working.

"It's just... You were talking to someone, and it wasn't me."

Storn was too tired to try and make something up. "I was talking to my wife." He smiled, turned back the way he came, and walked back up the stairs to the main floor. *Why is she on my mind more than usual? Was it that bard?* He had always thought of her, that was why he was always angry, but of late, she was *vivid* in his memories. He walked into the council chamber and sat upon the high table and got ready for the day's annoyances. He surveyed the people coming in to stand in line to ask him to settle this argument or that boundary dispute and had to smile again. At least he wasn't dealing with haughty nobles like Arian.

The Golden Palace, G'harr

SHE WALKED BACK AND FORTH, heels clacking on the deep golden tiles of the throne room. She had felt Egroan die in Keragan Hold and had seethed quietly for over an hour. She had lost seven such assets in the last tenday and it was getting tiring. He was supposed to stop Storn from warning his king about her presence, but that must've failed. Madam Ill'lyth G'harr stopped pacing and closed her bright green eyes, counting to ten. As an elven archmage, she was ancient in the count of years, but looked as fresh and young as when she had turned one hundred. Her long, bone white hair was tied up in a bun, held by a wrought-iron pin, and her long black dress was slit up the side revealing her shapely legs. It was not a good day.

"What's the matter, my bitch queen? Plans not going the

way you thought they would?' The voice came from the floor by the throne, and a face poked its head out from behind it. It was a man's face, and it was filthy. His long black hair was disheveled, but Ran'cian, Sorcerer King of G'harr was—for now—still alive. He was chained hand and foot, but Ill'lyth had kept him breathing for a reason. He just had to figure out what that reason was, very soon, before her temper gave way to violence. Still, he couldn't help but poke her with a stick now and again; after all he'd endured, it felt good.

"Oh please—please push my patience! I would love to just let go and make this whole city tremble." She turned on her heel and faced the wretched man, smiling her wicked smile. "I trust that those chains are still nice and tight?" Ill'lyth had enspelled the chains so he could no longer command the elements, effectively castrating the most powerful sorcerer in all G'harr.

"I never should have brought you back," he scowled at her smug, elven face and cursed her in his head for the millionth time. She was infamous as the elf that destroyed the elven nations. She had taught her human lover elven magic and had been banished for it. She traveled to the southern reaches of their great forest, there to make a community for herself and her disciples. They had brought their human slaves, and the ones who now commanded magic, and began teaching them as well. Thus, began the dynasty of G'harr. She had been slain decades ago by infighting, but Ran'cian had found her corpse. Of course, he didn't know *exactly* what he had found, as the body was buried with traps and deadfalls, but in the end, he brought her back. He had needed ancient power to break the seal on something even more powerful and had rushed without researching what he had found. Even after he realized who he had brought back, he thought that he could control her—after all he was the all-powerful sorcerer king, right? That backfired faster than he could say "Bitch Queen."

"That is correct. But you did, and now I have another shot at ruling Lythinall. Once I level the capitol, that land will be added to G'harr and I will be queen of both." She walked away, clicking across the floor to look out one of the massive windows. "Isn't it better here? Haven't I made everyone equal in the short few years I've been back? There is no poverty, no ruling class... just people. People working to better themselves and live their lives."

"Is that what you call it?" Ran'cain should just let her ramble, but he had found his old core of rebellion. "They all have to worship you, or they are killed in horrible ways. You rule by fear and pain, delighting in the suffering of the very people you helped create." Ran'cian lost all restraint. He was angry that his people were treated this way. G'harr was his home and she was ruining it.

Ill'lyth looked at him with mock pity. "You're just upset that I took your toy away from you. You were taxing the less fortunate and giving the so-called nobles breaks. The homeless were dying in the streets and you sat on your golden throne laughing at them; yet *I'm* the evil queen?" She honestly couldn't believe he was trying to take the moral high ground... he couldn't even spell morals.

Ran'cian sighed and lowered his head. She was right. He *had* been a tyrant, even plotting war against the peaceful folk of Lythinall, but this had opened his eyes—and possibly a vein or two as well. "Trust me Ill'lyth, I know. Yet heed this promise: if I ever get out of these gods be damned chains, I will be taking back my country and fixing it." The blow came unexpectedly. His head snapped around as a hardened gust of wind slammed into him, then lifted him as high as the chains would allow. Then he went a little higher. His wrists and ankles strained against the metal and started to sheer off the skin around them.

The room went deathly quiet, except for the pitter patter of his falling blood.

Ill'lyth's humor was gone. "That will be quite enough. You will forever be my pet, and you will never have this lovely piece of land back, you wretched piece of filth." The room grew colder as she spoke. "Now you will be silent as I contemplate my next move, or I will rip that tongue right out of your head." She let him drop to the floor and scramble back behind her throne. *Her* throne. Ill'lyth once again walked to the window, her favorite place to think. Through it, she could see the distant Barrier Mountains and sometimes, on a clear day, the Forest of the Lost. *Well, I guess they know that I'm alive, unless I can catch their messengers before they reach the king,* she thought quietly, tapping her foot.

"Ash'anti fra sistren eae oren alar!" she asked the air to deliver her words. She didn't say the name of her commander, but instead thought of him and pictured his face in her mind as she finished, then spoke to the wind. *Commander Ellis, I have another mission for you and your men. Split your forces and hunt down the messengers coming from Keragan Hold, and send the rest of your men around to attack the hold from the north. It's time to escalate things.* She cancelled the magic and sighed. She wasn't going to start this early. She would rather have had the incarnation do her dirty work for her. "Wait." She spun with amazing alacrity for someone her age.

"Oh, what brilliant idea does she have now? I swear elves think they know everything." Ran'cian spoke from behind the throne. His voice sounded weak, and he ended in a coughing fit.

"That's because we do, you sniveling mongrel. Now be silent while I think." Ill'lyth wanted the incarnation to do her dirty work, well why didn't she just bring him here? She would need to restrain him and find his weakness again. Obviously, it wasn't earth; even though that did hold him rather well. Once he had made his appearance again, she would capture him and keep him here until she could make him her puppet. She would just let the king and his hapless companions keep working on how to stop him and let her spy fill her in. Once she had his weakness, then she would bind him to her and have a weapon that no one could stop. "Oh, it is going to be a good day after all."

The High Grass, Southeast of Keragan Hold

COMMANDER ELLIS STARED at the packed earthen road and clicked his tongue. He detested hunting down spies. He would much rather be leading from the front of a massive engagement than scouting for three people on horseback. He raised his fist forward and the men behind him started moving once more. It was just an hour after sunrise and they had approached the road to Keragan Hold over the high grass instead of the road, hoping to catch the travelers off guard. He could see a small cloud of dust coming, but he had to be sure before he committed what forces he had left to the road; he didn't want a chase on his hands. He was in his fiftieth winter and his bones started to ache all the time now. Ellis had close-cropped, graying hair, and his broad shoulders held his southern cape very well.

"Think that's them, Commander?"

Ellis looked down at his second-in-command and tried not to smile. The man was hyper and excitable. Everything that he *didn't* look for in a second. However, the man had something that most others didn't. A spine. "Franc, you never cease to amaze me. Yes, I think that could be them. However, let's wait another moment and try to make sure before we spook them."

"Will do, Commander. I'll see if we have any good eyes back there and get you the info." Franc turned to the men seated on horses and cleared his throat. "Get ready to charge, but hold until the commander signals." He rode back among the ranks calling for eyes and the men just stared straight ahead.

Ellis chuckled and watched the little man ride away. He had curly hair and a bubbly attitude, but was never afraid to say what was on his mind, which was the main reason he never climbed through the ranks. The commander turned his own eyes upon the distant cloud of dust once more and sighed. He had received the message from his queen and had immediately dispatched half of his fifty men to circle around Keragan Hold. She wanted these messengers killed so that whatever message they were carrying to their king would never reach its destination. He wasn't privy to what that message could be, but he could guess it had to do with her being back from the dead and in charge of G'harr. He turned as he heard someone coming up behind him. It was Franc and a young man he had seen before but couldn't recall his name.

"Commander, this is Inbari, he says he can almost make out three riders from here." Franc looked skeptical but was still smiling.

"Well, soldier, how is it you can see them from here? That's not just good eyesight now is it?" Ellis had his suspicions on the young man's background at hearing this, and by the shuffling feet, he wasn't wrong.

Inbari hesitated, then spoke. "Well sir, I studied for a year at the Mysterium, but I failed, so I had to join the military." He scratched his head and shuffled his feet once more.

Now Ellis understood—another failed reject thrown at him. Failing at the Mysterium meant military or death. Easy choice, really. Not that the kid was a mistake, but more often than not, they weren't cut out for this life and got themselves killed in battle. "Well, show us greatness kid, or just see if that's them."

Inbari looked and used his *sight*, stretching out ahead of him and into the cloud. "There's three riders, two guards and..." His head exploded in agonizing pain. "Agh. Get her *out!*" He fell to the ground, bleeding from his ears and eyes, thrashing back and forth while holding his head. Three seconds later he was gone.

"Well, that can't be good."

"Shut up, Franc."

Janna was riding hard, and between her and the two guards at her side, they were making quite a scene kicking up this much dust. It would help if it would rain some more, as the roads were so dry it was horrible. They had already covered about thirty miles, but it felt like they were crawling. The two guards insisted that they flank her horse as they traveled, since she had the important message in her head to tell the king, but it was totally unnecessary. She had been around for a long time and could more than take care of herself, but she adored the attention. "We're about halfway to the split. Not bad, guys," she called out over the thundering horses.

Stard smiled at her and held on tight. He had never really ridden this fast before, and it was more than a little frightening. In the guard you rode in formation, and since he wasn't cavalry, he had never had to charge. He only used horses to get somewhere and he was never in this much of a hurry.

"He looks petrified," Dren called out over her head as he watched his friend white-knuckle the reins. "Imagine if we weren't on the road!"

Janna was going to throw a pretty lewd comment at that one, but then something grabbed her attention. She turned her head as the tingling magic focused on her, and she could almost see a young man staring at her through a faint mist in her mind. Someone was using their *sight* to spy on them and was untrained at grounding himself. "Oh, no you don't." She closed her eyes and threw up a mental shield, then pushed hard at the magic, sending it back at him. Not only that, but she threw her own mind behind it, riding the magic back at him like a battering ram. As she opened up her eyes and used her own *sight*—grounded of course—her magic slammed into his mind. It was crackling through the many pathways and burning them faster than he could scream, and scream he did. He dropped to the ground and she pulled back as he died. She had caught a glimpse of what he was a part of, and they were in trouble. "Enemy in the grass. Follow me!" She pulled the reins hard to let the men pass her then she yanked hard to the left and took the steed off road, kicking it faster and waiting for them to catch up before she used the air to speed them.

Stard sputtered at the realization that he would be riding that fast over uneven ground, but the soldier in him obeyed quickly. He pulled a little lighter, taking a much wider turn into the grass, and his horse was not pleased at the lack of control. "Come on girl, just do it and stop fighting me," he whispered to the horse as he bent over and hugged her neck for stability, not caring that he got a snort for a response.

Dren laughed at the sight of his friend hugging the horse, but his laughter died as a shout came up behind them. There had to be at least twenty men on horseback, all dressed in the black armor of the G'harran guard. "Crap. That is definitely not good."

"You think?" Janna laughed at the understatement. It was beyond bad. They were outnumbered at least six to one, and these men probably had fresh horses. She was no Karsis; these odds were death if they were caught. So, they couldn't get caught. "Hold on, I can make us go faster." She started, but was cut off.

"No!" Stard had caught up, but was bouncing something

awful, and his horse didn't feel too stable. Then his horse stumbled and went down, rolling over and over, finally coming to a stop and pinning him to the grass.

"Stard!" Dren pulled hard, stopping the horse and leaping off. He didn't have much time before they were on him. That's when he saw that the ground had been pocked, probably on purpose. Small holes were dug every ten to twenty feet or so, staggered here and there to make riding hard, and damn near impossible going that fast. He got to his friend and saw that he was still conscious. "Hang on buddy, I'm here." He looked at the massive animal and despair flooded him. There was no way he was going to lift this.

Stard coughed up blood and tried to get air into his lungs. He could feel that his ribs were crushed, and the lack of pain in his legs was un-nerving. He wasn't getting out of this one. Before he could tell his friend to flee, the horse moved and rose, slowly, then shifted to the side and rolled over. He could feel the wind swirling around the beast, and he looked at the beautiful woman that had stopped and tried to save him. At least now he could die on his feet, or maybe his knees, since his legs were currently not working on the count that he couldn't feel them.

Janna let the air lift the horse, but the minute she saw what the horse had done to him, she let the magic go and sobbed. She had seen enough death in her long life to know that this man was done. She couldn't heal that, maybe a little, but only enough so that he wouldn't bleed out. *Why did I have to lose another one, Ollian?* she asked as she pulled her thoughts in and set her mind rigid. "We have to go Dren! They're coming." She slid off and touched Stard on the legs, whispering to the ether to heal some of the damage to his body. She threw everything she had into it, and felt his nerves mend in his back. They wouldn't stay for long, but he might be able to stand and die on his feet. That's the way she wanted to go. No, that was a lie—she wanted to die naked, and in bed.

Stard's eyes went wide and he felt his legs again. Tears came to his eyes. She had given him what he wanted, without knowing. "Help me up old friend," he asked Dren, who was silently crying.

"It would... be my honor." Dren helped up his friend and steadied him. His whole midsection looked crushed. "I will always remember you..." He couldn't finish. If he finished, it would be real.

"Go. I will stay here and see if I can whittle down their numbers somewhat." Stard knew he wouldn't get more than two, maybe three if they stopped to interrogate him, but it would be something. He checked to see if his sword was still good and then he felt Janna wrap her arms around him.

"May your arm be strong and your aim true, my friend," Janna said as she handed him the twin daggers she kept under her dress. "The song I write about you will be glorious." She gave him a quick kiss on the cheek and ran to the horse. She could see them coming now, and without the air to help them, she could only hope that the horse would make it to Everknight without falling over dead.

Dren hesitated, pulling his sword halfway out of its sheath. "I could stay..."

"I'll kill you myself if you don't get on that horse. This is my song, damn you. Now get you gone." Stard laughed at the look on his friend's face, but he couldn't let Dren throw his life away.

Dren turned with a heavy heart and climbed onto his horse, kicking it into a canter and not looking back. *I will avenge you, Stard! On my life I will avenge you.* His thoughts were whirling with memories, and soon he heard steel clash with steel and the tears came again.

"He wanted to do this, Dren. I'm sorry." Janna was moved at

the loss that she was seeing. It was almost like they were more than just…. *Oh, my Goddess…I didn't even notice. That is why they never tried anything with me.* She rode in silence, knowing that it was a private matter. Most men never opened up about relationships with other men, especially in the guard. It was going to be a long hard ride; she just hoped that the ground would slow down their enemies as well.

Stard watched them ride away and his own tears fell slowly. He really didn't want to die, but he knew that it was going to happen. How come all the bards write about selfless sacrifice being so easy, when he was shaking in his boots? He just hoped that the end came quick, and that he didn't cry in front of the enemy. He saw the lead horses now, and he crouched behind his own. The poor thing had snapped its neck rolling, but it made for good cover.

As the first horse came into range, about thirty paces away, Stard stood painfully and threw a dagger at the rider, then threw another at the man behind him. Both hit, but only the first man was hurt enough so that he was out of the fight. All the horses were pulling up now, expecting more fighters to appear, and Stard used that momentary distraction to draw his sword and limp towards the second man. The dagger had hit the man in the chest, but he was still breathing. He knocked the man's sword away and after a quick thrust with his sword, the man was gone.

Stard was surrounded now by men drawing swords and pointing them at him. He didn't want to be taken alive. He took his own sword and stabbed the horse that he was next to. The poor animal bolted away, scattering the men on horseback that had surrounded them. As the beast took flight, Stard grabbed the saddle and let it drag him off though the ranks, slashing his sword at the horses as he went by. One two, then a third was hit before his grip failed and he tumbled to the ground

Commander Ellis rode up to the organized chaos, shaking his head. What could be tearing through his men and scattering them like this? He saw a solitary man, on the ground but fighting to stand, and had to admire him. The man was badly wounded, and by the look of the horse a few feet away, it seemed that he had fallen victim to these damned pock holes that had his men going slower than frozen syrup. "Let him stand." The men froze at his voice and that made him proud. He loved command. He got down from his horse and approached the man, his hand on the hilt of his great sword, but not drawing it. Yet.

"They left you to die," he said.

Stard grinned and rolled his shoulder, trying to work out his stiff arm. His legs were wobbly, and he could feel his body growing slower. His wounds were worse than he thought. He could at least breathe deep without a sharp pain in his chest. "No, they didn't. I stayed so they could get away and warn the king." He spat at the commander, but it never reached him. He lunged, all his training behind the thrust that should've caught the man flatfooted. It didn't. The man sidestepped and spun, pulling a massive sword as he did. When Stard tried to turn and get his sword up, it was too late.

Commander Ellis saw the man start to move and was again impressed, but he had training too. He spun drawing his great sword and swinging it around in a deadly arc. The blade sheered clean through the man's neck and took his head in a single swipe, then Ellis wiped the blade and sheathed it once more. "After them."

The Serpent River Bridge, Southwest of Everknight

They had ridden hard for the whole day, and the enemy was still behind them. Once the pocked ground had stopped, Janna could use the wind to speed them up—but the horses couldn't take much more. From the bridge, she guessed it was just a little over ten miles. She was hoping a patrol would be near the bridge when they got there. *But that would mean something going right... and I don't see that happening*, she thought as they followed the river south towards that bridge. Just then Dren's horse staggered and made a horrible sound. "Dren, it's gone." She stopped her horse and grabbed his arm to help him onto her horse. He leapt on and left his horse, watching as it slowed then stopped, gently lowering itself down to the ground, bleating out its misery.

"Think we can make it on one horse?" Dren asked, looking back for a sign of pursuit. He hadn't seen anyone behind them for a couple a hours, but he knew they were back there. The dust was still kicking up from their horses.

"We'll be fine on the one horse. She's holding up well, and I've been using magic to help her keep going without exhausting her." Janna couldn't get rid of the feeling that something was wrong. *Better check the bridge, just in case.* She sent out her *sight* towards the bridge, trying to keep her head straight on the moving horse. There, waiting for them, were at least twenty men and a commander of some sort. "Okay, that's not good. Dren, how is your sword arm?"

"Why? How bad is it?" As the captain of the guard Dren was pretty good, but he was no King Arian.

The question became moot when she saw them lift up their bows and ready a volley. Another couple of seconds and they would be in range. "Never mind, hang on." Janna pulled the reins to the left and angled the horse towards the river. "Ash'anti wan hadar dosit roan wanel!" she all but screamed at the water, begging it to keep the horse afloat. She wasn't sure if it would do as she asked, but they had run out of choices.

Commander Ellis had seen them coming, but couldn't tell

who was on the horse. He was confident that his plan would work, but he couldn't be sure till he saw them. Splitting his already weakened force to catch them here at the bridge was a gamble. They had ridden the horses almost to death to get here, but now there wouldn't be a chase. Then he saw them pull towards the river. "What in the hells?" He squinted and when they didn't plunge into the water, he all but choked. They were getting away. "Fire at the target! All arrows!"

"Sir, they aren't really in range." Franc wasn't usually the voice of reason but...

Ellis turned a hateful gaze upon his second and held his eyes. "I. Said. *Fire!*"

The arrows flew up and over in a high arc, higher than normal to reach such a distance with any sort of accuracy. They were moving farther away, and soon they would be lost. The horses were too weary to give chase; this was his last gamble. He would follow at a pace that the horses could manage, but only to the other side of the river. If they weren't there, he would have to go home empty handed. He didn't yet have the force for a confrontation with Everknight guards.

Janna couldn't believe that they were riding over the river's surface. The horse was panicked, but steady, and they were almost home free. Then she heard a small 'zip' sound and a sharp pain in her back. Dren gurgled behind her then another sharp pain hit her in the leg. *Arrows!* She couldn't fathom how they had hit her this far out, but at least three more splashed around her into the water to either side. *Lucky for them, but very bad for us*, she thought as they neared the other bank. That's when she felt Dren slipping off the horse. "Dren!" she called, turning and trying to hold him on. He looked pale and quiet. "Almost there, hang on." Janna was losing blood, but she would heal. She always did. They touched down on the other side and she immediately stopped the horse and slid off, helping Dren down as she did.

He had taken an arrow to the back, and it looked like it went into his lungs. She could guess this because of his labored breathing and she had seen this a time or two. Janna could heal things, but not that. She snapped off the arrows that were in her and draped him over the saddle. Leaping up next to him, she kicked the horse into a gallop and used the wind to speed them. "Hold on old girl," she whispered to the horse. "Just a couple more miles..."

Commander Ellis watched her ride away like some kind of demon. He had no choice but to head back to Keragan Hold and see how the attack had gone. The way his day was going he didn't plan on having much of a force left anyways. He turned his company around and headed back, cursing that message with all his heart, while he still had one.

"Think the queen is going to have us skinned?"

"Shut up, Franc."

7

REUNIONS

The wagons limped into the city of Everknight two days after their storytelling night. Everyone's spirits were high thanks to the music and stories of Karsis. The folk of Caerlyn Hold were looking forward to getting a nice warm meal, and Allissana had promised them all that and more. Both Graf and Rhoe were nervous, but for very different reasons. Rhoe was worried that once they arrived, Liss would be too busy with the affairs of the kingdom to have any time for him, and Graf just flat-out hated people. He had been uncomfortable the last two days, and often hid under blankets in the wagon when no one was looking. At one time, they lost him for three hours.

Once they hit the city gates, Karsis knew word would reach the castle and the parents of both kids would come running down that hill faster than dragons could fly. Scratch that, Rhoe's mother was a Fra'hir—or wind warrior, though they just used warrior now that she had been the last—so she would be even faster than a dragon. He looked over at Rhoe and frowned. The boy was in a funk over Liss being the princess. He probably had this absurd notion that she wouldn't bother with a farm boy once she was back in the courts. Little did he know that she had it worse than he did. He had watched them for two days, and now that there was no pressing danger their bond grew stronger. It bothered him more than a little. Mainly because he couldn't seem to detect anyone or anything influencing them.

"It looks just the same as when I left." Liss was staring up at the massive castle on the hill. It loomed over them like an over-protective father, ruling over all it surveyed.

"You thought they would change it?" Rhoe quipped nervously. He was trying to be witty, but it failed miserably.

"No. I thought that something might have happened. I've been worried since River Vale that they may have been attacked here, but I don't see anything." She knew he was trying to lighten the mood, but she was nervous about her father meeting him. *Oh, and finding out that we got married by the faeries. That should go over about as well as his daughter running off after an ancient incarnation of evil.* She laughed at her own thoughts, and nudged Rhoe to make him smile.

"Well, I for one am looking forward to the family reunion. I promised your father that I would get you home safe, and I'm a man of my word." Karsis put away his lute and straightened his longcoat as they started the long climb to the castle. This road was packed gravel and wound up in a "S" to prevent all-out charges by cavalry. Situated between the road were large mounds of earth to help prevent erosion from heavy rains. He knew that the reunion was going to be more than just the king and queen, he also expected Gareth and Tierra—whom Rhoe thought were dead. *Any minute now... and there she is!*

Tierra had seen her son from the high parapet and no one, not anyone, was going to stop her. She went by the king so fast that he almost drew his sword, thinking that they were under attack. Gareth just laughed and plodded after her, patting Arian on the shoulder and letting him know that the kids were home. She heard them, but was already gone. Down the stairs, around the courtyard, vaulting over the short gate despite the protests of the knights guarding it, and onto the road. *"Rhoe!"* she screamed, running full speed with tears streaming down her face. Her twin braids were flying in the wind and were as dangerous as daggers going this fast.

Rhoe looked up at the sound of his name being screamed like that. At first, he looked towards Liss, but her eyes were on the road ahead, wide with shock. He followed her gaze and saw her. His *mother*. Tears sprung to his eyes as he slid down from his horse, already running faster than most men could. *"Mom!"* He couldn't believe it. He passed Karsis and gave him a look, and the bard was smiling smugly. He was probably behind this, and enjoying it too. He would get a hug later. He closed the distance quickly, and they came together like a hurricane hitting land. Robes and hair tangled, mixed with tears and kisses as they spun around and around in circles trying to burn off their momentum. Not one person watching had a dry eye, except for maybe Karsis. He was laughing way too hard to be crying. Rhoe couldn't even think straight. Then he saw Gareth come down the hill as well and the tears started again. He hadn't lost them! He dragged his mother with him as he ran for his father, hitting that massive barrel chest at full speed and not moving the man once inch.

"I've missed you, son," Gareth said through misty eyes, as he hugged him back a little harder than usual, but he had to make sure he was real.

"I love you Dad! Mom! I can't... how?" He just couldn't fathom how they were alive.

"Plenty of time for talk. Let's get inside, there is a certain king that would like to speak to his daughter." Tierra was still crying, but she had composed herself enough to speak whilst doing so. Then she saw Rhoe's face drop at the mention of the king, or was it Allissana that made him look so? "What's the matter son?"

"Oh, nothing. We will talk later. You're right." He turned and waved to the wagons and saw that Caerlyn was frantically waving with both hands.

"You've brought more refugees; that can't be good news. At least Caerlyn is here. We were going to have to send for her anyway." Tierra didn't want to tell Rhoe about Innal and Rythal. Not yet. She tried to change the subject, but Karsis saved her at the last moment, as usual.

"Last one to the castle has to wash the saddles!" he yelled as he raced past on his horse. He saw their faces as he went by and it made his heart soar. This is why he had waited to tell Rhoe, and it was worth it. All the frustration and pain that the boy had gone through on this trip was washed away by the relief of seeing his parents alive. *Gods above, I'm in a good mood. I may even have to find Carana tonight,* he thought as he sailed into the inner courtyard. Just then a horse passed him and flew into the stables at a canter, barely stopping before it went through the back wall. He looked and saw Caerlyn laughing and trying to catch her breath. She beat him. Crap.

Below, Graf waited until the wagons had started again, then slid out of the wagon and slipped into the city unnoticed. He had no plans to go to the castle, and the voice had said to get the princess here safely. That he had done. Now he was going to find a nice filthy alley and hide from this incessant wind. It was worse here up on the hill and it was making his skin itch and his eyes water.

You have done as I asked. Enjoy your reprieve, for I will have need of you in the days to come, but for now... rest. The voice echoed in his head as he shook it back and forth, somehow thinking that he could make it stop by doing that. In the end he gave up and continued to walk in the shadows, looking for a pile of blankets.

Liss rode up to the gate in quiet awe. She had seen the raw emotion come raging out of Rhoe when he saw his mother, and it had overwhelmed her. For him to care so deeply for someone surely was a testament to his depth. Could she compete with that? *And she was so pretty!* she thought as she tried to climb out of the cavern of self-pity she was falling into. Then she forgot all about Rhoe's mother as her own came into view.

Maressa came through the gate in a rush. She looked around and then saw her daughter. "Allissana!" She ran over and all but pulled the girl out of the saddle, showering her with kisses upon her brow. "Oh, gods above, you're all right." She pushed her back at arm's length to really get a good look at her, then noticed how mature she looked. Maressa let her go and stepped back calmly. She was treating the princess of Lythinall like a child, and in full view of townsfolk as well. "I'm sorry honey, it's just that I was so worried." She never got to say anything else.

Liss was stunned that her mom pulled away. She had traveled so far to get back here, and this is all that she wanted to do; that and apologize to her father. So, when her mother started apologizing to *her*, she just tackled her in a big hug, squeezed her tight, and whispered in her ear, "I love you, mother. Never, ever forget that. No matter what I've done, or how I acted, I've always loved you." Tears fell as she let out her feelings, and then she noticed her father standing there.

Arian came out of the castle slowly. First, he saw Karsis and Caerlyn over at the stables but passed them by. They weren't the ones he was looking for. Then he passed Gareth, Tierra, and a young man that could only be Rhoven. He shook his head as he contemplated how fortunate they all were. He couldn't wait to catch up with them later also. When he passed the gate, he saw them: his wife and daughter. He stood and watched their exchange like a statue on a mountainside—vigilant and patient. When Allissana looked up and saw him, he smiled at her. *Look at her, so grown up. She really looks like her mother in those leathers and that damned sword at her side,* he thought as he stepped closer and placed a hand on his wife's shoulder. "May I?"

Maressa stepped back and let her husband in. He had been so strong in her absence, but he had been worried just as much. The queen patted them on the shoulders and walked down to the approaching wagons, which were having a hard time with a missing horse that Caerlyn had unhitched to race Karsis. She missed stunts like that. She waved to the people and got them calm and ready to enter the castle. After all, someone had to be responsible around here.

Liss slid into her father's arms and started crying. "I'm sorry father, you were right." She tried to control herself, but all of the stress of all of the time she had been gone rushed in and swamped her.

"For what, dear one?"

"For thinking that your job was easy. That I could do the same thing without even trying. I can't. I had to make decisions that made me want to curl up and just cry, and if Rhoe wasn't there, I wouldn't have been able to get it right." She was babbling now, through tears, and not even really thinking about what she was saying.

Arian held her tighter and leaned down to whisper in her ear, so that no one would hear him confess. "Little one, how do you think I do things around here? I have your mother's love to guide me. The fact that you made those decisions even when they were tough means you *can* do this—probably better than myself." He was so proud that it didn't sink in right away. Something was trying to tap his brain on the shoulder... then it hit him. "Wait, are you and Rhoven...?"

She knew she couldn't say anything else but the truth to him, and not just because he was her father. He had this way of knowing when he was being lied to, and the only one to get away with that was her mother. "I love him, and I'm fairly certain he loves me. It's a long story, but technically we're... well, married." She didn't close her eyes, she wanted to see the lightning bolt when it came out of his eyes to smite her down.

"I see." He swallowed visibly and kept his emotions in check. He was a master at concealing his anger at things that angered him in court, but this was something entirely different. "Well, I suppose we will hear all about it later. For now let's get you inside and cleaned up."

The parents walked into the castle with their kids, and Karsis watched them go with warmth in his heart. Things were looking up, now they just had to figure out what to do next. Unfortunately, he knew what he had to do, and the kids would have to go with him. He watched Caerlyn dote over the refugee's and couldn't help but remember the inner workings of her soul. Then he spied Ralavin coming out into the courtyard and laughed. This was going to be spectacular. *It's like it's my birthday!* he thought as he folded his legs under him, floating in mid-air and getting ready for a show. *If I only had some dried beef...* He checked his inner pockets anyway just to be sure, but found no food.

Ralavin walked by the king and Allissana and laughed a bit when she stared at him. He had tried to forget what had happened to him, but he was reminded about it whenever someone new showed up. Tierra just laughed and pushed the kids on saying that she would explain it later. He smiled at the looks, but he had heard that Caerlyn had come with the refugee's, so he thought he would bring Griff out and introduce him to Lady Caerlyn. "Don't worry young one. Believe me, she is the nicest person in all of Lythinall. You have nothing to worry about." He patted the kid on the shoulder and stood a little straighter. He hadn't seen her in years.

Griff swallowed hard and nodded, trying to stay calm. He was worried no matter what Ralavin said, but he would try. He breathed in deep and held it for a couple of seconds, then breathed out again. It was something that he was shown by Ralavin to find his inner light, but it worked in calming him down as well. Then he saw her. Griff had seen pretty ladies before, had even peeked into the brothel once or twice to see them without any clothes on. This was something altogether different. She was a vision. She was dressed simply, in a long white dress that had seen days of road travel, and adorned only with a gold belt. Her flowing blond hair was braided down her back, and her deep, emerald eyes shone like a nyad's pool. At thirty feet away, he already swore to himself that he would die rather than see her come to harm.

Caerlyn looked up and saw the cutest boy walking towards her with freckles, wavy red hair, and green eyes. The man escorting him however was completely new to her. *Who in Davalar's name is that?* she thought as her heart skipped a beat. He had shoulder length raven black hair and ice blue eyes. His pale skin accentuated those features and his cotton robe hung snugly on a well-muscled physique. He was no warrior, but he had seen his share of trouble to be sure. That's when she saw his holy symbol and she knew that he was sent from the gods themselves. It was identical to her own. "Well, who do we have here?" she asked, trying to keep the quiver out of her voice.

"You may not know me anymore great lady, but I've known you for many years." Ralavin chuckled at her incredulous look, but went on before she could ask more. "This is young master Griff, and he has the talent for healing. Actually, talent is an understatement; he is closer to master healer than I care to admit. He's healed broken bones in minutes." He saw her eyes go wide and nodded in unison. He had been there, and he still didn't want to believe it.

"Ralavin, I told you—I don't know how I did it. It just seemed natural." He didn't want this woman thinking he was that good. He was just new, that was all.

Caerlyn fell back and clutched the wagon. "*Ralavin?!*" It couldn't be him—he was closer to eighty winters than twenty. "Can it be you?"

He shook his head and laughed again to himself. "Yes, Caerlyn. I was struck down by a traitorous sorcerer and Karsis saved me with a strange potion. It brought me back and restored my youth, but I'm still the old me." He found that he felt a little uncomfortable standing next to her. He had never thought of her as pretty before, more like a little kid, but now..." Anyway, I wanted to introduce you two since he will be going with you when you go back to the hold for training. I've showed him all I can."

Before she could tell him about the fall of the hold, a cry went up in the western tower. They were shouting something about a wounded rider. Lady Caerlyn and Ralavin nodded to each other and ran off in that direction, with a scared but determined Griff right behind them. They ran down the hill and over the short fence that led to a rocky slope above the west gate. They saw a horse with a limp body behind a woman covered in blood ride in, but they couldn't get down there fast enough. The small rocks impeded them.

Western gate, City of Everknight

DREN WAS in a steady world of pain and bouncing. It was almost rhythmic, the bouncing, and it helped him concentrate on the pain of his wounds. *Poor Stard. Gods above am I going to miss that man,* he thought to himself. Then suddenly the pain was receding, and the bouncing was less and less. There was a brightness to everything, and he thought that they might actually be home. *Finally, Everknight. Now I can get a hearty drink or three and drown my sorrows in style.* His reflections were interrupted, however, by the absolute silence of his surroundings. He looked up and he was standing upon the battlements of the castle...with Stard! "This can't be good, huh?" he asked his dead friend. He had no illusions of his friend's demise; he knew that the man would die to protect the mission, so that meant...

"I'm afraid not, old friend." The man said, but then he turned as if listening to something. "Well, never mind. It looks like someone has other plans for you."

"What?" Dren started to ask, but the man was already gone. Vanished in a blink. Then he heard a voice over a great distance. It was saying something about punishing him and ripping out his very soul. Startled by this horrible threat, Dren looked around for an exit, or stairwell, but there was nothing; just a wall and a sixty-foot drop. *I thought I'd done good in my life, but if this is what I think, then I'm in more trouble than I thought.* He spun as the voice grew louder.

Come to us, man... we will rip your bones for fun and sip your marrow... pleasure is pain and we are but tools of the master!

"Well, sorry to disappoint you, but I'm not going anywhere without a fight." He looked around again, but this time he wasn't looking for an exit; he needed a weapon. Then another voice came through to him, sounding as if it were on the other side of the wall of the battlements.

"Come back to us and let thyself be healed!"

Dren stopped and looked out over the wall and saw a small figure on the ground. It looked like a white ant, but as if he could pull in the view, it grew bigger and bigger until he saw himself on the ground next to a young boy with red hair. He spun around as a flapping echoed from behind him. Figures came from the very stone he was standing on, passing up and through it as if it were clouds.

They were large and horrible, with leathery wings and rotting hair on dark dead flesh. Fangs dripped some sort of liquid, and a throaty growl was almost constant. There were almost twenty of them already and he could hear more of them in the distance. *Right then. The fall would be one-hundred times better than fighting these things, and at least I get to feel like I'm flying for a couple of seconds.* He leaped before his brain could argue, and he only had to scream a little before he sat up coughing and looked around with panicked eyes...

Janna had ridden full-out for gods above knows how long, and all sense of time had escaped her. She was almost at her limit, and that was saying something. Her wounds had closed, the one with the broken arrow still in, but her constant use of magic to keep both the horse and Dren alive was wearing her down. *I feel like a street beggar at the end of a busy day of rolling in filth,* she thought as she neared the gate. She wasn't sure the guards would move, but she wasn't stopping. It probably helped that Dren could be seen over the saddle, poor guy. She tried to wave at them, but it was tough to keep her arm up. All she could do was try to yell. "Wounded man!" She saw the gate go up as they echoed her statement to the guards behind them. Too bad she wasn't going to stop there either.

Caerlyn saw them but was at a loss. "Ralavin, it will take us forever to get down there without breaking our necks." She knew that the two people needed them, but couldn't see a way down.

Ralavin cursed under his breath. He hated that he couldn't see any way around this, until he saw Griff fly by them. "What? Griff!" he called after the boy as the kid went down the hill of small rocks on a broken door. He was kneeling on the board and holding on to the doorknob for dear life.

Griff knew that those people needed help and when the Lady and Ralavin seemed lost for ideas, he just went on what he knew. In the winters, he and the other kids used to find broken pieces of buildings and slide down the hills of snow. As he looked around, he saw a broken door by the stables. He smiled and grabbed it, running as fast as he could and jumping on it as he went down the hill. Now he was holding on for his life, regretting this decision with a fervor that is only found by the most decadent of religious fanatics. He was going to wipe out and get dashed upon the rocks, he just knew it. Then the rider saw him, and she pulled the reins and galloped in his direction.

Janna came roaring into Everknight and saw movement out of the corner of her eye. It looked like a boy, with red hair and apparently no sense of self preservation. He was careening down a slope of rocks on some sort of board, and if those white robes were what she thought, then he was being steered by the gods themselves. He looked like a healer! *Thank Ollian,* she thought as she pulled the reins hard and took the tired horse right to the young daredevil. That's when she saw the other two at the top of the hill. She shouldn't—she was too low on stamina as it was—but she never listened to anyone, even herself. "Ash'anti sonn cra'del lae kithens dwoen." She called to the stones to help them down, then proceeded to pass out.

Griff slid into the road and bailed from the door, rolling over and over ungracefully. He finally got to his feet as the girl— no, woman—slumped over in the saddle as she said something in a language he didn't understand. He rushed to her side and grabbed the reins to stop the horse, which looked like it was going to fall over any minute. She was a bloody mess, but he saw that the man over the saddle was worse. He tugged the man off, falling in a heap in the road, and rolled him over to look at his wounds. Arrows protruded from his back and they looked deep. He cleared his mind and took a deep breath focusing inward once more. *Davalar, God of Life and Honor, bless me with your wisdom and power to heal these wounds so that I may serve you.* He felt his hands grow warm, and he touched the man's back. A powerful glow surrounded both him and the man as the arrows suddenly burst into ash and the wounds closed in seconds. Griff felt in his soul that the man's wounds were healed, but he couldn't feel the man getting better. Something was wrong. "Come back to us and let thyself be healed!" Griff pleaded with the man, or more importantly the soul of the man, and he felt an invisible impact to the air around him, then the man drew a deep breath.

Caerlyn saw the stones start to rise and gather at the woman's shout, and they quickly formed a stairway down. Ralavin didn't hesitate, and Caerlyn was right behind him. She saw Griff pull the man down and cringed, knowing that if he had wounds they would open even more. Then she saw the glow. "By Davalar! Who is this child!?" she called out to Ralavin as they took the stone stairway down as fast as they could.

Ralavin saw the glow too, and his smile was one of love and pride in this boy. He was a true caller, that was for sure. Then he saw the boys confused look and a chill swept up the priest's spine. "No, he can't... he doesn't even know *how* yet."

"Is he doing what I *think* he is doing?" Caerlyn asked as she heard the boy plead. This wasn't happening. He was trying to prevent the soul from leaving the man, but if done without training... well, anything could happen. She had even seen someone else come back in the wrong body. That was a very bad day. The two healers skidded to a halt by the man as he sat up drawing breath, coughing and looking around with panicked eyes. Then he focused on the kid and hugged him.

"Oh, you little miracle worker! I think you're my new favorite person." Then Dren's eyes fluttered and he lost consciousness.

Inner Courtyard, Castle Everknight

KARSIS WATCHED Caerlyn and Ralavin rush off to help someone and knew that he was not needed for this one. Those two could probably put back together a dragon if it were in pieces. He got up and wandered towards the castle and saw someone walk out. It was a very small child, a girl if he wasn't mistaken, but it was no page. "And who might you be little one?" Karsis hadn't seen her on his last visit, or if he had, he had been drinking.

Sprout was daydreaming when she heard the sweet voice say something. The voice was calming and happy and it caught her off guard here at the stuffy castle. She had been having no fun of late, what with the big people worried about the almost big people. She looked up and her smile grew wide. "Oh! I'm Sprout. Who are you?" she called out, immediately interested in this happy man.

Karsis laughed at her youthful ignorance. This is why he loved walking the land. He loved meeting people like this, the ones that breathed new life into...well, life. "I am a traveling bard called Karsis. Are you someone's little? Does the king have a secret he hasn't told me?" Karsis was just teasing—he knew how loyal Arian was—and he would know if this was the offspring of that man.

"No silly, I has no parents. I grew up on the street, but the king found us and brought us here to help him. We're the king's messengers." She looked sad for a moment, but then smiled once more and bounced over closer to him. "I mean, I'm not one yet, but I will be someday."

Karsis frowned at her words, as if they could change his mood that quickly. Mainly because they did. He hated that children were abandoned to the streets, stealing or worse to make it through the winters alive. He had thrown down more slavery rings in the outlying cities than he could count... and he could count pretty damn high. "Well, I for one am glad to have met one so pretty." He looked up as others were approaching, sensing a tension even from this far away. It looked like a ragtag bunch of children, but they were already fanning out to attempt to flank him. He let them think they were doing good. "Ah, company. You must be the king's messengers I have been hearing about."

Lan saw the dandy and signaled to the others to move out around the man. When the man named them, he knew that Sprout had been talking again. "State your name and business in Castle Everknight," he called out, taking a stance to draw the man's attention.

"Oh, ho! Look at you all. Well, I will grant you a courtesy since the king is a dear friend of mine. I am Karsis the bard. You might have heard of me?" He bowed mockingly as he kept his eyes on the pretty girl to his right, and the big boy coming on his left. "However, the courtesy vanishes if one of you even tries what you are thinking." It wasn't a threat, but it had been a long tenday or two.

Lan stopped at the mention of the name. He knew that name. Gods above, *everyone* knew that name. "I'm sorry sire, I... I didn't realize," he stammered an apology, but then a strong hand was on his shoulder.

"Stand down students, this man means you no harm." Carana was trying not to laugh. These kids were so hells bent on throwing their lives at every bad guy they imagined was coming for the king that someday they were going to find one; then it would be too late. That's why she was trying to teach them everything she knew in such a short amount of time. Some would live, others wouldn't. It was the way of things.

Karsis bowed again at the sight of the high general, and then tousled Sprouts hair as she skipped away towards the others. "Stay out of trouble kids!" He looked at Carana and saw her smile as they left. "Having fun training the new kids I take it?" It was a guess, but he was very good at reading people after all these years.

"You have no idea." She beckoned him towards the castle as she turned and kept talking, "They are going to have a council meeting in the morning, so that the kids can catch up the king and their parents first. Care to have a little fun tonight in town?"

"My dear Carana, I will *never* turn down a woman that wants to have a little fun." He caught up with her and linked his arm with hers and walked into the castle. He never saw the figure watching him from the far side of the courtyard.

When they were gone, the man dressed in all black walked briskly back inside to do some more research. *If I can find what I need, I will have that pretentious bard once and for all,* he thought as he walked the halls, seemingly invisible. No one saw him unless he wanted them to. He got to his rooms, walked in, and locked the door. Time to get to work.

King's Chamber's, Castle Everknight

RHOE COULD HEAR his parents still arguing outside of the rooms as they walked down the hall, and it worried him more than a little. King Arian had wanted to speak with him alone, and it took everything that he had learned about control to keep from hiding under the bed. Maressa had taken Liss away, damn near kicking and screaming, and now they were alone. Rhoe's father had protested, but even Tierra had seen that the King and Rhoe needed to chat. They had all heard about the two kids becoming married, and they needed the facts before the servants spread it to all the other nobles in court.

Arian walked in and shut the door again behind him. "So young man, do me a favor first before we speak overmuch. Here, take this." Arian tossed the young man a small bundle of clothes. Simple white tunic and breeches so he could change. "We will wash that robe of yours or get you another in a little while." The boy wasn't much to look at, except that hair. It hung down to the boys lower back and was bone white. Then he saw the boy take off the robe hesitantly and almost gasped in shock. The robe hid more than anyone would know. The boy had a solid build, with a well-muscled frame and he looked like he had spent a good many years training. Not at all what the king had thought when he first saw him.

Rhoe stripped and got dressed in the clothes that the king provided. He hadn't worn anything like this in a very long time, and he felt weird. He finished and looked up as the king turned and poured two glasses of something. "No, thank you my lord. I'll have water if it doesn't bother you."

Arian laughed and turned with two glasses of water. "Don't believe the stories, Rhoven. Nobles don't just drink alcohol all the time." He handed Rhoe the drink and sat in a big comfy chair. "As you know, I may be a little concerned about the whole 'married to my daughter' thing. Especially since this is the first time we've met."

"You wouldn't have had any cause to meet me, sir. I'm just a simple warrior from the north," Rhoe said it before he thought about it. He knew he shouldn't interrupt a king, but he forgot where he was. Then he realized that the big man was laughing.

"Oh Rhoven, you remind me so much of your mother. She never let me prattle on either."

"Rhoe," The young warrior interjected.

"Ah, sorry. Rhoe it is." He cleared his throat then continued. "Now what can you tell me about your relationship with Allissana?"

Rhoe took a deep breath and let it out slowly. *How am I going to handle this?* he thought, then he just closed his eyes and started talking. "Well sir, when we met, I had no idea who she was. Once we were both conscious again, I knew her as Liss, and it wasn't till much later that she told me who she was." He stopped there to gauge the reaction from the stern man, and wasn't left waiting.

"So, you had no idea who she was—the princess of your own kingdom?" Arian was trying to treat this young man fairly, but his anger was simmering through a little.

"Well, no sir. I don't think I would've recognized you either if you were not dressed as a king. You see, up in Daelyn we are simple folk who value hard work and honesty above anything else. While we all *know* who our king is, we've never seen or actually heard from you. We don't have fancy courts and nobles."

No one had talked to him like this since his days with the Companions of Everknight. They never let him forget that they weren't noble and this young man's candid observations snapped him out of his overprotective father role just as quick. "I'm sorry Rhoe, you're right. That was wrong of me. Tell me then—what ceremony was this that you both were included in, that you are now married." It hurt to even say it out loud. Nothing against this young man, who by all respects was a decent hard-working young man, but he wasn't prepared for this at all.

"The faeries called it a Revel, and no I don't remember much of it."

"I thought you don't drink—or is this *why* you don't drink." Arian was still stunned that faeries were real. He never fully believed Karsis about them and now he would probably have to apologize to him as well.

"No sir, I didn't have any of their drink. It was their food. You see, it is just as intoxicating, apparently, and I was unaware of that. Before you ask: no, we did not do anything untoward with each other. That I *am* sure of."

"But if you don't remember, how can you be sure?" Arian wasn't angry anymore, now the story was pulling him in more than anything else. He missed this part of adventure.

"I rode a unicorn." Rhoe whispered so low that it was barely audible. He was embarrassed to say it in front of such an important man, but he felt compelled to be honest.

"What was that? I didn't hear you."

"I rode a unicorn," Rhoe said a bit louder.

Arian was so caught off guard he didn't hear the page announce the seneschal. "Oh, well, er... don't worry son. That makes me like you even more." He stammered before he regained his composure. He winked at the young man and turned to the door to see Othren walk in. "Welcome, Othren. Come, sit and meet Rhoe, son of Gareth and Tierra Whiteheart."

"So, *this* is the young man everyone in the castle is talking about." Othren sat down and couldn't help but stare at the young boy. He thought he would be taller... and more muscled. He marveled at the boy's hair though. Something about it was tickling his memories, but he couldn't quite put his finger on it.

Rhoe bowed to the older man and noticed that he walked with a small limp, but it was barely noticeable. Not bad for a man of his age. He also saw that the man wore a holy symbol of the goddess Ollian, seemingly made of pure silver, denoting that he was a high-ranking cleric of the goddess of beauty and songs. "Pleasure to meet you good, sir."

"So, what brings you here, Othren?" Arian hadn't seen the old man recently, and if he wasn't as busy as he was, he would've been worried. "Did I forget to sign something again?" The king noticed that Othren couldn't help but stare at the young warrior, something he wanted to do as well, what with all the stories flying about. This boy had done some amazing things, and coming from Karsis, that is no small feat.

"Well sire, as you may know, I have been charged with the first ever census of the castle. I have painstakingly compiled a list of everyone's name that has stayed here this year, and I am almost finished." Othren took out an ink jar and a quill. He set them on a small table and produced a piece of parchment, unrolling it and holding down the corner with the ink vial. "All I am missing at the moment are the newcomers. And, of course, the elusive Karsis."

"Don't you already know his name if you just said it?" Rhoe closed his mouth the minute he finished but it was too late. He didn't know any of the courtly etiquette and was used to just speaking his mind.

"Why, I guess you are right. But I would also need his last name, and he is quite unreachable for one such as I. Your name would be Rhoven Whiteheart?" Othren wrote as the boy nodded.

"I could always ask Karsis if you want?" Rhoe wanted to be could be helpful, and if that made him look better to King Arian then why not try.

"Why, that would be a tremendous help to an old man such as myself." Othren smiled to them both then put his tools of the trade away and got up slowly. The king had risen and walked to the window, looking out with a far-off glaze to his eyes. "I'll take my leave now, sire." He bowed and left unceremoniously.

Rhoe noticed the King lost in thought and walked over to him by the window. "Copper for your thoughts?" he said playfully

"My daughter is married, and I can't find fault with the man she chose. You would think that would be a happy thing, but you have no idea about the courts and treaties we have." He turned and looked at the young man—not a boy at all. "Don't worry though, I won't let anyone come between you two, if this is what you both want. They still fear me a little." He smiled but in the back of his mind he knew that the nobles would have a hissy fit you could see from the Northern Belt about the boy being a commoner. *Well, isn't that just too bad. The boy is a legacy from the Companions of Everknight, and that ought to count,* he thought, and right then he knew that he had found his loophole. They couldn't say anything bad about the companions, so the kid was in. Of course, that wouldn't stop them from trying.

Rhoe couldn't believe that the king was saying this. He was sure the man was going to hate him. "Why, thank you, sire."

"Please—call me Arian."

"Sorry. Arian." They both turned towards the door as it opened slowly, creaking as if mice were pushing it open.

Overlook Bridge, Castle Everknight

Liss couldn't help but scowl as her mother led her up to the bridge that crossed from the east wing to the west wing. She didn't want to leave Rhoe with her father—gods know what he could be saying right now. *He wouldn't hurt him... would he?* she thought as she felt the wind pick her hair up and spin it like a children's toy. She couldn't see but it felt so good.

"Don't worry, honey. Your father will be on his best behavior. He just wants to get to know the boy that married our daughter." Saying it still made her stomach do that funny upside-down thing. Maressa took a deep breath and felt the wind course by her. This is where she went when she needed to really think. Not "What do we do about this or that Lord?" type of thinking, but real serious issues like this. The overlook used to be where she would come to await Arian's messages, back when they had to sneak around his own father. "Besides, after this it's your turn anyway, so I would start thinking about how you are going to handle Tierra."

"Shouldn't I be worrying about the mountain she is married to?" Liss quipped while trying to fix her hair. She stared right into the wind and it blew her hair back like she was flying. This was so relaxing.

"You mean Gareth? No. He is one big teddy bear. The one that will be coming at you with daggers drawn will be the boy's mother."

"*Man*, mother. Rhoe is no more a 'boy' then I am a 'child.'" Liss was tired and just wanted some sleep before this big council meeting they were going to have. She couldn't deny that she loved being here with her mother though. Her mother had never brought her up here before, it felt really special to her. Now if she could just stop worrying about Rhoe.

"I'm sorry Allissana. It's just so weird to us. We know *of* him, but thanks to the feud that your father and Gareth had all these years, we missed seeing him grow. We don't know if he is a good man, or even what kind of man he is." She saw her daughter's face twist and knew a tirade was coming, so she just plowed on through without much of a break. "Don't get us wrong. He is probably the best there is, but your father wanted to talk with him alone." They both heard someone clear their throat politely behind them and turned to see Karsis.

Karsis smiled seeing them together like this. "While this is cute and all, and I'm sure there is a whole barrel of girl stuff to come, we are needed downstairs. One of your guards came in severely wounded with a very beautiful bard and they need either the king or queen. Arian is busy grilling my student, so you are going to have to do." He spun a full circle as he finished and bowed like a lord.

"Karsis, you never cease to amaze me." Maressa smiled and walked by him, slapping him on the shoulder playfully.

"He does that a lot. At least he has since I met him In River Vale." Liss laughed at his shocked face and followed her mother. They left him behind pouting all by himself. Once they were out of view his smile broadened. He had learned some things as he sat here listening to them. He was shocked that at least Maressa never heard him approach, or even saw him as he stood here. He really was getting better with age. Liss was still worried about Rhoe, but not as bad as when she was near him. Distance was a small factor, that much he had learned. *Small steps are what gets you to the destination,* he thought, remembering the old saying that his teachers used to tell him. He skipped after the girls and headed to see this supposedly beautiful bard.

Outside the King's Room, Castle Everknight

GARETH PACED BACK AND FORTH, wringing his hands in frustration. He knew the king would be angry—hells below, *he* was angry, and it wasn't even his daughter—but he also knew Arian wouldn't take it out on the boy. So, what was taking so long?

"Dear, if you keep doing that you are going to wear a hole in the carpet all the way to the foundation." Tierra was anxious too, but not for her son. She had taught him all the control that she had, and she had no worries about how he would handle himself with the king. The only problem would be him speaking his mind. No, what she was anxious about was getting that *girl* alone and finding out what made her tick.

"I know, but I need to be doing something, not just sitting here." He kicked the base of a marble column that held a vase and sent the expensive art object tumbling down. Before he could even try to reach out and miss catching the vase, steady hands caught it and lifted it back up onto the pedestal.

Tanan stepped out from behind the curtain and bowed. "Gareth, please be careful of the art. It is very expensive and I would hate to steal another one for Arian." Tanan laughed at the scowl on the big man's face. He loved sneaking up on Gareth. It never got old.

"Tanan!" Tierra ran over and grabbed him in a big hug. She hadn't seen him in days, what with one thing or another keeping them both busy. It felt odd at the same time to see her old companions together again. A good odd though. "What have you been doing these last couple of days?"

"I've been sneaking around the lower castle trying to see if I can pick up anything for Arian on these spies and assassin's he has lurking around." He was disappointed that he had found next to nothing, but that just meant he would have to dig deeper. He saw something out of the corner of his eye and reflexively ducked behind the curtain, stilling it and ceasing his own breathing.

Gareth didn't know what was happening. One minute he was talking to Tanan, and the next—when he turned to greet whoever was coming around the corner—he was alone. He saw Allissana meekly peek around the corner and smile at them, and he instantly loved her. She was the spitting image of her mother and father, and it swelled his heart that he could finally meet her. "Come over here and meet your uncle Gareth," he called out, trying to take the focus from Tierra, since he knew his wife was just waiting to get her claws into this young girl.

Liss saw the great big man and smiled, walking faster than she should have, but she saw the look that the woman gave her and it scared the breath right out of her. She knew warriors by looking at them, and this woman could eat half of them. "So nice to meet you. Rhoe has spoken highly of both of you."

"I doubt that. He thought we were dead until recently, remember?" Tierra was annoyed. No, not annoyed—she was livid. This girl had taken her son.

"Dear..."

"Not now, Gareth."

"Why don't I let you girls have some quiet time," he said, pulling Allissana into a bear hug. He brought her closer and whispered to her. "Don't worry, she hasn't killed anyone in almost ten years. You'll be fine." He let her go and turned to his wife to kiss her on the head. He wasn't getting anywhere near her teeth until she calmed down. "Be nice." He left them without waiting for his wife to answer. *I wonder if the Laughing Sprite is still there?* he thought as he turned the corner.

Liss had never been so worried in all her life. This woman was more than just angry. She had people angry with her before and she knew how to handle them. She knew if she tried to 'handle' this woman she would be on the floor faster than sunlight through a window. *And I thought Carana was scary,* she thought as the woman slowly walked towards her. "Before you start hitting, what should I call you?" Liss asked, getting ready to deflect incoming attacks.

Tierra stopped, honestly shocked at how the girl was standing. She went into this angry at the noble princess stealing her pristine baby boy, but she could see now that she was blinded. The girl stood with her feet apart and her right foot slightly back, better able to twist to the side if she had to move quickly. Her hands were open, but raised high to deflect anything that came within her range, and she had stopped her deep breathing and had gone into shallow breaths. This was a warrior, and was prepared to fight for what she believed in. "Mom."

"What now?"

Tierra took a deep breath and exhaled slowly, finding her center and washing away the hate and anger. "I said, you can call me Mom. If you wish." She moved in with her arms open and hugged the confused girl. "Come on, let's walk and talk about how adorable my son is. Then you can fill me in on how you got to be the warrior I just saw standing in front of me."

Liss smiled, still confused. She didn't know exactly what just happened, but she was going with it. "Oh, you would love Carana. She is the high general of Everknight and has been training me since I could hold a wooden sword." They walked down the corridors chatting for hours and after a time, they started harassing everyone that they passed. Once they had gone, Tanan came out and followed Gareth. He wanted nothing to do with women right now.

MARESSA PUSHED the door open slowly, not wanting to bother her husband. When she looked in, she saw them both staring at her. "I don't want to intrude, but we have a situation Arian."

Rhoe saw the man next to him go from easy going to king in an instant, and it awed him more than a little. Then he saw Karsis come in behind the woman and knew something was wrong. The bard wasn't making any jokes. "It's okay, we had pretty much finished up, haven't we sire?"

Arian took two steps and stopped at the young man's words. He sighed and smiled with his head down. "Yes, we have. He is a fine man, and I'll be proud to call him son. Now, you stay here with Karsis and I'll go with Maressa and see what we have." He put his arms around his wife and escorted her out. "You can fill me in along the way dear, let's go."

"But Arian, Karsis only told me just a minute ago..." Then they were gone.

"So—it must be bad if you're still not smiling, Karsis." Rhoe felt like he was the only one still happy around here.

"I'm not exactly sure right now, and that's the part that has me a little off balance, Rhoe." He was surprised that Arian and the boy had gotten along, but then again, he remembered that Arian had a soft spot for politeness, and Rhoe was raised to be very polite. It was a little sickening really.

"Oh, and by the way, Karsis. What is your last name anyway?" Rhoe wanted to get this to the seneschal and maybe score some points with the king.

"My last name?" Karsis had too much to think about right now. Normally he wouldn't give his last name out, but it was Rhoe, so he wasn't worried. "It's Eversong." He paced a couple more times, then snapped his fingers and twirled towards the door. "All right, it's been long enough for those two to talk about you and fill each other in. Let's go see this wounded man and find out what's going on *this* time." He dragged Rhoe out the door and down to the temple, praying for answers and not more questions.

"What wounded man?" But alas, Rhoe was ignored

Temple of Davalar, Castle Everknight

LAN SWITCHED FEET AGAIN, trying to get the cramps out of his legs. He had been standing guard outside the temple for hours and his legs ached to move. He glanced sideways at his counterpart and smiled. Kari had her long brown hair tied up in a single long braid today with pink ribbons entwined down its length. She was rocking from side to side to keep her feet moving, but she was smiling like it wasn't bothering her. "Did you hear if Griff was okay?" he asked her, trying to break the silence.

She turned her head, still bouncing on the balls of her feet to keep them from hurting and failing miserably. "Yeah, the nice lad —Caerlyn I think her name was—said he would be fine, just spooked is all." She grew serious as she thought about what they had been told. "Do you think that he was really touched by Davalar?" She had known him all these years and never had any clue that Griff was so special.

Before Lan could answer her, he heard footsteps coming down the long hallway and saw the king and queen. They were holding each other's hand and talking quietly, but in a serious tone. Lan snapped his feet together and almost laughed when he heard Kari try the same thing and almost fall over. "My King!" he exclaimed, holding his fist to his heart.

Arian didn't even notice the kids standing guard until the young knight snapped to attention. "At ease, young man. How goes it inside?" He was so proud of these children; they had done so well learning to get along in the castle. Another year and they would be ready.

"Nothing yet, lord." Kari spoke before Lan could get all high and mighty. He tended to use 'thee' and 'thou' a lot now when he spoke to the king. "It's been awfully quiet in there." She moved aside when they approached the door and bowed to the queen. "Radiant as always, my lady." Kari added as they passed. The queen just winked at her.

The King paused at the threshold and turned to Lan. "Oh, and Lan. Karsis should be here any moment. Try not to irritate him anymore. I'm rather fond of you, and would hate to lose your services." Arian almost laughed at the face that Lan made.

Somewhere between incredulous and horror. He slapped the boy on the shoulder and went after his wife. She was talking quietly with Ralavin and Caerlyn. He walked over, taking care to look around the room just to make sure they were alone. The only other people were Griff, sitting down in one of the benches, and of course Rythal, standing quietly by the statue of Davalar. They had tried keeping him in his room, but he showed up here every morning regardless of the guards posted at his door.

"Oh Arian, just the man we've been waiting for." Ralavin walked to meet the king and embraced his arm in a firm shake. "It's Dren, from Norhil Hold. You sent him and Stard to bring Storn to Everknight."

"Yes, I remember him, and his friend. They were good men. Is he going to be all right?" Arian didn't see any wounds on the man, but he was still out cold.

Caerlyn walked over and hugged Arian and Maressa without speaking. She hadn't been to the castle in over a year, and with everything that had gone on with Karsis inside of her mind, she just needed to let them know that she cared. "He is physically healthy," she started as she let them go and straightened her dress. "It's his mind and soul that have to come into balance now." She still couldn't believe that the young man brought him back. Not that it was hard, if you knew what you were doing, and had years of training... which the boy had absolutely none of. It should never had happened, yet here they were.

"What caused him to... get out of balance? Am I saying that right?" Maressa looked at the man but had no idea.

"His soul had started to move on, but was brought back. If not done right, then it takes a little time and energy to fix itself." Caerlyn looked over at Griff and smiled, knowing that he was hearing all of this. He probably felt awful, but he shouldn't. He was a miracle worker.

"You usually don't miss things like that, Caerlyn—or was it Ralavin this time?" Karsis said as he strolled into the temple. He had heard the end of the conversation and had figured out what had happened, mainly because he had seen this before.

Caerlyn scowled at the bard, and that made everyone laugh. Except her. "No Karsis, as a matter of fact it wasn't either of us. The savior of the day was young master Griff." She waved her hand over to the boy and everyone looked. "This boy did what took me years to master, without even knowing how, and saved this man."

Karsis didn't know what to say, and that was happening *way* too much lately. He just nodded to her and walked over to the boy, ignoring the king and queen entirely. He stared at the young red headed boy and finally smiled down at him. "You feel warm a lot, don't you?"

Griff was scared. This man wasn't just frightening, he was death come in person. He didn't know *why* he thought that. The man was dressed like a dandy, with a longcoat and ruffled cuffs, but that's what came to him just looking at this formidable warrior. "Ye... yes sir?"

"I'm not a *sir*, but thank you. Now, I'm also going to guess that when you slept at night you would wake up at dawn like clockwork?" Karsis thought he knew what was going on. He had heard of this from an elven priest decades ago. The elf was handpicked by Davalar and suffered for years before he came into his powers.

Griff nodded mutely. It was if this man could read his mind. "Yeah, but I thought I was just an early riser." He really wished he knew what was going on. He could do things that no one else could do, and it was making him feel distant and alone.

It's not his fault Karsis, the gods stir their fingers in us all.

Karsis looked up as the voice sounded in his head. That wasn't Griff. "Everyone stop what they are doing right now and move away from me quickly." He stood up and placed the boy behind him reflexively.

"Karsis, I'll be behind you shielding Caerlyn," Arian said as he moved with purpose. He knew that voice and had always trusted this man's instincts. It had saved both his life and the others time and again.

"I've got Ralavin, Karsis. We will be on the far side of the Temple behind you." Maressa longed to be with her husband, but knew that they had to protect the others. She hadn't heard him talk like that in many years, but her old habits just kicked right in. She looked around as well and the only ones that weren't accounted for, besides the two out cold on the floor, were Rythal and Rhoe.

Rhoe sat quietly in the back as they came in, so as not to disturb anyone. Now he got up and calmly walked to the other side of the room, to the front of Karsis. He didn't want to call out though; he felt like he was still intruding here at the castle. He longed for the dirt roads and fields of his village. He saw Rythal and wanted to run to him and hug him. They had finally broken the news to him about Innal before he talked with Arian, and it still hadn't hit him until right now. Silent tears streamed down his face as he watched his childhood friend stand rigid and unmoving. He used his *sight* to see if he could find out what was wrong, and immediately felt stupid. If Caerlyn and this other priest couldn't find out what was wrong, then how could he?

Ralavin had no idea what was happening, but the adrenalin coursing through his younger veins felt satisfying. He didn't sense anything outwardly evil, or malicious, but he had heard a great many stories from the young king in his days. "Could it be Rythal?" he asked as he watched the bard with trepidation.

Karsis heard them all as he scanned the room with his *sight*.

Nothing. When he heard Ralavin say Rythal's name he looked at the boy again and realized that he couldn't *see* him at all. Interesting. "Okay, I think we're all right, but give me a moment." He slowly walked to the boy and smiled at him. He remembered this one from when they left Daelyn. "Hello Rythal, are you trapped in there?"

Rythal saw everything; he always did. He screamed again for the millionth time for his brother, but Innal was still dead. His brother was still a pile of ash and dust, and he wouldn't hear anything anymore. It didn't keep him from screaming though. That's all he did now, inside this broken mess that was once his mind. That is, until this man walked in. Somehow, this man stabilized him enough so that he could try and think through the broken landscape of his mind. He heard the speech, and even thoughts of the man and with great joy he talked to him in his mind. With this moment of clarity, he could feel the divine presence in his mind, just not which one. Maybe soon he could sleep. *Yes, Karsis. I am. Somehow you gave me clarity and made the screaming stop, but I don't know how.* He didn't want this to end. Then the pretty lady walked forward and he realized it wasn't Karsis that cleared his mind. It was the angel!

Caerlyn knew the minute Ralavin said the boy's name that it was him. It was the boy that did something to Karsis to make him fear an attack. Ralavin had mentioned the boy before, but only in passing since they were trying to figure out what happened with Griff. This was her area—her bailiwick—and she *had* to reach out and sooth this boy. Once attuned to him, which only took a simple prayer under her breath, she could feel his fear and wonderment that her presence afforded him. "Rythal, I'm here. I'm coming over to you now so I can try and help you." She saw Karsis stare at her and smiled. "It's fine Karsis, this is what I do." She took Griff and handed him back to Arian, then reached out and laid a hand upon the head of the boy, gripping him in the power of Davalar.

"Caerlyn, wait!" Ralavin tried to say.

Caerlyn was stopped by a wall in his mind. Worse, this wall was getting larger and warmer in seconds. She had to trust in her friends now, she had no time. *"Run!"*

Karsis heard her scream and knew that he couldn't stop it. He still had his *sight* on and *saw*, as she did, the growing force within the boy come alive at her touch. He was closest though, so he simply grabbed her and spun. He threw her to Arian's arms, which were already reaching out to shield them both. Karsis knew he wouldn't make it, and neither would Arian. At this range, this much force could almost break him apart. Then he was astounded for the umpteenth time in as many days.

Rhoe still had his *sight* on when Caerlyn touched Rythal and he *saw* the growing heat as well. "Ash'anti fra sho la alar!" he called for the air and pointed at Karsis and Caerlyn. He didn't know the elven word for force, so he used the word for shove and prayed that he could get it to push them fast enough. Once he shouted it, he turned and started his roll around the seats on this side to get ready for whatever was coming out of Rythal. Then the room turned black.

Arian was the first to regain some sort of consciousness. The spinning in his head was keeping him from gaining his feet, but he pushed himself up with his arms and looked around through blurry eyes. The temple was a ruined mess, with large chunks of stone laying all over the place. He couldn't see his wife. "Mares..." he coughed and choked on her name as his dry throat refused to work through all the dust in the air. He cleared it and tried again, using her nickname. "Mar!" He got nothing back but groans and shifting rumble. It was then that he remembered the two bodies under him.

Frantically backing up so he could see them, Arian breathed

a sigh of relief when Caerlyn stirred. She seemed decent, cuts and bruises only, and even Karsis seemed unharmed. His jacket was a mess, and that wasn't going to go well once he saw it. He loved that thing almost more than Maressa loved her sword. "Karsis, are you all right?"

Karsis heard the king but his throat was full of stone dust, so he just nodded to Arian. He couldn't believe he was even alive. Then his mind started to clear, and he thought of his young pupil. "Rhoe!" He tried to yell as he stood and promptly fell over before even getting to his knees. He looked down and saw that Caerlyn had a death grip on his coat. Then he noticed that his longcoat was in tatters. He sighed, but knew that it would repair itself in time. Caerlyn wasn't that lucky. "Arian, a little help?" he coughed out.

The king pried her hand from Karsis, and that's when he saw the figure under her. She had covered Griff in all the commotion. "Brave girl." He pulled Griff from under the limp body and checked his breathing. Still alive but seemed to be in shock. He laid him down gently.

"Brave, yes. She also has a basic lack of common sense, but that's why we love her." Karsis gently pulled free and tried to crawl over the rocks to see where Rhoe was. He turned his *sight* over where he was last, and finally saw him in a corner, under a row of benches. *I can't believe that this young one saved me. Me, of all people. Not many on this earth can say that,* he thought as he rolled the boy gently to see if he was hurt.

"Can we not do that ever again?" Rhoe asked weakly. He felt someone roll him over and opened his eyes. That was a colossal mistake. "Oh, and maybe stop the room from doing cartwheels?" He was pretty sure he was going to throw up any second.

"I second that!" Maressa called out from the far side of the room. She had a huge slab of marble on her leg, but she had shoved Ralavin back far enough so that he was just bruised. She fell into a coughing fit the minute she shouted, but it was worth it. She looked out over the room and realized that the area around the statue of Davalar was intact. Not only intact, but untouched. And there in front of it—in the eye of the storm— was Rythal. The boy looked unconcerned and distant. "Well, the boy is all right at least."

"He was the last time this happened as well." Ralavin chimed in, standing up and limping over to the two bodies on the floor. Nothing had hit the woman except dust, but Dren had taken a hit to his head from falling rocks. *Not too bad, but it will need a bandage. We got lucky—the whole roof could've come down with that one,* he thought as he checked them both over again.

"Ralavin, what do you mean the *last* time?" Arian asked in his 'I'm a King, so answer me' voice.

"When I tried to break through the boys mind a couple days ago." He shrugged at Arian's intense stare. "I tried to warn her, but I was too late."

Caerlyn got to her feet slowly, using Arian for balance. "It's all right, Ralavin. I'll get you for it later. As soon as my head stops pounding at least." She turned at the rushing footfalls coming down the hall, and saw Carana, Tierra, and Allissana burst into the room ready for anything. Behind them were the two children that were guarding the door.

"What in the deep hells happened in here?" the high general asked. She hadn't seen devastation this bad since the year that the dragon had hit the castle.

Liss rushed past her and searched the room with fear. Then she saw Rhoe and leaped over the rubble to get to him. "Rhoe, you're all right! Thank the gods."

Tierra was right behind her and wrapped her son in a fierce hug. "Can't leave you alone for a minute, can we?"

Rhoe smiled at her as she let him go, then he wrapped his arms around Liss affectionately. "This time it wasn't my fault. Caerlyn did it."

Tierra tilted her head at the unusual display, but smiled nonetheless at her son with a girl. She was about to tease him when a strange voice called out through the rubble.

"So... do you bring all of your visitors to warzones, or just the pretty ones?" Janna said timidly. She was awake, barely, and feeling like she was hit with the pointy side of a mountain. That's what she gets for drawing constant magic for that many hours. She looked up at the impressive figure coming over to her and smiled. "You must be King Arian. I have braved the very gates of death to get you a message from Lord Storn." She paused to catch her breath, clearing her throat of dust.

"Yes, I see that you have. What is the message, dear..." He didn't even know her name

"Janna, my King. I am a bard of no small skill and fame in the southern reaches of this great lan—"

"Get on with it!" Carana yelled. She knew what this woman was and wanted to run her through with her sword. It wouldn't put her down, but it would make her feel better. *I'll deal with her later; right now I need to know what is going on if I'm going to protect the city.* Her thoughts were running away from her. Storn was always the most practical of the Companions, she remembered him well. If he stayed behind, then it was something to do with G'harr.

"Fine. The message is simple. Madam Ill'lyth G'harr is alive and in power." She counted to three and watched their reactions. Not everyone would know that name, but that woman would know. Janna knew what she was, and that meant that her own cover was probably blown. She was about to be worried when she saw him. *Karsis was here.*

"Well, there goes the party. Right, Arian we need a private

council meeting and we need it *now*. Get all of the Companions, the kids, and everyone in this room. This is bad. I don't mean 'There's a dragon coming' bad... More like, 'The earth is swallowing us' bad." Karsis honestly couldn't have envisioned a worse thing to happen, and he was very creative.

"But the wounded?" Ralavin wasn't used to being caught up in all this epic hero stuff. Even when he was young and adventurous, it wasn't this bad. "We will need time to heal them still."

"You and I, Caerlyn, and Griff can handle that in about an hour, maybe two, if I'm *seeing* what I think I am *seeing* in that young lady there. Janna was it?" He watched her nod absently, staring at him like he was a leg of lamb and she hadn't eaten in a tenday. "For you, my dear we may need a potion to balance your magic energy. You used a lot of it over a long time, didn't you?"

"Yeah, it was a long flight out of Keragan Hold. Their armies wanted to stop this information from getting to you." *Gods look at him, he is amazing,* she tried to hold back her thoughts, just in case he could read them, then smiled. *Screw that, I hope he can see what I'm thinking.*

"All right everyone! Council chambers in three hours, and please don't make me come looking for you." Arian wanted this time to digest everything he had taken in over the last couple of days. Things were getting out of hand, and It seemed that it was all tied together somehow.

A Darkened Room, Somewhere in Castle Everknight

THE MAN SAT in the dark room and went through his contacts in his mind. *Who could've caused an explosion that big without me knowing?* He couldn't think of anyone. Everyone he had left was very low level in the magic department, unless there were infiltrators here that he was unaware of. No, he would've *sensed* them. It had to be something else—but what was a mystery to him. Then he heard his new apprentice coming and straightened up a bit. "Come in," he called right before the woman knocked.

Belenna froze with her fist inches from the door. She hated when he did that. She was new to this conspiracy thing, but desperately wanted change to come to Lythinall. She was one of the maids and had seen firsthand the abusive power of the so-called noble lords. She had lost her best friend to one of them, after they raped her and left her for dead in the city below. She opened the door and walked into the darkness. She hadn't been permitted to see her lord yet; she had to earn that privilege. "My Lord, the newest rumor has it that the explosion was caused by the inert child." She didn't really believe it, but she always reported the rumors no matter how bad she thought they were.

"Actually... that would make sense. I have *sensed* something within him, but never really thought about what that might be." He smiled, feeling a lot better knowing that there might be a better explanation than another sorcerer that he didn't know about. "Now, have you made any progress into finding out about the young warrior?" Karsis's protégé was whispered about in his circles as powerful, but he hadn't seen anything to back that up.

"Well, believe it or not, I have." She smirked in the darkness to herself, thinking that if she hesitated she would seem like she had some of the power finally. She was wrong.

"Then spit it out and stop with the smirking. You are my student and if you ever want to learn anything other than what I have taught you, you will show respect."

"Forgive me, my lord." She was used to bowing and scraping, but she hated it. He had taught her how to use the air to bring whispers to her, to lower the flame on the torches to darken rooms, and to use ether to cast illusions of lesser creatures; but she needed more. "It is whispered that the young man has somehow married the princess and is also able to cast magic as the elves do."

"Impossible!" This couldn't be right... Was Karsis teaching him that much? He had assumed that he could do little things, but to be on par with the elves... that was just inconceivable. And he never used that word.

"I can't say one way or another lord. That's just what they say in my presence."

"Well, then we may have to start looking a little closer at the young man. Follow him and see what he does." He would watch the boy himself and keep an eye out for anything that the young warrior could do. "You are dismissed." He waved her away and shut the door behind her with air.

Belenna walked down the hallway with an angry stomp, and Barris watched her go quietly from the corner. He had been there for almost thirty minutes, but he had yet to see who she was talking to. He shrugged his shoulders and faded away down the hallway. He would tell his queen about the women, and hope that it was enough. He just wished he was brave enough to get a good look at the man in the room.

8

REVELATIONS

Lord Tanan Norhil walked down the city streets and breathed in the late spring air. It would be getting warmer soon, and he would miss the northern climate. He turned a corner and saw what he was looking for: The Laughing Sprite. How he had missed this little hole in the wall tavern and the nights spent drinking with his friends here. He had followed Gareth through the city and thought he knew where the big man was going. This was where they came to drink when they got sick of the politics of the castle. Before he could get twenty feet from the door, movement caught his eye. He didn't turn right away; that would startle the little thief. Instead, he yawned innocently and stretched his arms out wide, showing the cutpurse his belt and pouch without anything in the way. Not many urchins could pass this target up. When he felt the tiny, expected tug of the drawstring being cut, Tanan whipped his hands down and grabbed the wrist of the thief and spun to confront the little one. Imagine his surprise when it wasn't little at all.

Graf was surprised that this well-dressed lord caught his hand and spun with the grace of a dancer. He usually never got caught, so he was frozen for a minute. They stared at each other and then a smile spread across the man's face. "What's so funny?" Graf finally asked.

"Not funny, dear sod, but rather amused." Tanan let go of the man's hand and bowed, keeping his eyes focused. The man was about six feet tall, but whip lean, and his black hair was long and tangled. He wore rags and smelled slightly like old wine and urine, but it was his eyes that made Tanan smile. He had eyes that had already looked all around to see who and what was near and had probably mapped an exit from this encounter. The man was good. "My name is Tanan, and I recognize talent when I see it. If I may ask—why were you stealing money? Debt? Tithe to a more powerful entity?"

"I wanted to have a drink or two. It's been a really long set of days and I can't seem to find an alley that suits me," he said it as a matter-of-fact, but the minute he said it the man was roaring with laughter.

"Well, good sir you can have that drink—on me of course —and we can tell stories whilst we ponder the bottom of many a glass." Tanan always got uppity when he was entertaining others, it was just what he did. "Now let's go inside and meet my good friend. He will enjoy some of those stories as well. They walked in and some of the patrons stopped talking at the sight of Graf, but Tanan ignored them with practiced ease.

Gareth saw Tanan come in and was pleasantly surprised that he was here too. He thought that he would just come and have a couple of drinks and relax after all the fuss at the castle, but now Tanan was here. This could turn dangerous, but Gareth was still smiling. "Tanan, come sit and have a drink. Who is your... friend?" Gareth could smell him now, and so could everyone in here, no doubt.

"He's... well, we haven't gotten that far yet," he turned to the man and waved him to a seat. "And what would your name be, good sir?"

"Graf. And who might you two be?" he said mockingly. He pulled out the chair, turned it around, then sat down straddling the chair the wrong way. The place had resumed talking amongst themselves once more, no doubt more gossip about him. It never stopped. He saw the other man stand up to shake his hand and he reflexively inched back. The man was a mountain!

Gareth smiled knowingly. He had that effect on people. He held his hand out anyway. "The name is Gareth. Pleasure to meet you, Graf." He saw the man tentatively shake it and then grimace like he expected Gareth to crush it. "Any friend of Tanan's is... well, I've never met any of his friends, so I wouldn't know."

"Laugh it up, big man. Nice to meet you, Graf. Been in the city long?" Tanan signaled the girl behind the bar as he talked.

"Nope, just got here a couple days ago with a wagon." He looked around nervously. *At least there wasn't any wind,* he thought as the girl came over to bring them three mugs of ale. He grabbed a mug and downed it in one shot, as did Gareth. They locked eyes and smiled. The unspoken contest was on.

It had been a long time since Gareth had seen someone drink like that, and he knew it was going to be one of *those* nights. He smiled at the man and was about to wave the girl back again when he saw a young boy walk in and scan the crowd. The boy had the official jacket of the king and Gareth just knew the jig was up.

Barris didn't come down to the city very often. In fact, this was the first time in at least eight months that he had been out of the castle. He was on urgent business and had to find Lord Tanan. He stopped outside of the Laughing Sprite and grimaced. He really didn't want to go in there. He drew up his courage and walked in, scanning the crowd for the lavishly dressed man he had met just days ago. He was sitting at a table with the other man he had to find, and apparently a homeless person. "I have a message from Karsis."

"What does he want now?"

"What does he want now?"

Gareth stared at both Tanan and Graf as they both spoke at the same time. His head hurt already. Now they were babbling at each other trying to find out how each of them knew Karsis. "Page, why is the message from Karsis and not the king?" He had a real bad feeling about this.

"Well, sir—"

"Gareth. Please, call me Gareth. I am not a *sir*." Gods above he hated that title.

"Gareth, then. The king is meeting with the queen about the damaged temple, and Karsis is handling the emergency council meeting that he called."

Tanan stopped arguing with Graf long enough to hear that and turned his head. "Emergency meeting? What happened now?" It couldn't have been him; he was down *here* causing trouble.

Graf took a deep breath and let it out slowly. "Boy... what is the message that you are patiently waiting to deliver?" He wasn't going to get involved but they would be here all night if he didn't.

Barris sighed in relief. He wasn't about to tell them they were wasting their time. He cleared his throat and assumed an indignant posture. "Karsis calls an emergency council meeting in light of desperate news. All Companions of Everknight are needed, as well as any other person so involved with them in *any* way or manner." He bowed and took his leave as fast as he could before they asked him any other questions. Heroes could be such a bother sometimes.

Tanan got up and threw some coins on the table, eyeing the patrons next to them with that look that said 'Don't think about touching them', and walked to the door. "Come gentleman, the castle awaits!"

"Can I come too?" Graf got up and eyed the coins, but thought better about it for once. He started walking, not realizing that Gareth wouldn't get the joke.

"Of course! Why would you think...? Oh, the gentleman comment. You're just as bad as Tanan, for all of the gods' sakes."

"Thank you, Gareth!" Tanan called from the open doorway.

"It wasn't a compliment, jack ass."

Ruined Temple of Davalar, Castle Everknight

THEY HAD another hour or so before the meeting, and all the injured were finally fixed up. Dren was lounging in the council chamber already with a bottle of spiced wine, and Janna had gone looking for Karsis. It was just the three of them now: Caerlyn, Ralavin, and Griff. Make that four, as Rythal stood impassive in front of Davalar's statue. "Now that we are alone, there are some things that I wanted to talk about with you, Griff." Caerlyn was worried about the power that lay within this small boy. *What was he, eleven winters? Twelve?*

Griff knew this was coming. He hung his head down and waited for the lecture. "I know, I wasn't supposed to bring him back. But you don't understand." How could he tell them that it just felt wrong?

"Then tell us, son. Trust us, we've both seen some pretty weird stuff." Ralavin caught the look that Caerlyn shot him and laughed out loud, not even trying to hold it in. "Okay, she has seen some weird stuff." He turned to Caerlyn though and smiled. "But to be fair, I was brought back from near death by a magical potion that turned me young again."

"We will have a weird story session later. Now, Griff tell us what we don't know." She needed more insight into how he was doing this and why.

"Well, when I was trying to heal him and realized that he was gone... it felt wrong. What I mean is, it felt like the man was supposed to be here and if he wasn't, it would've been wrong." He saw their faces grow pale and knew that he had said too much.

"Dear Davalar—can it be?" Caerlyn couldn't fathom what she had just heard. Even Ralavin was taken aback, so he must've known what the boy was just as she did. The boy was an Oracle. She reached out and laid a comforting hand upon the boy's shoulders and sent warm tendrils of healing into his mind. He had nothing broken, like some of the people she helped, but it would make him feel better, nonetheless.

"I think he is, dear lady." Ralavin had heard of this before, but had never met one in his lifetime. An Oracle. They were healers in tune to the flows of not only the present, but the future as well. They could tell if someone was going to have a boy or a girl, if they were going to have complications later in life due to illness, and even sometimes if they were supposed to die now or much later. The later was rare, and Ralavin was fairly certain it was for bardic stories more than factual... until now. "That would explain a couple things, like why the arrows turned to ash. They weren't supposed to be there."

"Yeah, that was a new one for me. I've never seen that." Caerlyn had seen some other very strange things, but that one was impressive to be sure. "You Griff, are going to be one of the best healers in all of Lythinall—better than myself or even Ralavin."

"You mean I'm not in trouble?" Griff was overjoyed. He

thought for sure they would be angry about those things with wings. He hadn't seen them up close, but as the man came back, he caught a glimpse of them. They wanted to come over too.

Ralavin saw that something was till troubling the young boy. "Tell us Griff, what is it?" He wanted the boy to trust them, especially if he was going to be as good as the stories said oracles were.

"Well, I think I know why you're not supposed to bring people back like I did." He swallowed hard and closed his eyes. He was going to sound crazy he just knew it.

Caerlyn beat him to it. "Let me guess. They were large and horrible, with leathery wings and rotting hair on dark, dead flesh. Their fangs dripped a corrosive bile, and their throaty growl was almost constant—like they were talking amongst themselves. Does that sound about right?"

Griff was frozen. That was them. She knew of them. "Yes, Lady Caerlyn. They wanted to cross over and leave him behind." He wanted to curl up and cry. Worse was that he only had a fleeting glimpse and he felt this way. *No wonder that man said I was his favorite person.*

"Yes. They are called Reapers, and they do the bidding of the Dark One himself. I've seen someone brought back with a Reaper inside, instead of them, and it never ends well." She looked at this young charge with a new understanding of his strength. This child had done something on instinct that most trained healers would blanch at trying. "I can teach you how to deal with them—it's a simple charm. When all this is over, I'll take you back to my hold and your training will really begin." She caught Ralavin smiling at her and felt almost ashamed at her flagrant lack of protocol. "I'm sorry, Ralavin. I should've asked first. I..."

"Caerlyn, it's fine." He cut her off before she got going. "I agree. I've started teaching him what I know, but it is plain to see that the young master would benefit more from your expertise than mine." He couldn't imagine a better teacher than this woman.

"Well then, it's settled. Now let's get to the council chambers so this meeting can start. I for one am curious as to what this all means." Caerlyn led the way, tousling Griff's red hair as she walked.

Ralavin watched them go, and for the first time in a very, very long time he thought about something other than Davalar. He shouldn't—he knew that—but she was everything he had always wanted in someone. It helped that she was a priestess as well, but it wasn't just that. He looked up to the statue of his god and closed his eyes. *This was your work wasn't it? Well, if it was, then I will approach it like I would any other task you have led my way. With patience and restraint.* He walked after them whistling a merry tune and none of them noticed that Rythal's head had turned to watch them go.

Inner Courtyard, Castle Everknight

OTHREN WAS FUMING. They had called an emergency council meeting and hadn't invited him. Worse still, it was that incessant bard Karsis that had called the meeting—not even the king. Hero of the free land or not, that was a breach of protocol that he could not ignore this time. Besides, maybe it was time. The only good news was that a page had come delivering Karsis's last name from Rhoe. He stopped and called for a page, then waited as one of the boys came trotting over. *Where do they come from?* he wondered as the boy seemed to appear out of nowhere. The boy came to a stop and did not make eye contact, like he was trained to do.

"Sir." Fenton had been watching Othren for an hour, bored out of his mind.

"Young page, I want you to find Karsis and tell him to meet me near the East guest room corridor as soon as he can. Tell him that it is a matter of grave import, and that the fate of the land is at stake." He flipped the boy a coin and the young man was off like lightning.

Frenir heard the exchange and made a mental note on where Karsis would be heading. As the councilor of foreign relations, he had his suspicions on who was feeding G'harr information, and who could be trying to kill the king. He had been laying low for the last tenday learning what he could from what spies he had left, and he hadn't learned a whole lot. He would be there when Othren met with Karsis and then he would see the old man's true colors. He walked the other way, avoiding Othren and disappeared into the castle.

Othren smiled and walked on, knowing that Frenir was there. He had outlived his usefulness as a decoy and would have to be eliminated. He strolled the rest of the way inside without his customary limp and turned a corner. Once inside and out of the view of the guards, his worn robes turned to a burnt black, flaking off like dead skin, and his hood came up all on its own. The man in black walked without a sound down the corridor to where he would meet Karsis—and now that he knew the bard's last name it would be quick—then he would take out the others in the assembly without their beloved savior. That was Trost's mistake: he tried to take on a man like that without plans. He missed his old student, but he had a new one now. He laughed at his own cleverness in this devious trap and hurried to where he would end it all.

Fenton rushed all the way to the council chamber. He knew that Karsis was there, and with what he had for a message, he knew time was precious. Sliding into the room, out of breath and panting, he held onto the large table for balance.

"What is it, Fenton?" Karsis saw the young boy come in, and just knew that things weren't getting any better. Some days it seemed that he couldn't win with an army.

"Message for you... from Othren... grave import." He couldn't get his breath back. He inhaled deeply and let it out slowly, then opened his mouth to try again. He didn't need to.

"Ah, got it. It's fine, Fenton. Rest here and wait for me." He started for the door, but he wasn't done with Rhoe. They needed to speak before the meeting. Him and the girl. "Rhoe, Liss, with me. We will be back in time for the meeting. There are some things that you both need to know before everything gets hectic in here."

Rhoe stood quickly and grabbed Liss with a smile that said he was glad to be doing something besides sitting here. "Goody, field trip," he quipped, laughing at the face Karsis made at his remark.

"Be nice Rhoe. I'm interested in what could be so secret that he has to tell us ahead of time." Allissana was no novice to castle intrigue, but this man elevated it to a whole new level. And from what she had seen already in their brief travels, he wasn't done.

Karsis led them out and walked the hallways quickly, avoiding people with fluid grace. He talked as he went as to save time. "So, what everyone doesn't know is that prophesy speaks of the three of us taking a long trip after this meeting." He knew they would question him, and he was ready. Then they both surprised him yet again.

"I'm in." Rhoe said, keeping up with no problems. If there was one thing that he learned young, it was how to walk fast to keep up with his mother. Those short legs could seriously move.

"Me too. Where are we going?" She was grateful to be

home, but with all that was going on, she knew that her father would have to concentrate on that instead of her and Rhoe.

Karsis didn't slow as he turned and walked backwards and looked at them with his intense stare. "We have to go persuade the elves to help us fight G'harr." As he dropped this fireball of a plan, he turned back and kept walking, waiting for what was coming next.

"The *Elves!*" Liss screamed, scaring half of the people around her into getting out of her way. "Sorry! Sorry, it's... okay. Really, Karsis? The elves?" She had dreamed of meeting an elf almost all her life. Well, except recently, then her dreams changed to meeting Rhoe. Thinking of those dreams got her thinking; she hadn't had them since she met him on the bridge.

"Yes, well, calm down a little. We're not there yet. It's going to be fun persuading everyone that we can even get in to see them without dying immediately. Good thing I know an easy way in. Even before we get to where it could go wrong—it is a long journey and I want to take a small side trip to see the faeries." Karsis went down the side stairs quickly, worried a little on what this new 'grave danger' was going to be about. Othren better be lying, he didn't think he could take any more bad news.

Rhoe groaned at hearing about visiting the faeries. They made his head hurt, but elves! He had always wanted to meet one in person. It was then that he slowed his steps. He had a feeling growing in his stomach, not unlike butterflies or a twisting knot. It had never happened before that he knew of, and he almost yelled for Karsis. The bard was walking fast and was already way ahead of them, but then the decision was taken from him. He was going to yell for his mentor, but he was hit with an extremely solid clump of absolutely nothing. He didn't even notice anything out of the corner of his eye so he couldn't even roll a little bit out of the way. Rhoe hit the wall and was pinned there, presumably by air itself, and it was crushing him slowly. He fought consciousness as he tried to breathe with compressed lungs, and he saw someone fighting Liss. He couldn't pass out, she needed him!

Liss saw Rhoe take the hit and even though she was watching, she had no idea what happened. It looked like Rhoe just lifted off the ground and hit the wall, except he just stuck there, pressed against the unyielding stone, fighting to get free. "Karsis," she tried to yell, but the air whooshed out of her in a rush. Gasping for anything to fill her lungs, she turned at the sound of the only person still here. She drew Deathsong in a clean sweep around her, coming to bear at an opponent that was dressed in all black. The sword rang with a clear bell that seemed to echo for much longer than usual. Liss noticed that everyone had run off at the first sign of trouble, so there was no one to get in the way, thank the gods.

"Darling, you can't begin to stop me." The man reached up and lowered his hood, revealing the close-cropped white hair of Othren, and his clever smile. He could see what it had done to her as her sword dipped to the floor and almost slipped from numb hands. He waved his hand and commanded the air to pin her firmly to the ceiling. She flew up and slammed into the marble ceiling with a sickening thud and stayed there, her tears falling slowly. He let her breathe again though; he didn't want her passing out and missing the grand show he had planned. The death of Karsis the bard.

Frenir had waited for this moment. He had hidden here after taking a shortcut, and his alacrity had paid off. He stepped out and whispered words to the air to free the Princess, but before he could the air whooshed out of his lungs as well and he fell to the ground gasping. He rolled to his knees, expecting this all along. He knew that he would be outmatched by magic, so once Othren had commanded the air on a third target, he knew he would be taxed. He threw the dagger with everything he had left and saw it bury itself in Othren's shoulder. Just six inches off the mark. The world went dark then as he slowly suffocated, and he fell over onto the stone floor.

Othren was more angry than hurt, but he left the dagger where it was. "Poor Frenir—you were never more than a distraction for these pathetic fools." The man in black looked down at the unconscious man and almost laughed. This was too easy.

Liss sucked air in hard and tried to steady her lungs. Every part of her was trembling or in pain. "Othren... why?" she forced out. Her ribs were killing her, probably bruised or broken, and she could only cry as the man she grew up knowing was trying to kill them. She saw Karsis turn way down the hallway at the commotion and tried to smile. Now that old man would pay.

Othren was in his glory. He was going to destroy the princess with the truth. The glorious truth that his Lady was going to bring this land under her exquisite rule, but then he saw Karsis running back to them. "Obren ethir, sistren Karsis Eversong's shiran!" He uttered the command that the ether take his very life. By using his true name, the bard couldn't hope to counter it by any means known to man. He saw Karsis slide to his knees and scream in agony. Othren laughed as he watched his dreams coming true... then it all fell apart.

Karsis felt the walls shake and turned back to look. Nobody was behind him. Then he saw Liss hit the ceiling and as he started to run and noticed Rhoe pinned against the wall, along with Frenir's valiant stand. This wasn't good. The sorcerer had three separate commands going without breaking a sweat, and the only other person here that could do that was himself. The other problem was that he couldn't just kill the man, because the princess would fall, and he wasn't sure if he could catch her with air from this distance. He would have to get much closer.

"It can never be easy can it?" he asked no one in particular as he started to run at the sorcerer. He saw who the man was and did a double take. *Damn, that one slipped by me.* Othren was always there, in every decision and plan. *No wonder we have been getting surprised at every turn,* his thoughts were fleeting though, as he needed his wits about him to fight a sorcerer this powerful. Then he heard the man cast and knew that all his hard work was over. He tried to brace for it, but it hit him viciously, knocking him to his knees. He continued to slide forward with his momentum, screaming in pain. Then it was over... but Karsis was still alive.

The bard's smile was fearsome—once he could smile through the pain—and Othren, Rhoe, and even Liss could see the auburn curls slowly melt away. His tanned skin lightened to a pale color and his ears grew longer, more pointed at the tips. His hair was now a long bone white and spilled out down his back, past his waist. His fingers lengthened as well and as he stood, very slowly, they could see that even his eyes were different. Before them stood an elf.

Of all the gods in the heavens... Liss thought as she watched the being that was Karsis stalk towards Othren.

Karsis threw out a focused blast of air to stun his opponent, then smiled. "That was very good, Othren. You almost had me. But that's *not* my name." He drew his sword and flung it out asking the wind to carry it swiftly. He had to use the surprise to finish this before the man got his wits about him. Othren was dangerous. The sword buried itself in the sorcerer's chest, and in a blink of the eye Karsis was right there, pulling it out sideways in a fountain of blood. He looked up and asked the air to catch Liss as she fell, then checked the traitorous old man. Dead. He cut off his head for good measure, then used a torch to light him on fire. *You just never knew sometimes,* he thought as he turned to find the two young kids staring at him. He knew what was coming. He never wanted anyone to know, but at least these two could be trusted to keep quiet... he hoped.

"This isn't a spell, is it?" Rhoe asked, already knowing somehow.

"No. The other image was a glamour, something that I use to blend in with humanity. When Othren cast that spell and tied it to a name, it killed that image, but that's all it could do." He felt naked without his curls, but he did feel a little better with someone knowing after all these decades. He prodded Frenir and saw that he was starting to breathe normally once more. Gods above, that man would have one hell of a headache tomorrow.

"So, you have always been an elf? Even back with the Companions?" Liss was trying to wrap her head around so much, that it felt like her head was going to pop off.

"Yes, even before that. No one has ever known, except you two." He motioned for them to walk and talk. "I'm very old, but I enjoy being Karsis, so no one need ever know." This was said in that "I will kill you in ways that you couldn't even think of" voice," and he continued without waiting for them to acknowledge. "It will only take me a couple minutes then we can get back to the council meeting. Anything else?" He knew that they would be a ton of questions, but if he got the important ones out of the way, they could wait till later.

"All right, I've got one." Rhoe was already thinking of what he was going to ask him once they set out on their trip, but this one needed to be asked right now, he was too curious. "If your image was a glamour, then how did you maintain it for so long, and even when you were unconscious?"

Karsis stopped walking and smiled at this young prodigy. "Good one, Rhoe. That is a fine question. You see, most wizards cast a glamour for short term use. To get by a guard, or to deceive a patron in a bar. But when I cast it, I tied it to my soul."

"You did what now?" Liss was so lost in this conversation that she swore she was asleep.

"I tied it to my soul, so that even if I was hurt or lost concentration, it would remain. Effectively always being on without constant use of magic," as he finished, he asked the ether to form his glamour once again, mentally tying it once more to his quivering soul. His hair curled up and turned a deep auburn once again, then his skin darkened back to a nice tan. His eyes turned back, and his ears shortened. Karsis was back. "Ahh. Now then, not a word from you two. Is that clear?"

"Yes, and might I add—that was creepy." Liss was limping, and her ribs were killing her, but in better spirits. She still couldn't believe that Othren was behind this attack.

"Not a word, Karsis. You can trust me." Rhoe was stunned by the fact that Karsis was an elf, though it did make a lot of sense with some of the things that he had heard. Long life span, his magic, his skill with a blade. "But what about the body, and Frenir?"

"Frenir is all right and I'm sure the guard will be here at any moment, what with all the screaming and dying and such." He waited for a second to see if there were any more questions, "All set? Good, now let's go make Arian's day even worse by telling him about Othren." He waited for Liss to laugh then patted her on the back. "I even think his own daughter should do it." It was his turn to laugh as she blanched at hearing that.

❧

ELSEWHERE IN THE CASTLE, a tired page was just getting back to his rooms after escorting three men back from the city. Barris walked into his room, rubbing his eyes, and almost tripped over the pair of black cats staring at him. He froze in horror as he knew there hadn't been any cats in the entire castle for years.

Then the cats faded away, and a woman stepped from the shadows to close the door behind him.

"You, little one, have been spying on me." Belenna smiled a wicked smile. She had seen this little vermin watching her and had followed him until she was certain that he was alone. The cats were just a diversion, in case he wasn't alone. She had learned that trick from Othren; thankfully she was linked to him. It gave her power a little boost. "Now it's time for you to—" Pain burst into her head and agony shot through her whole body. Her chest started to seize and she bent over. The last thing she saw before she felt Othren die was the look on the young boy's face as he swung a steel bookend into her head with both hands.

CARANA WAS on her way to question Janna when she heard the rumble. She had been in this castle for more years than she cared to remember, and when something happened out of the ordinary, she knew. She was running when she saw the boy inch backwards out of his room dragging something, and her hairs stood up on the back of her neck. Some days she just couldn't win at all. "Barris! What is going on?" She almost certainly did not have time for this.

Barris froze at the sound of her voice. He was trying not to cry, and failing miserably. "I... ki-killed... he-her," he sniffled, trying to drag her out into the hallway. "She... she was..."

"Oh, gods above stop talking." Carana grabbed the body and threw it over her shoulder and grabbed the page by the hand and walked, almost dragging him along in her wake. "We will sort this out later, once you can talk without swallowing your own snot." She just knew that the rumble she felt was bad news, what else could it be with her luck.

Barris said nothing as he tried to keep up with the wild woman dragging him, and when they wound down a side stair case and saw guards coming as well, he felt her go even faster almost pulling his arm out of its socket.

"Um... High General?" One of the unlucky guards tried to stop her, concerned about the body on her shoulder and the blood trail she was leaving through the hallways. Then her fist was in his face. He never even felt the stone floor cradle him as he fell into unconsciousness.

"Anyone else want to question me?" She saw the guards moving out of her way and stormed past them, still dripping blood from the body over her shoulder and still oblivious to it.

Lan skidded around the corner as she continued and saw the blood. Not bothering to ask, he just hurried past the stunned guards and fell in step with her in silence, giving a look to the page that conveyed condolences for whatever it was that got him mixed up with an angry Carana. They came upon the burned and decapitated body not more than a minute later, and the guards that were looking at the body faded away, back to the stairway. They knew trouble when they saw it. Frenir was propped up against the wall. He rubbed his head and nodded to the high general when their eyes met.

"Sorcerer?" Lan asked, in a matter-of-fact tone. He was trying work on his problem with the knights, and he figured he would practice a serious approach to anger to see if he could diffuse it. He couldn't.

"Did I ask you to speak, trainee?" Carana was angry, more so since she was carrying a dead body around her castle. "Now, let me just catch my breath."

"But you're not out of breath."

"It's an expression, Lan. Now shut up," She knew he was only trying to be a grown up instead of a kid, but she needed to think. "Please," she added so that he wouldn't feel *too* bad.

Carana set down the body she was carrying and turned over the burnt one on the floor. It had dark black robes and a wicked looking dagger, but naught else. She went over to the decapitated head and rolled that over then sucked in her breath in surprise. Othren. Crap. "Right. Lan grab young Barris here and please follow me. We are going to the council chamber right now and I'm not going to let anyone stop us. Anyone." She stacked both bodies and hoisted them up over her shoulder, then looked down at the head. "Someone want to help?"

Barris blanched at the prospect of touching the severed head, so Lan reached down and picked it up, handing it to her gingerly. He closed his eyes and tried to breathe through his nose—he didn't want to get sick in front of his superior.

"Thanks, now let's go. You too, Frenir. We will want to hear all about why you're here with a dead body as well." With that Carana, Frenir, Lan, and Barris made their way to the council chambers, and all of the guards let them pass while trying to help the one on the ground be more comfortable.

Council Chambers, Castle Everknight

THE ROOM LOOKED MUCH CLEANER since Maressa was last here. She looked around and tried to remember the charred walls and flame-scarred table, but saw only the shine of new wood and walls. They were all here. Well, almost all of them, and soon they would hear what Karsis had to say about that name. "Nice of him to be here and not make us wait," she mumbled under her breath. She looked over at the recovering soldier, Dren, and the beautiful new arrival, Janna. They had risked their lives to get that message here form Keragan Hold, and quite possibly had saved everyone, depending on what Karsis said about that name. *Why does that name bug me so much? It's like I should know it,* she thought as she saw the other kids file in.

Kari, Vance, Tomas, and Sprout all walked in looking like they were in a place they weren't supposed to be in. They claimed seats in the far back, usually reserved for witnesses or guests. Arian stood when they came in and gave them a nod of thanks as they sat. That's when Karsis, Rhoe, and Liss came in. The bard looked like he had wrestled a bear, and Rhoe and Liss looked like they just stole cookies from the kitchen.

"Karsis, I take it the meeting with Othren went well?" Arian asked sarcastically, glancing to Fenton to let him know that it was all right. The boy didn't want to tell anyone where Karsis went, but when the king asks...

"As a matter of fact, my Liege, it did not." Karsis sat with a flourish, fanning his coat out behind him as he slid into the chair with grace. "Othren is dead, killed by my sword after he attacked both the princess, Frenir, and my charge." He was being formal on the count that Othren was the castle's Seneschal. "Turns out, my lord, that Othren was in fact the sorcerer behind all of this. Possibly even Trost's superior."

"I shouldn't have to ask, because I trust you, but with everyone here we may as well be formal. Do you have any proof?" Arian was getting another headache. He hated this political dance; he missed the days of hitting things with his sword when they attacked him.

"He doesn't need it, sire," Carana called from the doorway as she came in with the two bodies over her shoulder. She dumped them on the table and watched most of the people around the table smile. "One of these bodies—the woman—attacked page Barris in his quarters, and the other body—Othren himself—was found in the east guest room corridor like this." She forgot that she was still holding the head, so she placed it by the body. It rolled away off the table and no one made a move to catch it. "You can see by the robes that they are of southern cut and make, and the knife in his pocket is also of G'harran steel." She nodded, then glanced at Karsis. "Nice work, by the way."

"Why thank you, my dear."

"My show was better. I put my dead body in a rug." Maressa pouted in her chair. She hated being out done sometimes.

"I would've loved to see that, my Queen—I'm sure it was very stirring." Tanan kicked her under the table and she laughed, kicking him back.

"It was. I was there. Very stirring, lass." Frenir said, still rubbing his head.

"Must we?" Gareth interjected. This was why the bad guys got away so much back in the days of the Companions. They were always poking fun at each other and not being serious.

"It's fine dear, relax," Tierra placated him, all the while she kicked Tanan under the table as well.

"Hey!" Tanan shouted, not knowing who did that one.

"And *I* get in trouble for being sarcastic?" Rhoe loved seeing his parents in this situation; it became them somehow. He turned to Liss and saw that she was staring as well, but for different reasons.

Liss couldn't believe what she was seeing. "Now if council meetings were all like *this*, I would've gone to every last one of them. Every. Last. One!"

Ralavin actually laughed out loud at that. As the old man at the table for all of those stuffy meetings, he could imagine how it would've gone. "Here, here! I agree with the princess. Now wasn't there something that Karsis wanted to fill us in on?" He was all for some steam blowing, but he wanted to know what was going on.

Karsis stood, with an acknowledged nod from the king, and

cleared his throat. "All right, first. Madam Ill'lyth G'harr is an ancient elven archmage. She is credited with the downfall of the elven civilization and the teaching of magic to her human lover. She is the bad wolf in all of the stories, the proverbial woman behind the curtain, and our worst nightmare come to life." He paused for dramatic effect—like there was any other kind of effect he wanted right now anyways.

Caerlyn sat forward with a frown upon her face. "Is she actually worse than the incarnation of death?" She heard murmurs around her, all wondering that very same thing. When Karsis nodded, she exhaled the breath she didn't know she was holding. "So, on top of dealing with *his* return, we have to fight this mad woman as well?"

"Wait, one moment. What is this about the incarnation of death?" Janna sat straight up. She was happy to lounge in the back and stare at Karsis, but when she heard that name her world was pulled out from underneath her feet. She felt sick.

"Sorry, have to catch you up. The incarnation of death has broken free and has decimated the northern towns. He was stopped by the northern bridge by the princess and Rhoe some time back." Carana was staring at Janna the entire time she was recounting this. She knew what the woman was, but couldn't call her out here. She had planned to find her before the meeting, but then dead bodies started popping up like rose bushes.

"I thought it was an elf that attacked Norhil hold?" Janna looked at Dren but he was just as lost. "Oh, good gods above I need a drink." She was getting up to leave the meeting, and to flee the city while she was at it, when Graf came in. Both Janna and Carana turned as one to stare at the doorway as he stood there mouth agape at the two of them.

"That's it!" Carana turned back to the assemblage and slammed her fist down. Hard. "I want the pages, Frenir, and the king's messengers out of this room *right now*. That goes for you too Dren. I know you are still recovering but this has to happen."

"Carana, what is—" Arian started, but the look she gave him shut him up mid-sentence.

"Ari, sit down and let me do this," she said, mentioning his childhood nickname that she used to call him. She had trained him since he could lift a sword, and she could see the realization on his face as he took his seat. The rest of the Companions looked at each other and even Karsis seemed a tad lost. "Move!"

The kids filed out and Dren and Frenir followed them, talking to them about their training. Fenton took Barris out by the shoulders; the poor kid was still staring at the dead body of the woman he had killed. Once they were out, she sealed the doors—as was customary with any private court—then took a deep breath and turned to them. "All right, I don't know how, or why, but the gods have chosen this time to speak. Janna, do you want me to, or should you start?"

Janna sighed. There was no way out of it now. "Fine. My name is Janna Suris, and I am the Incarnation of Beauty. I have served the great goddess Ollian for almost fifty years, and I come in peace." She stood proud and strong, radiating an aura of compassion and calm. She nodded to Carana and sat once more, enjoying the stunned looks from around the table.

Before anyone could interject an opinion or outrage, Carana continued. "My name is Cara Annalan and I am the incarnation of protection. I have served the honorable god Davalar for the past one-hundred and some odd years and I come in peace." She felt a wave of panic at her naked proclamation, but saw the queen nod with a smile on her face. Of all the people still in the room, only Maressa and Ralavin weren't floored right now, and even Karsis only arched an eyebrow. Yet that might change. "Now it's your turn, stranger." She said to Graf.

Graf had no idea what was going on. He had walked in late,

on purpose. He had wanted to just sneak in and find a place in the back and hide. Then he felt those two girls and knew they were connected. He heard what they were saying, but he had no idea what they wanted him to say.

They want you to proclaim yourself, Grafton. I've kept your shattered mind aside for all these years because it would've meant that I would have to replace you, but now there is one that can fix you.

Graf stopped and stared at the ceiling for a second as the voice in his head rambled. "So, who is it?" he asked out loud. He was used to being alone when the voice talked to him. After all, he was crazy.

It is the healer, Caerlyn, that can fix you. Close your eyes and hold on to the table. I will restore you now.

With a flash of pain, all his memories came rushing back to him. He grabbed the table and his fingers dug into the polish as he screamed. As quick as it happened it was over. "Sorry... sorry, it's all right." He took a deep breath and steadied himself. "I am Grafton Jalmes, and I am the Incarnation of Shadows. I have served Norar for the last thirty years, and I come in peace." He shook his head slowly, feeling the madness coming on. "Caerlyn, the voice in my head says that you have to fix my mind. It hid my mind away for all of these years, but you have the power to fix me."

Caerlyn rose without hesitation, holding out her hand to forestall any objections. "I can feel your pain from here. Come out back and we will fix you Graf." She led him away to the private chamber the King used to deliberate as the other two sat down.

"Now that the drama is over," Karsis said as he slowly rose, "I can honestly say that what I have to propose won't be that much of a shock after all that." He looked at Arian, then at Tierra. Those two would be the barricades he would have to break down. "Madam G'harr will declare war with Lythinall any day now, if she hasn't started marching already. I know you will send forces to Keragan hold, but I need the princess and Rhoe to come with me."

The King sat back—not too shocked, but still wary. He was trying to process all that he had heard. Carana was the same woman that had trained him, and probably trained his father as well. "All right Karsis, where are you going?"

"Well, Arian... I have to go to the elves and ask them to help us fight G'harr." He closed his eyes and waited for the screaming. When it didn't come, he opened his eyes slowly. Tierra was scowling but remaining silent. Arian was smiling.

"I figured as much, Karsis. And as long as the room is sealed, I can tell you all that I was going to send Allissana anyway. My father—and his father's father—have had a deal with the elves for many years. The new king must journey to Tir-Lanan and meet the high king to reforge the treaty we have with them. Your timing is perfect."

"You never told us you met with the elves!" Tanan was trying to stay with it all, but even his quick mind was finding it hard to stay afloat.

"I couldn't. Now, let's not get sidetracked. There is still a lot to go over, including the dead bodies, and what the hell we are going to do with three of the incarnations." And that was when Rythal appeared in the room out of nowhere.

"He told me to save you."

Rhoe was out of his chair and on his feet, as was his mother and Carana. Liss drew Deathsong, which was eerily silent, and went to stand by her father. Karsis yawned. It was Ralavin that was the first to speak.

"Hello Rythal. How are you today?" he asked in that nice sing song tone. As usual, he received no response.

"Well, that is not creepy at all." Rhoe said through almost

clenched teeth. He heard Graf stifle a scream in the back room, and pictured Caerlyn giving him a treat for being a good boy, which made him laugh. Then Karsis laughed. For whatever reason, he always found any given situation funny. Soon most of the friends relaxed and giggled and sat back down. Rythal continued to stare at the table with nothing to say.

"Now is there anyone *else* that wants to just pop in for a visit?" Arian asked the ceiling. He got a disapproving look from both his wife and Karsis on that remark, so he cleared his throat and continued. "All right, Allissana. Take Rhoe and get your-selves ready to leave in the morning with Karsis. We want the night with our daughter, however." This last remark was made at Rhoe, and the young man looked away blushing.

Tanan snickered and punched Rhoe on the arm, then got another kick under the table. "Hey I was just—"

"We know what you were doing, Tanan. Please don't." Tierra said with an icy stare and elbowed Gareth before he could say anything.

"What was that for?" he asked, his pride wounded more than anything else.

"Just in case, that's what."

Arian sighed. This was why he had appointed his friends to far away holds. Nothing would ever get done with them in court. "Carana, can we get the kids back in here with Dren? We still have to figure out Storn's plea, the two dead bodies, and how we are going to hold the city."

"Can I sit next to Karsis when we do that?" Janna said, bouncing up and down in her chair like a kid awaiting presents.

"I'll go get the children. You deal with her," Carana said, giving the Incarnation of beauty a scornful glance. *It isn't because she is flirting with the man I slept with... that was just fun.* Her thoughts tried to placate her, but it just made her angry.

"Ow!" Tanan jumped up, holding his shin.

"Tierra, stop kicking him. We're trying to have a meeting here." The king pleaded.

"Sorry Arian," Gareth said sheepishly. "That one was me. He was looking at her funny."

Carana shut the door and shook her head. She might take her time finding the children just so she could have some time to think.

The Golden Palace, G'harr

THE LARGE VASE smashed against the wall with such force that the shards embedded themselves into the walls around the impact site. Madam G'harr screamed again and picked up another vase with air and smashed it against the throne this time.

"Having problems, my Queen?" Ran'cian ducked behind the throne as another piece of valuable art smashed against the chair. He hated that she was destroying his prized art, but seeing her this frustrated was reward enough to compensate.

"They've slain all my spies within the castle! Now we won't be able to know if they figure out the incarnations weakness!" She was furious, and was not used to being on this end of any confrontation. "Generals!" she called out to the men waiting outside of her throne room. They were always there, on penalty of death, and answered only to her.

Five men came in wearing stylized jacket with many embellishments on the shoulders signifying their rank, deeds, and favor. None of it mattered now that the sorcerer king was thrown down.

"Yes, Madam Ill'lyth?" They all looked down at the floor. There used to be seven Generals.

"General..." She squinted at the name on his arm and scoffed when she read it. "General Pondar. Ready the troops at once we are marching upon Lythinall." She smiled and started walking away, but a cough drew her attention back to the five men.

"Madam, we can't declare war upon another nation without the vote of the merchant leaders." He knew he was going to be killed, but better now than when he looked weak to the people he chose to serve. He cringed as she walked back over, her heels clicking across the tiled floor like angry insects.

"Then bring me the merchant leaders—or if they resist, their heads will do. I will force them to accept, then we can get on with this." She saw that another general was going to try to be brave; General Braslen, an older man damn near seventy. She held in her rage, mainly because she really did need them. "*Don't* even try to tell me that you cannot kill them because of their importance. Find replacements first then drag them here in chains. If they acquiesce, then they live; if not, their replacements will have to be promoted." She turned again and vowed that if any of them said anything now then they asked for it. She smiled at the sound of shuffling feet.

"One of these day, Ill'lyth, you will understand that structure can't just be replaced in a tenday." Ran'cian called out from behind the throne once more. He wasn't going to show himself to his remaining generals; he had some pride left.

"We shall see, fallen one. We shall see. In days, my armies will march upon Lythinall, and then soon we will have the capitol. Then it will be mine." She closed her eyes and envisioned the armies crossing the river and swarming into the gates of the city, slaughtering any who stood in their way. Nothing would stop her now. All that was left was to trance and see what their defenses looked like, maybe even hear their plans.

Northern Belt, Somewhere Close to the Watching Woods

DAR'KRIST COULD FINALLY SEE the distant trees without his *sight* on. He used it anyway, peering into the clouds hovering low over the Watching Woods and relishing in the view. He pulled back his *sight* and walked on, weary of all these rocks. He had been walking so long that time had ceased to exist for him, just a methodical step by step. Once he was down out of these gods forsaken mountains, he would resume his inexorable march towards the castle and that irritating bard. He would also have to track down that youngling as well. He originally thought it was a young elf back when he first caught a hint of his power, but upon seeing him on the bridge for the first time, he knew he might be wrong. He realized that this was the first time that he had, to think on the events that had transpired since it all happened. That stopped him in his tracks.

He looked up at the dark clouds gliding silently by and scowled. How had he not taken even a little time and thought of any of this? Had he really been that driven to destroy everything in his path that he was blinded so easily? He shook his head and started walking again, this time going over the details of each encounter that he had with the various heroes that had tried to stop him. He remembered the fight at the village with that big man and the woman with the hair, the sneak at the hold that stabbed his foot, and even the faerie and the unicorn that had impaled then banished him to the far north. He replayed the bridge over in his mind and had to laugh at how easily he was tricked into getting angry. It wasn't all luck; these heroes were good. It came to him why he was finally thinking of these things. He wasn't angry anymore.

Dar'Krist turned his head up and laughed at the sky. He wasn't angry! All the walking he had done, and the healing that he had to go through had drained him of the intense anger that he had stored up. It wouldn't last—his temper was legendary—but he had time to think things through so that when he arrived, he would be ready. "Then they will all be sorry," he said without malice. His steps picked up, more determined this time instead of just plodding along. Soon he would be back on level ground, then he would make up some time.

❧ 9 ☙

THE COMING STORM

Storn stared out from the battlements and shook his head as he watched the line of people coming to Keragan Hold for protection. He couldn't shield them anymore than he could hold back the tide that was coming. His men had repelled the G'harran forces that came against the hold after he sent out those two soldiers and the woman. He had seen the cloud of dust coming and knew that it had to be a force to stop him. His archers rained down a hail of arrows and cut their forces in half before they got to the walls.

The commander called for a retreat right then, so as to spare his men. Storn admired that. A day after they left, runners had come and given Storn the numbers of troops marching from the G'harran border and he knew that he was in trouble. They hadn't even waited for the report from this commander before they marched. They really meant business. He had sent his fastest runners out to both the southern town of Alrin and to Everknight to tell them of the destruction that was imminent. He heard a slight cough behind him and turned to see his steward standing there. "Yes, Thanier?" He smiled despite the grave circumstances at their doorstep. Thanier Gles was one of his favorite people. He was short, only about five feet tall, with a shaved head and grey robes, but the man was whip smart.

"Well, lord, I was just wondering where we were going to bed down all these people I see coming here." He wasn't really serious, but he was trying to distract Storn from worrying too much. Give the man a problem to work out and he focused much better. Thanier was a pro at coming up with problems for his lord.

"Right you are to worry, Thanier. We don't have the room, nor can we hold back this tide that is coming." He looked out again and judged that the refugees from Alrin would get here within the hour. The G'harran's were a day behind them. "I was going to call a meeting for you, Ellen, and I to discuss this very thing."

"I heard my name again." The voice came from the slight woman coming up the stone stairwell. Ellen was dressed in traveling clothes of earthly colors and had her favorite bow slung around her shoulder. Her short brown hair was more boyish than stylish, and she took nothing from no one. Ever. "What did I do this time?"

Storn turned and regarded the girl. He had always thought of her as the daughter that he could've had, and it was hard not to show it. "You did nothing Ellen. I was just telling... oh, never mind. Come over here and lend us your inspiring thoughts." He waited until she was closer to begin, then let out his ideas. "So, the problem is that if we try and evacuate the hold, we will be overrun. We can only move so fast with the women and children, and that army out there is going to move faster—especially over the road. If we stay here and try and defend the hold, we will be overrun as well. This hold was not designed to hold off those numbers." He leaned back against the battlements and looked to his trusted advisors.

"So, rock and a battle axe, huh?" Ellen could see the frustration etched on his face. He was a fighter, used to just putting an arrow into any of his problems. "Is there any way a token force left here could hold their attention long enough for the women and children to flee?"

"No." The chances that they could just divide their forces and hunt us both down is too great. They may have sorcerers. If that happened, the forces here would be powerless to come to the aid of those fleeing.

Thanier scratched his head. "As I see it, there is only one other option. The good news is that the G'harran forces won't even consider it as an option, mainly because it would seem like suicide." He was pleased with himself, as he had been thinking about this for hours.

"Well, don't let us die of old age man! Fill us in." Ellen liked the thought of a plan that consisted of danger and possible death. She was only truly alive when she was being tested.

"Sorry. Yes, well, first we take the women and children and lead them back behind the hold onto the old trail. Then from there, we bring them up into the Shield Mountains and find a cave or something similar to shelter in. The rest of us will stay here and try and hold off the G'harran's until help from Everknight arrives." It was truly a perfect plan, except that the lower Shield Mountains were home to ogrann, and not just a couple of them.

"Thanier, that is the craziest thing I have heard in months... and it just might work." Storn wasn't thrilled with it, but the alternatives were much worse. It also saved him from coming up with something else just as crazy.

"Thank you, lord."

"Don't thank me just yet, old chap. Someone will have to lead them and find shelter, and I want the both of you to go." Not only would that spare them from the forces coming, but it would give the women and children a fighting chance. Thanier couldn't fight, but there was no one who was quicker thinking on his feet.

"Chances of fighting ogrann? I'm in. I'll have to take a couple extra quivers of arrows though. Can you spare them with that many coming?" Ellen was bouncing on the balls of her feet. Finally, a chance to get out there. It had been more than eight months since her last scouting patrol, and she was getting itchy to shoot something. She looked at Thanier and the man was pale. He wasn't saying it, but she could tell that he didn't want to go.

"No, but guarding the women and children come first. We went through a lot of arrows in that last engagement, but we're making them as fast as we can." He looked out at the coming line of refugee's once more, this time with a little more hope. "Well, with that settled, let's get the women and children ready. We can separate the others from Alrin when they get here. You two should be ready to leave as soon as they are situated. The runners estimated that the G'harrans would get here within two days, and that was a day ago." He smiled and clapped them on the shoulder as he went down the stairs to rally his defenders and give them the news that they would try and hold this place. The runners also estimated that there were almost two thousand G'harran soldiers coming. Against his paltry one hundred, that seemed bleak. If they could whittle down their numbers with archers, they would last longer. Hopefully long enough for Everknight to send help. It had been five days since his message left here for Everknight and no one knew if those two soldiers and that beautiful woman got through to the king. He had to have faith that they did. There was something about that girl that reminded him of Karsis, and that man *never* failed.

Elsewhere, just South of Alrin, Commander Ellis reined in his horse and stared at the army in front of him. There had to be two thousand soldiers bivouacked outside of the empty town. He and his men had ridden straight out to get to Alrin so that he could send a messenger back to the new queen, but by the looks of it he didn't need to. He was down to fifty men, and they were exhausted. He spied the general coming with his retainers and slid off his horse to engage the man, but Franc beat him to it.

"Greetings General Pondar. What brings you to Lythinall on this late spring day?" Franc was limping badly—as he had taken an arrow to his leg—but his smile was bright and his salute unwavering.

"Silence your pet, Ellis. I am not in the mood." Pondar was an older man, with close cropped grey hair and broad shoulders. Gone was his stylized jacket, replaced by a more practical field jacket. It still had most of his awards on it though.

"Forgive him general—we've had a long run. The messengers got past us but were severely wounded. We circled back and attacked the hold, but were decimated by archers before we even got to the walls. Reports on the number of archers at the hold were greatly under exaggerated and it cost us dearly." He glanced at Franc and was relieved to see the man keeping quiet for once.

"Yes, well, the report is moot. Queen G'harr wants Lythinall right now, and Keragan hold is the first stop on the way to Everknight." He knew that the hold would fall; he had brought two sorcerers that guaranteed it.

"Is this all the men you're bringing to invade the capitol city?" Ellis seemed unsure that they could pull that off. Sure, it was enough to decimate the hold, but Everknight had more than two thousand soldiers.

"Generals Haldir and Kasson are behind me by two days, and they each have another two thousand—not that I have to explain our plans to a *commander*." He gave Ellis that look that said the conversation was over, and then gave the same look to the little one with the mouth. "Now get some medical attention and rest up. We march back towards the hold in the morning; in three days, it will be rubble." He turned on his heel and stormed back towards his tent leaving Commander Ellis alone with his second.

"Bit of a wind bag, don't you think, sir?" Franc didn't much care for Pondar, especially after serving with the pompous ass two years ago. The man didn't have a solid thought in his head that didn't come from higher up.

Commander Ellis smiled and turned away so that Franc didn't see him. Unfortunately, his second was right. Pondar *was* a windbag, but he was his general and he had to follow him into the hells if need be. "Shut up Franc."

Western gate, City of Everknight

TANAN HATED the fact that he was charismatic. It made him the perfect choice to lead the force sent to help Keragan Hold. That and how resourceful he was when it came down to the wire. Lord Tanan smirked at a female soldier as she rode past him and then turned to look at the horizon. The council meeting yesterday was long and boring, but they had gone through everyone's assignments and where they were going to be during the attack. Lucky for him he got picked to lead this suicide mission. Then the runner from Keragan Hold had arrived and with the news that G'harr was already marching and that really made Arian's blood boil. The king hated when Karsis was right. So here he was, the Lord Norhil at the head of five hundred men and women ready to ride into danger on his word.

You would think I would be used to this after the years

making the hard calls up north, but somehow this feels worse, he thought as he held his hand up to give the signal to march. There was no fanfare, no send off from the king, and no last-minute speech. They had to move quickly so they could help the people at Keragan Hold survive. The plan was to break through, grab whoever was left to save, and fight a retreating battle back to Everknight. Five hundred men against an army. Not great odds, but then again, he loved those types of campaigns. Going with him were the beautiful bard, Janna Suris and Dren. The Guard captain was almost fully recovered, but shouldn't be anywhere near a saddle—never mind a fight—for at least three tendays. He should know, as Caerlyn had told Tanan that for over an hour.

"Drop the hand already. By the time we get there Storn will be old and grey." Dren smiled through the stiffness in his arms and legs and shook his head as Lord Tanan dropped his arm in a spectacular fashion. No horns blared as they left, just the quiet clip-clop of the horses. It would take them a day of hard marching to get to the hold, and by the runner's account the G'harran's would be getting there slightly before them; they had to hurry. Dren wouldn't miss this for the world.

Janna couldn't believe that everyone was in such good spirits. The hold was more than likely going to be in pieces when they arrived, then they would probably get ambushed and be killed. Slowly. They had told her that Storn was resourceful and that there was a good chance that they would get there in time, but she still had her doubts. It didn't help that she was grumpy. She never got a crack at Karsis, so she was pouting. She had sat next to him and tried every trick in the book to get him under her spell, but to no avail. Sure, he had said that if they made it out of all this, he would take her up on it, but it still felt like he turned her down—and she hated rejection. She might as well ride behind this handsome rogue for the trip.

"Smile Janna—we're going to kill a lot of G'harran's very soon." Dren tried not to sound eager and failed miserably.

"Sometimes I just don't know about you people. Then there's the other times that I do and that scares me." Janna smiled at him. She knew that he was doing this to avenge Stard and she couldn't fault him for that. She had lost her fair share of friends over the decades, and she knew all about revenge. "Well let's go then and I'll even write a song about it afterwards." She laughed and rode on. To glory!

Graf watched the column of soldiers march out of the West gate and shook his head sadly. He had wanted to go with them, but Arian needed him in the city. His job was to go through the streets and listen to the word rumbling through the people. He was to listen for any traitors that may have been left behind and deal with them. Once that was done, or the fighting at the gates started, he was to head to the East gate and help Caerlyn, Gareth, and Tierra hold that section.

He turned and headed back into the city. Now that his mind was healed once more, everything had become clearer. He remembered everything that had happened. From when he had been captured those many years ago in G'harr and the Sorcerer King broke his mind, to when he heard that voice—Norar's voice—telling him who he was.

He had been in such deep reflection that he had almost missed the fact that he was being followed. He stepped into an alley and spun around into a ball, pulling his ratted cloak down over his head. He heard slight footfalls enter the alley and shuffle past him, then he counted to three in his mind. When he got to three, he heard the slight scrape of the foot as the someone turned around. He leapt up, threw the cloak off, and kicked out. His surprise was complete when his foot was blocked, and he was thrust back against the wall with a kick.

"Now, why would you want to kick an old lady?" The

woman smiled and bent her head downward so that this vagabond couldn't see her face. She pulled off the 'Old Lady' bit rather well since her hair was bone white.

"Maybe because the old lady was following me?" Graf sized her up in a minute and knew something was wrong. You can't con a con. She looked old, but her legs showed no discoloration of her veins and her back was as straight as you could get on one leg. She was still holding him against the wall with her leg. "You, madam, are not what you appear to be, and it's my job to root out all traitors to the crown. So, what will it be? Going to tell me what you're hiding—or do we have to dance?" His eyes gleamed with eagerness. With his mind whole once more, his fighting prowess had all come back to him, and he was deadly before this.

She could see that he was no ordinary vagabond, and she cursed herself under her breath at her folly. She had stayed hidden for over fifty years in this city, living on the streets and caring for some of the children, and now she would have to be discovered. *All things must end, but it's up to me how they end,* she thought as she lowered her foot and backed up a bit. "Very well. My name is Illiyana, and I live on these streets. I have no intention of harming any king or queen, I just want to be left alone." She widened her stance and gripped her dagger in her belt tightly, just in case.

Graf cocked his head to the side and looked at her hair, then saw what had caught his eye. Her ears were pointed. "Oh, good gods. You're an elf?" He laughed out loud and the fight went out of him. "Don't worry—I don't care about your heritage, just your allegiance." He still wanted to know why she was following him though. "So, why are you so interested in me?"

Illiyana didn't trust him completely, but she saw that he had relaxed. "I was interested in the new guy in town, so to speak. I've seen you sleeping in the alleys and walking the streets here and there." She stood up and stopped pretending to be an old lady. She showed him exactly who she was. Her short white hair fell to her slim shoulders, and her silver eyes sparkled in the sun. She was almost five feet tall, and her slight frame was very lean and rugged.

"Well, to warn you, war is coming. G'harr is marching upon this city and we are all preparing to defend it. Women and children are being moved up into the castle and all able-bodied men are going to be holding the gates." He brushed off his cloak and straightened up, "But it seems like you could hold your own." He nodded to her and started walking for the main street.

"You're not going to bring me to your king?" She couldn't believe that he was going to just walk away. It wasn't every day that you saw an elf. Would she have to flee the city and start over somewhere else?

Graf stopped at the mouth of the alley and smiled back at her. "He's not my king, just a friend, and I see no traitors here. That being said, if I find out that your intentions have changed... Well, I've always wanted to dance with an elven blademaster."

"I'm not a—"

"Oh, don't even try. Your feet are spread apart for optimum balance, your shoulder is dipped just enough for pivoting, and your grip on that dagger is almost perfect for any style." He was flattered that she thought she could hide it from him.

"*Almost* perfect?" Illiyana didn't know if she should hit him or buy him a drink. Never had she been so transparent to anyone, even her fellow elves. Who was this man?

"Tell you what. If we all live from this attack, I'll come back down and find you and we can go over this then... unless you end up joining me at the East gate during the fight." He walked out into the street, blending in with the people heading up to the castle.

She was left with her mouth at her feet. She smiled and got

back into her 'Old Lady' persona and hobbled back out into the street. Yes, times were changing, but could she keep up this time.

The Bent Shield, City of Everknight

LAN WALKED into the popular drinking establishment called the Bent Shield and waited a moment for his eyes to adjust. It was dark in here and he couldn't see anything. The note that was left in his quarters said to meet here, and he wasn't sure who he was meeting; then he heard their voices and his heart fell. It was the castle knights having one last night before the attack. Fantastic.

"Well, if it isn't the young *knight*." Trav had a deep voice, not quite booming, but close. He was shocked to see the little upstart here. Shocked, but not disappointed. "Come in here for another *lesson,* did we?" The others behind him laughed and lifted their mugs in salute to the funny quip, and he turned and raised his own mug in response.

Lan sighed. This was not what he wanted to go through on the eve of what could be the end of Everknight. If there was only someway that he could prove to them that he wasn't trying to show them up. "No, Trav. Actually, I received a note to meet someone here." He saw the man come closer and could've hit him low to disable him early, but that wouldn't be honorable.

Trav smiled at the kid and raised his meaty fist. Couple of hits to his shield arm would make training real difficult. He didn't want this young upstart showing them up, especially in front of the high general. They had worked hard for their post as knights, and it just wasn't fair that this kid was sailing through this easy. Trav's fist came down and stopped an inch from the kid's shoulder. He didn't know what shocked him more: that the kid never flinched, or that someone's hand had stopped him. The hand that was holding his wrist was like a carpenter's vice and wasn't even shaking.

"Well, well, well. I see that you boys are having fun." Carana let the big man go and tossed his arm aside. She stepped back and lowered her hood, letting the other knights see who was amongst them. Carana smiled at the horror on their faces. "I thought that would be the reaction I would get." Without waiting she lunged at them and set about beating them with her bare hands. It was four to one, and they were no match for her at all. She connected a left hook on a knight sitting at the table and spun his head clear around, sending him out of his chair and on to the ground. Trav hit her in the face and she spit blood at him as she kicked him in the sternum. He stumbled back and two others took his place. "That's right boys, come and test me. I'm not the high general tonight, just sport."

Lan watched Carana take the knights apart, and not like in the training room. She was really hurting them. The two that went at her fell quickly, one with a broken leg, the other holding his throat after she hit him with a knife hand strike. Then she advanced on Trav, hitting him again and again, no matter how fast he tried to put his guard up. Her fist was always where he least expected. Lan swallowed hard. He couldn't believe this was happening. He was shaking with conflicting thoughts, but as she raised her hand to strike Trav one last time, Lan rushed in front and shielded him with his arm. "Wait, High General Carana!"

She hadn't let loose like this in a long time, and by the gods they had it coming. She stepped over the two sprawling knights and advanced upon the ringleader. Trav was despicable. To think that he was hurting this kid purposefully to keep him from being better than them. She smiled at the big knight as she hit him over and over, finally hitting him back into his chair. He had a look of horror upon his guilty face and she raised her fist to bring her wrath down upon him for a final blow, then Lan was there and she had to blink a couple of times to figure out what was going on. He was actually shielding the man! "Lan, what are you doing?"

Lan closed his eyes and counted to three. "Lady High General, I evoke the knight's honor code." It was a gamble, he knew, but he couldn't just sit by and do nothing. The city was going to be under attack any day and it needed all of the warriors it could find.

Carana tried to hide her utter surprise. She failed of course, but she tried. "The honor code? Really?" Carana had invented that code decades ago, so she knew what it meant. Lan would bind his fate with Trav's and be held accountable for his actions, as well as his own. This lasted until the death of either of the participants. "I have to ask Lan—with what this despicable knight was doing to you, how could you vouch for him?" Carana knew the answer, but she wanted Trav to hear it from the boy.

Lan took a steadying breath and looked her in the eyes. "Because It's what any knight would do for one of their own."

"But we were horrible to you, kid." Trav tried to say through a swollen face.

Lan turned around and faced Trav, giving him a worn smile that said he knew exactly what they had done. "Yes. I know, but I have to ask myself if I would be any less of a knight if I stood by and let it happen. You are a fellow knight and no formal charges were filled, so that means you were in distress. A true knight always helps those in distress." He turned back to face Carana and saw that she was smiling.

It wasn't her desired effect—she was hoping for more of the 'grovel while being beaten' approach—but it worked out the same. "Very well, young knight. Trav and you shall be honor bound together until the death of either one of you. Now, let's get a round of drinks over here."

The barkeep, who was fingering the pouch of gold that the high general had slipped him for any disruption tonight, merely whistled and the serving girls brought over mugs of warm mead.

Lan was still puzzled though about the note. "Lady Carana, was it you who left me that note then?"

Carana looked at him with a questioning look and simply turned away. "What note, Lan?" She had turned so that he couldn't see her smile. She stepped over the bodies of Trav's friends and sat down wondering if any of these knights would survive the attack.

Elsewhere in the city, Kari walked in silence with Sprout, Vance, and Tomas. They were heading to their old alley to discuss what the king and queen had gone over with them. She missed Lan and really needed him right now, since all the kids were looking to her with his absence. Sprout was the only one that seemed happy, bouncing as she walked down the familiar streets. Kari shook her head at the little ball of energy. "Try to cheer up Sprout."

Sprout stopped and turned to the others, confused. "But I *am* happy..."

Vance laughed despite the butterflies in his stomach. "No Sprout, she was being funny again because you're *too* happy." They arrived at the alley and they crawled over their old wooden pile and slid down to their old hideout. They hadn't been here since that fateful night and weren't sure it would even still be here.

Kari didn't know where to start. The king had wanted them to help defend the city, even though they weren't fully trained yet. He had said that they would have the North gate with what guards they could spare, and that they didn't expect any forces to hit that gate with the other two more accessible. She didn't believe that for a second. "All right, so we have to guard the North gate when the G'harran's come. Does anyone have any thoughts on this? Suggestions?" She had a knack for speaking to people, but she was at a loss for words on this subject. She was terrified.

Tomas, usually very quiet had waited for his cue to speak this time. "I think this is the perfect opportunity to prove ourselves to the king." Short and to the point, that was the blacksmith in him. They were told that they would be outfitted with the proper weapons on the morrow, and any armor that they could wear without impeding their fighting ability would be theirs as well.

"You *would* say that. We can't prove ourselves if were dead, Tomas." Vance was skeptical. Though with the right bow in his hands, he could do a lot of damage at a distance. "If those bastard G'harrans swing around, we will be in real combat and serious trouble." He wished Griff was here, though the king said the young healer would be at the North gate with them tomorrow.

"He did promise that there would be a contingent of guards there too guys." Even as Kari said it, she knew it wouldn't help them feel better. They had to be prepared for anything, no matter what the king said. They were street kids first, so they knew all about promises that went sour, or plans that went south when you least expect them to.

"Don't forget Lan will be there. He is almost a knight!" Sprout added, kicking her feet back and forth from atop the crate she was sitting on. "Why did we come down here again anyway. Can't we talk about this up at the castle?"

"Hush, Sprout. So, do we vote?" Vance didn't know what he was going to do. The king had been so good to them, but he didn't want to die.

"Yes, the three of us. Sprout is awesome, but a little young to cast her voice in something like this yet." Kari had a bad feeling that she was the swing vote, and that their lives were in her hands. Either way, their lives would change forever after this day. If they voted no, then they would flee the castle at first light and not look back. If they voted yes, then they would stay and hold the gate. Gods above, she missed Lan right now. There wouldn't even be a vote if he were here. She didn't want to be responsible for their fate, so she just blurted it out. "I'll go first. Yes." She held her breath.

"No." Vance was quick and precise. There was no doubt that if he stayed, he would die. He had that bad feeling in his gut, like back when Meri died.

Tomas looked around at both of them with a hurt look on his face. Now he was the vote that could damn or deliver them. He scowled and shook his head to clear it. Like that ever helped. "Yes." He saw Vance's face fall and had to look away. "I'm sorry, but I can't leave after all this city has done for me Vance." He turned and looked at his old friend and tried a weak smile. "You could leave though, we won't say anything, will we Kari?"

"No, Tomas, it was all or nothing. It's all right, I understand." He shivered and it had nothing to do with the chill wind. "So, it's settled. We will stay and hold the North gate."

"Yay! We can be heroes!" Sprout was excited to be a hero. She had always been too small before to be one. *What should I use as a weapon?* she thought as she jumped down and got ready to go back to the castle.

Kari laughed as they started back, but her mirth was forced. Sprout would be crushed when she found out that they were leaving her at the castle with the other littles. She would hate them for a while, but she would be alive. She remembered King Arian saying that the G'harran's would be here soon, so they had to be ready in two to three days. She knew they had to get fitted for armor tonight or tomorrow morning, so she picked up the pace. Once this was over—and if they lived—she was going to have strong words with whatever god was responsible for her life.

"What are you thinking about Kari?" Sprout asked as she bounced alongside her friends.

"Nothing, Sprout. Just thinking of who I get to blame for all of this."

Northern Bridge, Central Lythinall

RHOE STARED at the gap where the bridge used to be, and a shiver ran down his spine. He remembered plunging down into the swollen river like it was yesterday. It wasn't all that long ago anyway, but still. There was a half-finished structure in place, but with the threat of war, the workers were called back to the city to prepare. He looked at Karsis and saw that he too was in some sort of contemplation. *Probably enjoying the silence. Gods above know we bugged him long enough,* he thought as he chuckled to himself. They had left Everknight two days ago, and he and Liss wasted no time in pelting the bard with questions about his secret identity. They had asked all the things that they could think of, then five more just for good measure, and like some sort of saint, Karsis just smiled and answered them all. The big one was how old he actually was, and the answer seemed unreal. The man—or elf—was over three hundred years old!

After that, they had started going over more magic studies. Karsis went over more on Rhoe's *sight* and what not to do, and Rhoe told him some of the things that happened in the castle, like when Othren attacked. He seemed intrigued about that one, but said he had to think about it before he commented more. Rhoe also noticed Liss paying close attention to whatever Karsis had to say on the subject of magic.

"Long way down now that the waters have receded, huh?" Liss nudged Rhoe out of his silent thoughts and smiled as he turned to look at her. When they had fallen down to the river before, it had been swollen with the spring rains. Now it was a bit calmer as it neared summer. "How we getting over that anyway? Air?"

"She thinks she knows magic now?" Karsis laughed and spun away towards the horses. "Well, do us all a trifle and call us up some air to walk on, would you dear?" He really didn't mind her enthusiasm, but he needed her to know that it wasn't possible. Worse than that, he couldn't tell her why without more hidden things coming to light, and he just wasn't ready for another question-and-answer session.

Liss straightened up and squared her shoulders. The defiant streak in her was from her mother, and she embraced it fully. She turned and looked out over the chasm and closed her eyes.

"Karsis maybe we shouldn't let—"

"Quiet, Rhoe, and watch." Karsis admonished quietly. He was impressed with her determination and wanted her to really try. It had to be real, so when she failed, she knew it wasn't anything else.

Liss tried to remember the elven words that they used when they were training, but didn't want to guess wrong. She only could recall the beginning word for please. She took a deep breath. "Ash'anti air, hold me up." She felt a breeze and took a step off the edge, and promptly fell forward.

Rhoe saw that she was going to step off, even though he felt no strong wind coming to her aid. Strangely enough, he *did* feel the air stir in response, but it was like they couldn't quite hear her. He lunged as she fell and grabbed her arm, pulling her back before she went over. "I've got you."

"Now that was actually quite good, princess! Good form indeed. Now please mount up and let's get moving." He patted her on the back sincerely as she tried to catch her breath, then vaulted up into the saddle and called for the wind to hold them as they crossed the gap. He urged the horse forward and the great beast stopped at the edge. He sighed and placed his hand over its eyes, then urged it onward again. Reluctantly it took a step, and then another, finally walking across the span.

Rhoe jumped up on his horse and saw Liss do the same, then they both covered the horses' eyes and followed Karsis. Once across they pushed the horses a little faster following the River Winding northwest. Karsis knew of another faerie ring where the river splits just south of Havenar. They were travelling to the faeries to pay their respects to Lurien, then from there they were taking another faerie ring to the far northern Watching Woods. This part was going to be difficult, as they had no way of knowing where Dar'Krist was—other than coming south out of the Northern Belt. After that, they were going to take something Karsis called the "Silversword Pass" to cross the Snow Peak Mountains.

"Karsis? Can the horses go through the mushroom rings?" It hadn't occurred to Liss that they might not fit until now. She felt stupid asking, but she was always curious about things that were new to her.

"Actually, that is a good question Allissana. Yes, they can. Once they step in, they will be magically transported as if they were completely in the ring. But we're not taking them with us. When we get to the ring, I'm going to send them back to Everknight." He looked at her as they rode and smiled. He remembered all the stupid questions he had asked back when he was learning. Boy, were there a lot of those. They rode for the rest of the day, asking him about how the city will fare, and how the G'harrans will act when they get here, and he tried his best to lie to make them feel better. If they didn't get the elves to come fight, then the city was going to fall, and it would be a horrible fight to survive after that.

Rhoe was about to ask if they were there yet, just to break the tension of the past couple of hours, when Karsis held up his hand for them to stop. Rhoe reflexively slid off his horse and took up a wide stance, ready for anything. Then her heard Karsis laugh.

"Rhoe, while I appreciate your vigilance, all I meant was that we were here."

Rhoe shot Karsis an aggravated look, but ended up laughing when he saw how innocent the bard seemed. "All right, so I'm the paranoid one now. It happens when you get slammed into a stone wall."

Liss looked around but didn't see any signs of a mushroom ring like she used the last time. "Is it disguised by some sort of concealing spell Karsis?" She dismounted and walked around trying to see if it was hidden.

"No, nothing so sophisticated, my dear." He slid off his horse and held the reins as he patted the great beast affectionately, then turned back to watch her inquisitive search. *This she inherited from Arian, and it makes me feel very old indeed watching her,* he thought as he let her wander a bit more in search of something she just wasn't going to find. "It's placed in a out of the way location so that passersby can't stumble upon it by accident."

Rhoe smiled at the challenge and started to look himself. It was like a treasure hunt, and it took his mind off the journey ahead. Then he smelled rotting meat and saw something move just out of the corner of his eye and dove for the water. The wolvren just missed him and clamped down on a small bush instead. The beast ripped it free and Rhoe saw it spin towards him once more. The young warrior was horrified to see two broken spears sticking out of its shoulder and back. This was the same monster he'd faced before!

"Rhoe, back away and don't use magic!" Karsis yelled, drawing his own slim sword and racing to get in front of the beast. He saw how mangled it looked and the evil determination in its eyes. How it found them was anybody's guess. "Not today, foul beast!" He challenged as he slid in front and slashed quickly, catching it on the snout. He saw Liss frozen with fear, a first time to be sure by all the accounts he had heard, but after seeing Rhoe taken apart by this thing, he didn't fault her. A wolvren was twice the size of a large wolf, and had the temperament of a one-armed, blind beggar on an empty street. They are mean and cruel, but should never attack a force stronger than itself, and this one was still wounded from the fight with Rhoe and Liss outside of River Vale.

Rhoe made his way around Karsis to Liss, but saw the beast follow his movements precisely. This wasn't good. Hells, this wasn't even bad—it was worse than that. "Liss, can you hear me?" he called, staying where he was. "You've got to pull Deathsong."

Liss couldn't breathe, could barely stand. The wolvren was there again and it was tearing into Rhoe. She was powerless to stop it and could only stare, as the one she had started to love was ripped from her. Then she heard Rhoe calling to her and she came out of her daze. He wasn't lost yet! She gritted her teeth and pulled the sword, hearing it almost howl in anticipation of battling this thing again. "I'm all right now, thanks." She started to move closer with measured steps, still shaking but in control. *Gods above, what would Carana think?* she thought as she tried to stop the tremor in her hands.

The wolvren started backing up a bit faced with them all, and that's when Karsis pounced. He slashed once, twice, then a straight lunge that took the beast in the eye. "Have at thee!" he yelled playfully as the beast shook its head to free it from the sword. Blood sprayed on the air and it howled a deathly song of murder. Karsis fell and rolled backwards as it swiped a claw at him, then came up to his feet, only to see it had turned on Liss. "Come back, I've only just started!" As it stalked the princess, he looked at Rhoe and wondered again what the boy had done the last time. "You said you didn't cast magic at it last time, Rhoe, correct?"

"Correct. I asked the water to hold us up so we could walk on it to get away from this thing, and then cancelled it before he could use it too." He couldn't explain why he never tried magic on the wolvren; it just didn't seem right at the time.

"Now think hard, Rhoe... did he sniff the water afterwards?" This could be bad. And not the fun kind of bad, where he had to leap out of a second story building because someone's husband came home, either.

I remember that the beast skidded to a halt on the opposite bank, howling its rage, then it sniffed the water and grinned. "Would it be bad if I said yes?" He thought furiously as to what could've happened when the wolf sniffed the water and grinned. It grinned! "Oh gods, Karsis, it has my scent!"

Karsis was too worried to be impressed at his young protégé. This thing had sniffed the boy's magic on purpose so that it could find him again. *What am I missing?* he thought as Liss swung again at the wolvren and nicked its shoulder. He thought about what he had seen when he first saw signs of the beast and then it hit him. "It's not a wolvren!"

Liss heard him, but had no time to capitalize on the revelation—not that she knew what the hells that meant anyway. She backed up once more, taking a claw to the side as Rhoe launched a kick to the thing's face, snapping its head around. Her father's ring would keep her alive, but it still hurt something awful. "Does this mean that you can make this thing stop trying to kill me now? That would be great."

Rhoe leapt and came down with a knife hand to its neck, then barely rolled back as it came around with another claw. It hadn't tried to bite them yet... odd. The next time that it howled from the sting of Deathsong, Rhoe looked in its mouth and saw why. It seemed that a small piece of spear was logged in its mouth, preventing it from really biting down hard. "If he doesn't, I can." Rhoe said with determination. Fighting this thing once was bad enough, but twice...

Karsis needed more time. "By all means, my young friend. If you can finish this, go right ahead. I need to think." He remembered the remains of the hunter. Start there. Why did he assume it was a hunter: because it was deep in the woods? Probably. Novice mistake. He mentally kicked himself for assuming anything, but conceded that he was still in shock from Irilyn's death. Was it wearing a black cloak? Was there even enough remains for a whole body? They don't kill for food, just for the sheer evil pleasure of killing. Then Karsis heard Rhoe scream and had to stop his contemplation for the moment.

Rhoe waved Liss back, knowing that this thing had his scent. It wanted *him*. "Come on then, you want me that bad? Come and get me." He waited and spun out of the way of the first and second claws, pirouetting and coming around with his foot, but not across. Instead, his foot came down in an arc and hit the wolvren—or whatever it was—right on the head. Hard. Its head hit the ground and it whimpered, but before it could rise, Rhoe came around and brought his fist straight down on its head with a scream of fury. The sound of the small spear piercing through the beast's head was like seeing a rainbow for the first time; you never forget something like that. He felt the body go limp beneath him.

"Was that all it took?" Not that Liss doubted his fighting

prowess—she had seen him stand against the incarnation of death—but that seemed too easy.

"Hopefully it will stay dead this time." Rhoe said a little breathlessly. It took a lot of footwork to not get hit by those wild claws. It helped that he remembered being mauled by them before so there was some extra motivation.

Karsis almost had it, then he heard Rhoe. "Stay dead?" He looked at what he suspected and saw the tail twitch. "Oh, I don't think so, sir." He stepped forward and slid his sword into the thing's neck and out its face, then slid it sideways just to be sure. "Now burn it with normal fire, just to be final."

"So, what is it Karsis?" Liss wiped her blade on its pelt and slid Deathsong into its scabbard, leaning on Rhoe for a minute. He was trying to get a flint out of his sling bag, but she just wanted to rest.

"Well, I suspect that this used to be a sorcerer. Rumor has it that years ago a group of magic users were delving into lycan-thropy—with horrible results. The last I heard they had abandoned it all together. Until I saw how this thing focused on Rhoe. No wolvren would've acted like this one had, both times in fact. Add to the fact that it sniffed up your scent and survived to track you down and I have to think that someone finally figured out how to become a were-wolvren."

"That's it, now I've heard everything. I thought it was bad enough that we saw a unicorn, but a were-wolvren?" Liss was stupefied. This was almost beyond her comprehension, but she was trying to understand Rhoe's world. The world that she had always read about as a child but now, impossibly, she was living. Magic, faeries, and even monsters that stalked you in the night, and she wouldn't trade one minute of it all. *Though if I find out that there are talking animals, I'll feint,* she thought.

"Well, nothing to be done about it now." Karsis said as he watched the beast start to burn. It caught quickly and burned like it was soaked in oil. He turned to the kids and smiled. "Now let's be off to see Lurien. I owe her my condolences." He walked to the edge of the river and whispered so that his steps would be held aloft and crossed the fast-moving flow to the middle of them both. Once he was between the two rivers, he walked to the point where they split and beckoned to Liss and Rhoe.

Rhoe grabbed Liss and asked the water to harden so that they could both cross and saw Karsis raise his brow in surprise. He smiled and walked to where the bard was waiting.

"Well done, Rhoe. Quick thinking and intuitive. She needed to cross as well and that was the best way for the both of you to do so. I would ask how you came up with that idea, but you would just say 'It came to me,' wouldn't you?" He watched the boy nod sheepishly and smile. This one was going to be fun when they got to the elves. "Anyway, were here."

Liss looked at where they were stopped and couldn't think of a more mesmerizing place to be. The River Winding came out of the north like a fury and split right here. The main flow headed towards the Misty Woods, and the other spilled down a short fall to the Shield Mountains. They stood there under that short fall and saw Karsis wave his hand at the waterfall. It moved as if it was a curtain and a glorious cavern unfurled beyond, glittering with sparkling stones and hanging moss. "Gods above Karsis, it's breathtaking!"

"That it is, hurry now—secrets and all that." Karsis ushered them under and looked back at the horses. "Ash'anti ethir tol lea roans travar ta Everknight." He told the ether to make the horses go, then ducked under the water as he closed it behind them. He saw Liss staring at the cavern, and Rhoe staring at her. More and more he thought that something was behind their infatuation, but he had to admit that they were great for each other. "Right. Well, get moving. Don't want to stay here any longer than we need to. That's the thing about a secret entrance—you loiter, and it isn't a secret anymore."

Liss laughed and stepped into the ring, then Rhoe followed. Karsis smiled and stepped through as well, thinking about what awaited them on the other side.

❧

PANALIS WAS WALKING through the Revel glade when the girl popped in from the mushroom ring and scared the hooves off of him. He was an aging satyr, and his heart just couldn't take things like this anymore. "Oy! Watch it girl!" Then he had to laugh as she jumped up and screamed. *Serves her right, scaring an old satyr like that,* he thought as another one came through, a boy this time, and bumped into the girl, sending them into a tumble. "Oh, but surely this made my day. I thank you both for the entertainment this eve." He was going to say more, but then a familiar figure came through the ring. "Karsis! As I live and breathe!"

Karsis looked up and saw Panalis the satyr. He honestly couldn't remember the last time he had visited, but age had not been kind to his old friend. "Panalis, how fare thee?"

"Do you know *everyone?*" Rhoe asked, standing up and dusting himself off. He helped Liss up and dusted her off too, even as she smacked his hand away.

"We met ages ago when he came to save us from the dark wizard. Now, what do we owe the pleasure of this visit?" He looked at the two kids and something was vaguely familiar about them. "Hey! You two are the ones that were just here with Avaryn weren't you?"

"Yes, we were. We heard about the sacrifice that Irilyn made for everyone." Liss reached out and placed her hand on the aging satyr's shoulder as a tear came to his eye. "Know that I

244

hold her in my heart as one of the greatest heroes I have known."

"Yes. Well, before we all sit down and have a good cry, I would like to go give my thoughts to the new queen."

Panalis wiped a tear away and smiled at Liss. "Bless my heart, a human that can care." He turned to Karsis and bowed deep. "My King, follow me." He walked across the clearing and towards the Council Tree with the three of them in tow.

Lurien sat on the throne with a heavy heart. She had been doing her best, but she couldn't get the faeries out of their funk. Even Liana was unusually quiet, and that was saying something. Since they had hidden away here in the vale, they were sort of stagnant—stuck. She wished she could find a way to get them out in the world again, but the fear of humans was too great. Maybe it was time to see the elves once more and work things out. Though she wasn't there when the faeries left the world, she knew the stories. They had been pressured by the elves to fight against the humans and when they refused the elves tried to banish them out of their forests. So the faeries left everyone behind for safety and seclusion. The elves regretted it immediately.

Lurien shook herself out of her contemplation and laughed to herself. She wouldn't even know where to look for them after all this time; she had never been out of the vale. She looked up as someone was crossing the revel clearing and saw the two kids behind Panalis, then she recognized Karsis and she darted straight up into the air with a shrill cry. "He's back!" She flew at him with a smile and he laughed as she came at him.

Rhoe ducked under the queen and saw that faeries were coming out of the trees and bushes to see what had their queen in a tizzy. With excited whispers and fingers pointing, the faeries came out in *droves* to surround them all. Then he heard a sound that made him flinch.

"Ohmytreestheycameback!" Liana came out of the treetops like a rampaging dragon—a fourteen-inch dragon. She circled once then came down at high speed to land on Liss's shoulder, almost knocking the princess over. "Iknewyouwouldn'tforget me!"

Breathe young one, they probably can't even understand you. Avaryn was surprised to see the humans again, and even more surprised that they brought Karsis with them. He walked over and bowed to the king of the faeries, then backed up to stand at Rhoe's side.

"It's good to see you Avaryn." Rhoe said, wondering if he should pat the unicorn. He really wanted to pat the unicorn.

Karsis raised his arms up and the leaves rustled loudly in his summoned wind. The faeries all 'Oohed and Ahhed,' then shushed quietly. "Thank you. Now, please give me a moment to talk with Lurien, then we can have fun. I warn you though, we leave on the morning rays of the rising sun."

"His speeches get all old style here huh?" Liss remarked to Rhoe quietly. She still saw Karsis give her that look though, like he actually heard her. The faeries dispersed and soon the only ones left were Avaryn, Liana, and Lurien. They went to the throne and Karsis pulled his feet up underneath himself as he hovered in the air. "I'm so sorry about your mother Lurien. I felt her death and would love to know exactly what happened."

"And I would love to sit and tell you Karsis, but I wasn't there. Avaryn knows pretty much what happened though." She smiled through fresh tears, remembering how much her mother cared for this man.

I would be happy to tell you all I know Karsis. How about we do a campfire memorial tonight while the children sleep. I assume you still require no sleep. Avaryn knew that the bard was different, but didn't want to pry too much. His power was familiar, but he couldn't place it after all these years. It was just too... different.

That sounds perfect Avaryn, and thank you, Karsis thought to the magical beast. He truly missed this place sometimes. *We can even chat about your time with my young wizard in training.*

Indeed, we can.

"So, tell us Karsis. Other than coming to see me, what brings you to the Hidden Vale once again?" Lurien was grateful that he came to see her, but she wasn't so naive that she didn't know that he had an ulterior motive.

"Funny you should ask. We are travelling to the realm of the elves to enlist their aid in the coming war against the incarnation of death and the forces of G'harr." He smiled as he finished, knowing that the news would shock them. In fact, he was counting on it. *Five, four, three, two...*

"I—want—to *go!*" Liana said loudly and slowly, then she lost all her composure in a rush. "Ohmytreesiwanttoseetheleves!" She was flying in small circles, getting herself dizzy.

Lurien laughed and tried to catch her, then gave up and let her spin herself sick. That would calm her down for the night. "Karsis, I think you have a traveling companion." She couldn't believe the timing. This was just what she had needed, and it was as if the goddess Syll had heard her silent plea. She laughed. Maybe it *was* time. Maybe her people needed to go back to their roots after all. Her mother always told her that she would lead her people to new things. "I may even send her as an ambassador to the elves."

My Queen, I will go with them as well, to keep her calm and see that it goes smoothly. Might I add, it is about time a queen took the first step to mend the fence—so to speak—between our two peoples. Avaryn was proud of this young faerie. No other queen had ever thought about it as an option before.

"Then it is settled. We all leave on the morrow. Now, let us all retire and have some fun before we get some rest." Karsis took the queen's arm and escorted her down from the throne and away to the waiting faeries. "Rhoe, do play nice and stay away from the food over much this time all right?" he laughed as he called out over his shoulder.

Rhoe smiled and watched the bard walk away. Faeries flocked to his side and flew around his head like a wreath of excitement. "Well, looks like we have some time to relax before we start again." He looked at the princess and she was smiling right back.

"Time to ourselves? That sounds pretty good indeed." She laughed and ran ahead of him, calling for Liana and spinning in the glade with her arms out wide. This time she would stay sober, and when they slept, maybe she would take advantage of this young man. *Not just a man, but my husband,* she thought and immediately it sounded weird to her. She hadn't said it out loud till now; somehow it became more real.

Rhoe looked on and found himself turning inward. He felt his center, but something else was there too, trying to force its way in. It had been there this whole time, but every time he worked through a problem with his magic, it lessened. Now it was trying to pierce his center in a last-ditch effort to corrupt him. He was too strong for that. He smiled and called to the air to spin the fallen petals lying on the ground in a swirling pattern all around him, sending the faeries near him in a dance of giggles. Spreading his arms out wide, he felt the darkness within him break like fallen glass, spilling out of him like expelled air. He felt it now. He had claimed the power for his own and was a wizard in truth.

EPILOGUE: THROUGH A VEIL OF
DOUBT

Sunlight beamed in the myriad of windows dancing on the marble tiles of his work room. The elf sat at his worktable and gazed out those windows with a wistful look on his face. He loved his tower, and he could think of only three other things he would rather be doing, and at least two of them involved him being naked. The tower was the highest in the entire city and it was made primarily of glass. Here, he could see for hundreds of miles on a clear day with his *sight*. Even without it, the view was spectacular.

Adrilian Everence sighed and wrote something down in an oversized book, smiling to himself. He had been following the events of Lythinall—and in particular: the rise of the incarnation of death. He brushed a strand of long white hair out of his face and stood, smoothing out his bright red robes that hung loosely on his lithe frame. *Time to check on the kids,* he thought as he walked across the marble tiled floor, his bare feet slapping loudly in the pervasive quiet of his chamber. He headed over to his scrying pool and looked into the water. Its surface was calm and reflected his face back at him as he leaned over the edge. He didn't look a day over one hundred, not bad for being the oldest elf in all of the realm. He chanted softly and the water moved to please him, showing him what he mentally wanted to know. More reliable than *sight*, this was one of his secret treasures.

The image of Karsis and Rhoe became clear in the pool and he heard their plans to visit the elves, and they were even bringing a representative from the lost faeries. Interesting to say the least. He clicked his tongue and walked back over to his worktable. He had to think. He was debating on warning the elven council about the arrival of guests. On the one hand, it would do well to make preparations for their meeting that would inevitably occur. But on the other hand, the various factions would try and catch them alone and badger them about their initiatives. He laughed at the thought of the look on the council when they just showed up... but he couldn't do that. He would have to tell someone. He reached over and pulled the long red rope by his table, ringing the bell that would summon N'vea his serving maiden.

It took her only seconds to appear in his doorway. "Yes, Adrilian?" She gazed at her master with her soft silver eyes.

"N'vea, please prepare a writ to the council if you would dear," he started, waiting for her to walk over to the table where he kept his parchment and ink. She was short, even for an elf, standing at only four and a half feet. Her white hair was a little shorter than shoulder length, to show her stature in society, and her long dress was silver to match her eyes. As she sat and readied herself, he began again. "To the Council of Tir-Lanan, from Archmage Adrilian. Visitors are currently making their way here to parley with you on the recent dealings in the south. I urge that you make preparations for them as the group includes the human princess of Lythinall, and a representative of the lost faeries." He hesitated to tell them who was leading them here, as that would cause even more problems.

N'vea looked up from her transcribing with a look of amazement. "Truly master? The faeries are still around?" She wasn't even born yet when they disappeared from the world, and she honestly always thought they were... well, a fairy tale.

Adrilian smiled at her youthful display. "Yes dear, they are very much around. I'm the only one in the city that knows that, and I've kept it to myself for reasons I'd rather not discuss." In truth the other elves might have found them if they cared enough to look, but no one really did after their departure. Pity, really. Their absence was the reason that the elves were so dour —at least that's what he believed. He frowned, having doubts about how the factions would receive the news. The Sran'en Kith would be the most aggressive towards them, as they were for the isolation of the elven people, and they had a lot of influence on the council. Yet the Yaw Worl'aren was a persistent faction that wanted to see the elves go out into the world once more.

N'vea waited patiently for her master to start once more. He seemed to be in reflection, but not the nice kind. "Is there anything I can help with Adrilian?"

He snapped out of his morose thoughts and smiled at her. She was so good to him. "No, my dear, I've decided that the council can be surprised after all. Cancel the writ." He just couldn't see a good outcome to letting them know.

"Won't they know they are coming anyway master?" She was confused. How could anyone even find this hidden city, never mind getting here without the council's wizards *seeing* them from miles away.

Adrilian chuckled and turned away to stare out the glass windows once more. "They won't even know what hit them, N'vea. The person that is bringing them here knows ways into the city that most elves don't even know about."

"That sounds dangerous Adrilian. Shouldn't we at least

warn the guard?" She had a bad feeling about all of this. This wasn't like her master in the slightest.

"No... no, my dear, you misunderstand. The person bringing them here is my son. And while he is reckless and arrogant, he would never cause the people harm, and he does so like to make an entrance." He turned towards her and saw her soften at the mention of his son. "Now, you go and make sure that your best dress is ready for their arrival. I have some more things to prepare." He winked at her and turned away.

She watched him walk over to a shelf full of scrolls and other stacks of parchment and start picking out some of them to put under his arm. N'vea left quietly and worked her brain over and over, trying to think of the right outfit to wear. She could imagine the council's outrage when they were surprised with guests they didn't know about. She just wished she could be in the room when they found out.

Northern Watching Woods, Northern Lythinall

DAR'KRIST CAME out of the mountains with a sense of purpose. It had been a very long twenty days of running and it felt good to feel the soft earth under his feet. Odd that he would feel that way, but he hadn't been through something like that in almost two hundred years. He looked back at where he had come from, and even he was surprised. It should've taken him months to get here, considering how far north he was, but he had pushed himself once he was fully healed. He took a few steps, already thinking of which way he wanted to go, when he stopped cold. Someone was watching him. He closed his eyes and stood very still, feeling the air itself for any hint. It wasn't the same as when that elfling, or whatever that boy was, had spied on him. No, this was *old* power. He turned around and suddenly he felt the eyes on him. Turning coldly at where he had finally sensed the distortion of magic he smiled. "You cannot hide from such as I —" he began, but stopped as some force came towards him quickly. He threw himself to the side and rolled, coming up to his feet in seconds; ready for whatever ambush they had for him. Nothing came.

He waited then turned once more to the mysterious person watching him. Powerful indeed. "So, you think to impress me with a show of force?" He brought his hands around in a great arc, clapping them together and released a wave of death right at the spot where they watched and felt it flee high up in the air. *So—you can be hurt in this form, good to know,* he thought as he followed the distortion up with his eyes. He focused his *sight* and tried to pierce the veil of magic, but as he suspected it was too strong. Then it was gone. He sighed and shook his limbs out to release some of the tension. Whoever that was they would be back, and next time he would be ready. The incarnation of death and corruption set out at a steady pace back towards Lythinall, and he was more than ready to take on any heroes that came at him. Just not on any more bridges.

FAR AWAY TO THE SOUTH, in her special meditation room, Ill'-lyth G'harr smiled as she came back to her body. The trip had proven fruitful, to say the least. Not only had she seen the council meeting in Everknight and knew their defense plans, but she had also found the incarnation of death. Now that she knew where he was and what he was capable of after all these years, she could move forward with the next step of subduing him and bringing him here to her palace. She got up and walked to the door, still stark naked from her trance.

She walked out, not caring that she was indisposed, and

called for the generals to meet with her. Some unwitting servant tried to tell her that she was naked and found himself gasping for air as she walked by him. She held the breath from his lungs until he died and dropped to the ground with a heavy thud. Yes, this was going to be an easy victory now that she knew what the defenders planned to hold the city gates. Her laugh echoed throughout the hallways, and no one else dared say a word.

To be continued in **The Darkness Falls**

ABOUT THE AUTHOR

Born in the usual way, Michael D. Nadeau found fantasy at the age of 8 with Dungeons and Dragons. He loved being different people and casting magic. By the late 90's, he discovered his love for reading. His favorite teacher gave him her personal books to bring home, and he couldn't get enough. He had even more ways to explore the great worlds out there, and it was harder and harder to come back. When he was much older, and had created and destroyed more worlds than he could count, he decided to delve into the literary realm. He created Lythinall, a place where he could tell epic stories and invite his readers on the journey with his characters. The Darkness Returns is the start of that journey, but certainly not the end. You can learn more about his works at SkullgateMedia.com as well as his personal website, KarisTheBard.Wordpress.com.

 twitter.com/Salen_Valari

 instagram.com/michael_d_nadeau

 amazon.com/Michael-D.-Nadeau

Tales From The Year Between, Volume 2
UNDER
NEW SUNS
A crew of intrepid space marines...
A pregnant ship trying to get home...
And freaking space sharks.

SKULL
GATE

Available now at Amazon,
Skullgatemedia.com and
WHEREVER BOOKS ARE SOLD.

Tales From
The Year Between